STORM DAMAGE

TOM BOXLEITER

To my faithful readers who inspired me to keep writing.

CHAPTER ONE

I was all alone, just me and the road. No other vehicles near me on the four lane, and not another living soul in my bus-like motor home. I was headed west with no goal in mind and no purpose beyond escape. Behind me was an empty house, a destroyed medical career, and a buried wife. On the positive side, I hadn't had a drink in more than a year. So, at sixty-five, I was starting all over with less vitality but considerably more wisdom. Or at least I hoped that was the case.

The miles buzzed by with unchanging scenery. Rolling hills of brown earth showed the first sprouts of spring planting. Every now and then, there was a little town just beyond the horizon, only its steeples and grain elevators visible. The last actual city of any size was many miles behind, and the next even further ahead. This was the Midwest; my home for most of my life, and yet this part of it was unfamiliar to me. I'd never been on a farm. I couldn't imagine living in a small town where there was nothing to do but keep track of your neighbors' doings. I needed a city, big but not too big. One big enough, so there was a lot to do, but not so big that I'd get lost in the masses. I'd always wanted to be someone and in a small city, that wasn't hard to do. Unfortunately, my misbehavior over the years and, especially in the last two, had made me too much of someone. I'd come to be known for my mistakes, not my accomplishments. Hence the need to escape.

The long drive gave me plenty of time to think. Possibly too much time. I had to admit to myself that all of my problems thus far had been the result of my arrogant self-absorption. Only in the last few years, since my wife died, had I started to see myself clearly. I hadn't been happy with what I saw but had not been able to do much to change it. So I was on the run...from the person I had been. Or maybe I was running to the person I wanted to be. Either way, I had no plan and no destination. Just the hope that I could find a way to be a better person. I owed it to myself and to Marie, my wife. The brass angel dangling on a string from my rearview mirror had once adorned her headstone. I looked to its gleaming wings and sparkling green eyes every time my resolve slipped. It reminded me that Marie had seen something worthwhile in me and had encouraged me to find it for myself.

The previous night, my first on the road had been spent in a state park just a few miles off the highway. I'd been lucky enough to get the last RV site with an electric hook-up. I backed my twenty-six-foot behemoth on wheels into its spot with only a little guidance from the guy camped next door. I say "camped" because that was what everyone else wanted to call it. Camping to me had meant pitching a tent and finding a spot for your sleeping bag that avoided the inevitable rocks and tree roots. It meant relieving yourself in a hole you dug and refilled. It meant building a fire to keep warm, to heat water to rehydrate your supper and to scare away whatever lived in the shadows. I'd been a boy scout for much of my youth. An RV is not camping. It's hauling all the comforts of home to the woods so you can pretend you're roughing it while drinking cold beverages, grilling steaks and sleeping on a soft mattress.

But that first night had been a little claustrophobic. I ate a gas station pizza at my compact table for two, washed my plate in the single stainless-steel basin and showered in a fiberglass broom closet where I had barely enough room to turn around let alone pick up a dropped bar of soap. The piece de resistance was climbing into my bed through the narrow-angled doorway at one corner of the mattress. Though the mattress was actually queen-sized, it felt considerably smaller with it butting up against four walls. It felt like I had squeezed into a cave to hibernate. After watching a little satellite TV on the wall-mounted screen, I was able to shut my mind off enough to fall asleep. The night had gone well except for a few stumbling trips to the toilet.

In the morning, I'd pulled together a cold breakfast and a couple of cups of instant coffee and got back on the road. The sky was gray and the wind had picked up, making my big vehicle sway nautically. I was a newbie behind the wheel of the RV, so I kept my speed well under the limit, much to the irritation of other drivers on the road. I turned my radio off to pay more attention to driving and proceeded through traffic that grew progressively more sparse until I was essentially alone on the road. A fine grit, driven by the wind, started scraping against my windshield. As the sky grew darker, I switched on my head lights. Their beams highlighted the grit in the air, further reducing visibility. I switched the wipers on when large drops of rain began a random assault on my windshield. Before I knew it, the random drops had evolved into a steady thrum, then a downpour. I slowed down and switched my radio back on but got only static. Keeping one eye on the road, I played with the tuner until I got a semi-clear signal with a garbled message about severe storms. I couldn't make out what location the radio was referring to, but I suspected I was there when pea-sized hail started to mix with the rain. I was then crossing a bridge spanning a half-mile wide shallow valley, with no way to turn off or to safely stop.

I could just make out a highway overpass about a mile ahead and sped up to reach its shelter. Pulling under it, I edged as close as I could to the concrete abutment in hopes of reducing the effect of the wind on my sail-like vehicle while giving other vehicles space to get around me. Just as I did, the sky went black in front of me. I was enveloped by a deafening roar, and something slammed against my windshield, leaving a small web of hairline cracks. I unbuckled and rolled out of the driver's seat and under the dashboard. The RV was buffeted by the wind and slammed against the concrete abutment several times but thankfully remained upright.

As I lay curled on the floor, I was struck with the irony that my life could be snuffed out just as I was trying to set it on the right course. I don't usually believe in signs or fate, but at that moment, I had to wonder. Was someone trying to tell me that it was too late, that no amount of exploration or penance would buy me the redemption I sought? I had survived not one but two heart attacks. So why now? I didn't pray...ever. But I almost wished I could.

The worst could only have lasted for two or three minutes at most but it felt like an eternity. When the vehicle stopped rocking and the sky started to lighten, I climbed back into the driver's seat and surveyed the scene through my cracked windshield. The road ahead was scattered with debris, vegetation, soil and pieces of broken wood. It looked impassable, with torn sections of pavement and larger pieces of wreckage. I got out of the RV and walked to the edge of the concrete abutment. The rain had stopped, so I climbed up the slippery hillside to the top of the overpass. From there, I could see that the way I had been driving was blocked for several hundred feet. The other direction was mostly clear. Looking to the north, I caught sight of a funnel cloud, half a mile wide and heading north east. Left behind in its path were the remains of a farm, half of the farmhouse simply gone. The course of the storm led it to a wooded valley. Beyond it, I could make out a water tower, several grain elevators and a church steeple but the rest of what was obviously a town was hidden by the rim of the valley. I could only hope that everyone in the town had already taken shelter.

I slid back down the embankment, returned to my vehicle and climbed behind the wheel. Marie's golden angel swung slowly back and forth from the rearview mirror. somehow sparkling even in the shade of the overpass. My wife died three years ago and this little trinket had graced her tombstone until I accidentally broke it off. It was just about all I had left of her. I was momentarily mesmerized by it. It was not only a reminder of Marie but also of the commitment I had made to her. The posthumous promise to be a better man. I knew I could just drive back the way I had come and continue my rambling. But Marie would have wanted me to do better. She would have wanted me to lend a hand, to put other people first for a change. To be a human being.

I started the engine and backed the RV out from under the overpass to the off ramp I'd passed before taking shelter. I took the exit, drove up to the two-lane roadway above and followed the storm. By the time I'd gotten there, the funnel was nearing the horizon. The grain elevators and the water tower were gone. The church steeple had acquired a precarious tilt. Because the tornado had torn a path of devastation through the treed hillside as it passed, I could now see a little of the town below. What I saw reminded me of the aftermath of war. Buildings leveled or at least torn beyond recognition. Columns of smoke snaked into the air here and there. I was too far away to make out people or vehicles, but I feared that no one could have survived such complete destruction. I didn't know what help I could be, but I was ready to try. Marie would have wanted me to.

I headed down the slope of the overpass and followed the road north, hoping to find a turn-off to the town. But first, I saw the driveway to the ruined farmhouse I'd seen before. I took the right and drove toward the little mound which the house had been built upon. I passed the scoured foundations of what had been several outbuildings. Eventually, debris made it impossible to stay on the gravel driveway so I veered off onto the lawn, taking a circuitous route to as close to the house as I thought safe. I exited the vehicle and walked toward the halved structure that looked like it could collapse at any moment. I called out, "Anyone here?" and waited a moment before stepping closer and calling again. In the wake of the storm, there was absolute silence. I stepped forward to what had been the front porch. Afraid to set foot on what could be unstable, I leaned in and shouted again.

From somewhere inside, I heard a small voice squeal, "We're here, help us, we're here!"

I carefully stepped onto the porch. It creaked but didn't give. Using my elbow, I punched shards of glass from the frame of a shattered window. I climbed inside and found myself in what had been a dining room. The east wall was missing and most of the furnishings had been sucked out. The rest lay shattered and scattered about. Except for an old-fashioned breakfront that stood against the west wall, its glass doors somehow still intact and protecting the treasures inside.

I called out again. "Where are you?"

Another voice sounded. Deeper and more insistent. "We're in the cellar. West corner."

"Can you get out?" I shouted.

"The door is jammed," the voice returned. "Please, my family is in here."

"Okay," I called. "How do I get to you?"

"Stairs. Off the kitchen."

Feeling a surge of heroic fervor, I quickly located a doorway from the dining room. Stepping over what had probably been a family heirloom side table, I headed into the kitchen or what was left of it. A large piece of farm machinery, a plow or manure spreader, how would I know, had been thrown through the back kitchen wall and into the floor, taking most of the cabinetry with it. A small passage led off to the left. I entered and found a door leading to the garage. Opposite it, another opened to a flight of wooden stairs going down to the old cut-stone basement. I stepped down cautiously. The riserless stringer squeaked but it held. I descended slowly, scanning the space. It was undamaged, except of course for the large metal machine hanging down through the ceiling. On landing, it had sheared several of the joists that held the floor above.

I called again. "Okay, I'm in the basement. Where are you?"

"West corner," the man shouted, though he hadn't needed to. I could tell that he was quite nearby.

I noticed a cinder block cube, built into the corner of the cellar. Its metal door was cracked open a few inches. Unfortunately, a large tire on the farm machine was wedged against the door, preventing it from opening further. I pushed against the tire a few times, knowing beforehand it would be futile. I pulled my phone out, but there was no signal.

I spoke into the crack of the door. "A big piece of machinery came through the floor and is blocking the door. I can't budge it. I'm going outside to use my phone to call for help. How many of you are there?"

The answer came from inside. "Four. My wife, our ten-year-old son and six-year-old daughter."

"Anyone hurt," I asked.

"No, not really. Pretty shaken up, though."

"Great," I said. "I'm going up to make the call. I'll be right back."

"Okay," he said. "And... thanks."

I climbed the stairs cautiously and left the house through the kitchen door. My phone still had no signal, though. I scanned the horizon for a cell tower. There was none. If there had ever been one, the storm had probably done it in. Hearing distant sirens coming from several directions toward the devastated town, I suspected that, even if I'd been able to call them, the emergency workers had plenty to do already. I was on my own. I hurried back into the house and down the cellar steps.

"Who's there," the trapped man said.

"It's me," I answered. "My name is Hank."

"Hank, I'm Bob. Is anyone else coming?"

"Fraid not," I said. "I get no signal on my phone. I suspect the cell towers are down. And it looks like the town got hit bad. We can't expect any help from them."

"Oh my God," a woman's voice came from inside. "How bad?"

"'I can't say, but let's focus on one thing at a time. We've got to get you out of there."

"But my mother lives in town," the woman shouted.

Bob interrupted her. "Like the man...like Hank said. First things first."

"Promise me, as soon as we're out of here," Bob's wife sobbed. "We help her. All of us, you too, Hank."

"Yes of course," I said, "But first, we get you guys out of there."

I again scanned the green metal monster in the center of the room. The end that had crashed through the kitchen was buried several inches deep into the dirt floor of the cellar. It was firmly wedged in the ceiling above. There was no way I would be able to move it alone. I explained this to Bob.

"Do you have a sledgehammer or anything I could break into you with?" I asked.

"This place was built to survive a direct hit from a tornado," Bob replied, sounding exasperated. "There's no way you can break through without machinery.

"Okay, then what," I said. I scanned the cube again and caught sight of a detail I'd missed.

"The door hinges," I said. "How are they installed?"

"Foot-long bolts, cemented in," Bob said.

"But the pivot," I interrupted.

"A heavy metal pin comes down through holes in each of the halves of the hinge."

I walked over to the door and examined the three heavy-duty hinges closely. The pins were as thick as my thumb and had even larger flat heads that kept them from falling all the way to the ground. I could see nothing sticking out of the bottom of the hinge.

"Are the pins welded or glued or anything," I asked.

"Course not, otherwise they wouldn't be able to turn," Bob said.

"Sure," I agreed. "Where do you keep your tools?" A plan had formed in my mind.

"Shed," Bob responded. "Outside."

"Where outside?" I asked, holding my breath.

"Just to the east of the house."

"Shit," I said, thinking I kept it under my breath.

"What, what is it?" Bob yelled back.

"Any other place you might have tools," I asked, knowing that anything east of the house was long gone.

"A few screwdrivers and that kind of stuff in the kitchen," Bob's wife said. "Nothin' very heavy duty."

"Okay, I said. "Wait here."

"If you say so," Bob chuckled nervously.

I headed back up the steps and into the kitchen. Though most of the wall cabinets were gone, the bases were still there. I hurried to them and began rifling through the drawers. In the third one I hit the jackpot finding several medium-weight screwdrivers and a pair of pliers. Unfortunately, there was no hammer, so I kept searching until I found a drawer full of cooking utensils and amid the ladles and spatulas rested a meat tenderizer, as close to a hammer as I was likely to find. I grabbed it and the other tools and headed back downstairs.

Hearing my return, Bob shouted, "What are you going to do?"

"Set you free, I hope," I replied. "Now pull the door shut."

He complained but did as I asked. I approached the door and, using the pliers, attempted to pull the middle pin out by its head. I wouldn't budge, which didn't surprise me. Setting the pliers aside, I grasped the biggest of the screwdrivers and the tenderizer. With the screwdriver against the bottom of the pin, which was recessed slightly and gave me good purchase, I struck the handle a firm blow with the makeshift hammer. The pin didn't budge but the plastic handle of the screwdriver shattered. I tried to grip the shaft but, when I struck it with the tenderizer, it slipped in my hand. I dropped it and examined the other tools. One of the screwdrivers had a wooden handle but it wasn't as thick as the first one. I had no choice though and positioned it at the base of the pin. I stuck it more gently. The pin didn't move but the screwdriver remained intact. I hit it several more times, each a little harder, until the head of the pin started separating itself from the top of the hinge. A dozen more blows and the pin popped out. With similar effort the remaining pins were also removed.

"Alright, Bob," I said. "Now push on the door at the hinge side while I pull on the knob. I want to get it off the hinges and drop it on its side. Got that?"

"Got it," he said and before I could get hold of the knob, he had already pushed the door loose on the other side. I pulled the knob, but now the door was jammed with all of its weight on the knob side. I instructed him to push from inside while I stepped back, not wanting the heavy door to land on me. I could hear him grunting on the other side until the door burst from its frame and landed with a loud thud on the earthen floor. With some effort working together, Bob and I were able to push the door to the side, clearing the tire that had blocked it. It fell to the floor, raising a cloud of dust and a round of cheers.

I saw Bob for the first time. He couldn't have been much beyond his early thirties. Stocky, unshaven, and dressed in a flannel shirt and coveralls, he looked like an image out of a Grant Wood painting. He stepped out of the storm shelter and while I was offering my hand to shake, he enveloped me in a crushing bear hug. Uncomfortable with such spontaneity, I froze in place.

"I don't know how to thank you," he said. I tried to pull away, nodding self-consciously. Then Mrs. Bob, whose name turned out to be Charlotte, joined in the embrace. She was a trim redhead in jeans and a T-shirt. The kids ignored us and ran from the shelter and up the stairs. A second later, we heard a scream.

"Dad, Mom,' the little girl screamed. "The house."

Bob and Charlotte released me and bounded upstairs after the kids. I followed and found them all standing frozen in the dining room. I reached my hand stiffly to Bob's shoulder.

"I'm so sorry," I said.

"Sorry, hell," Bob chuckled, "We're alive, ain't we. This is just stuff."

"So, let's get going," Charlotte said.

"What?" I said, confused and mystified.

"To town," she said, pulling the kids through the dining room to the window I had used to get in. "We got to check on my mom."

Bob and I followed, and we all piled into my RV. I backed around and drove out to the highway, turned right out of the driveway and headed toward town, following Bob's directions. About a mile down the highway, we turned right again at a sign that read Amber Creek, one mile. We descended slowly into a river valley, passing the remains of a trio of grain elevators. In the passenger seat, Bob whispered, "Holy shit." We crossed a small river and entered a war zone of flattened houses and upended cars. A few people dug through the debris listlessly in apparent shock. After a left turn and then a right, we started to see standing homes, windblown but intact. Charlotte pointed out her mom's home, and I pulled up at the curbless side of the road. Charlotte burst from the vehicle and made a beeline for the front door. Before she reached it, the door opened, and a trim gray-haired woman stepped out and pulled Charlotte into her arms. Seconds later, the two kids were beside them, all embracing and all crying.

Bob leaned across me and shouted out the one window, "You all stay here. We're gonna check out the rest of the town." He pulled back to his seat and looked at me. "Let's go."

I followed instructions and got back on the road. After turning left at the next block, we started seeing heavy debris again and then complete devastation. It was like a bulldozer had gone through. There were intact houses with minimal damage and then, bang, there was nothing but rubble for the next several blocks ahead and to the right and left as far as the town limits. There were people everywhere, pulling up bits of broken wood and metal, digging for survivors. I pulled the RV to the side of the road, and Bob exited.

I joined him.

CHAPTER **TWO**

Bob and I stood awed for a few minutes. Where to start? The wreckage extended two or three blocks to the north and south and as far east as we could see. The mostly wood frame structures were flattened or scattered. The storm had crossed what appeared to have been the town square. On its south and east sides stood lines of early twentieth-century brick and stone buildings, windows shattered, and signage ripped but otherwise intact. The north and west sides of the square hadn't been so lucky. Half-collapsed walls and stripped foundations framed those sides. On the northeast corner stood the remains of a large stone church, its roof gone, windows shattered and a steeple leaning precariously, the belfry clipped unevenly away. Beside the church was an open space hidden by a low stone wall. To the north was what remained of a large brick building, the twisted metal trusses suggesting the wide span required of a gymnasium. To the east of the open area, a nearly flattened structure, probably of mid-twentieth-century construction, was barely standing except for concrete block towers at two corners that I suspected were stairwells.

In the center of the town square, a group of people had gathered inside a large octagonal wrought iron gazebo that had withstood the storm heroically. We headed in that direction. Sirens sounded in the distance.

In the gazebo, we found two police officers, a cluster of volunteer firemen, and an assortment of other people. Bob extended his hand to the guy who looked in charge. "Dan," he said. "This is Hank. What can we do to help?"

"You're safe!" Dan, a stocky, balding man in an ill-fitting uniform, shouted, wrapping his arm around Bob's shoulder. "Charlotte and the kids?"

"They're fine, thanks to this guy," Bob said, planting his free hand on my shoulder. "We were trapped in the storm shelter, but he got us out. 'Course, the house is a total loss."

"Sorry to hear that," Dan turned to me. "But thanks to you. Bob here is pretty special to us around town. I'm Dan Gilmore, the police chief. That sounds more impressive than it is." He shook my hand vigorously.

"Hank, Hank Pressman," I said. "I was just passing by on the highway when the storm hit. I saw what a mess it made and hoped I could help."

"That's good of you," Dan said. "We can use your help." He shook my hand and then turned back to the crowd in the gazebo. "OK folks. I've got a group walking the northeast side of town, surveying the damage and initiating rescues. The phones are out but I've got a dozen or so walkie-talkies. I distributed half of them, and the rest is in that box over there. I need a group to take the southeast and another to head out to the hospital. Thank God it wasn't hit, and it's got emergency power. We need to help the staff set up for casualties. What do you say?"

The crowd split into groups, grabbed walkies, and headed out. I tapped Dan's shoulder. "Hey, where's the hospital? I'm a doctor."

"You're shitting me," he said. "Bob, show him the way then get your ass back here."

Bob grabbed my arm. "Let's go. Anybody else going to the hospital, come with me." We took a walkie from the box, jogged back to my RV with two other men and a woman in EMT jackets. In a town this small, I knew they had to all be volunteers with other jobs, and with families of their own. They inspired me and made me feel a little guilty at the same time. I had never been as community-minded as them. Maybe this would be my chance to start.

We all climbed into the RV and Bob directed me around the town square, north through three blocks of debris and into a relatively unscathed residential neighborhood. The hospital was a long, low one-story modern structure with open fields behind it.

"There it is," Bob said. "Amber Creek Regional. That's the new building. Old one was one of those piles of brick on the square. I'll take you around to the emergency entrance and introduce you."

We couldn't drive to the entrance because of a dozen or so cars haphazardly parked around it. I stopped the RV and, jumping out, told Bob to drive it back to the town square. I showed him the walkie. "I'll call you when I need a lift." The other three piled out and Bob drove away while we made my way to the open doors of the ER. Inside was chaos, injured people on the floor and in chairs with desperate family members calling for help from the few staff members I could see. Two of the people with me scattered into the crowd and started interviewing and assessing the injured. One took me by the arm. "I'll take you to Doctor Sparks," she said.

I followed her through a set of swinging doors into the treatment area, where each curtained bay held one or more people, sitting, standing, or on a gurney. In the third of four bays, a tall blond woman in her forties and dressed in a blood-spattered white coat stood over a supine form. The woman leading me walked in and said, "Doctor Sparks."

The Doctor turned and I could see the form on the table, a young man with his pants torn open and a long jagged gash to his groin. "Sandy, I'm kind of busy," she said.

My escort didn't back down. "I'm sorry, but this guy is a doctor, and he wants to help."

Doctor Sparks turned to me. "Really. Well, jump right in."

"Let me explain," I said. "My skills are sort of specific. But I was good with suturing in med school, and I can do the basics. Free you up for the more complicated stuff."

"Ok," she said. "I just finished closing this man's femoral artery. We've got fluids going and all he needs is to have this wound stitched up. You up to that?"

"Sure," I said. "I'll need to clean up and gown, then I'm on it."

Doctor Sparks turned back to her patient. Over her shoulder, she said, "Sandy, show him to the dressing room." My escort showed me the locker area where I could wash up and get into a gown. Then she left, diving into the emergency.

I returned to the treatment room and found a suture kit spread out on a tray beside the gurney when a very anxious young man lay, his groin draped and covered with a surgical towel.

"Hi," I said. "I'm Doctor Pressman." I hoped that my anxiety was not too evident on my face.

"Hi, I'm Jeremy," the young man said, voice quavering. "I heard you talking to Doc Ellie. Have you ever done this kind of thing before?"

I smiled and nodded. "Do you have any allergies?"

"Ah, no."

"Okay then," I said, "let's get this show on the road."

I carefully donned plastic gloves, picked up a syringe marked lidocaine and began injecting around the open wound, which had already been thoroughly cleaned and sterilized by Dr. Sparks. After a few minutes to let the medication take effect, I opened a packet and removed the needle and attached suture using a needle holder that looked like an off center, very dull pair of scissors. I took a deep breath before punching the needle into the flap of skin that I was holding steady with forceps. Jeremy didn't twitch and neither did I. As I continued, pulling the suture through and then into the skin on the other side of the wound, the technique came back to me and so did my confidence. An hour later, the wound was closed and clean. I was sure Doctor Sparks could have done the job in considerably less time but in that hour I'd freed her up to see at least half a dozen other patients. So, all things considered, I was doing a pretty good job. I felt like a doctor again. Of course, I would have to eventually admit to being unlicensed, but that could wait until the emergency had passed.

I spent the next thirty-six or so hours remembering all the emergency care I'd learned in med school and internship. I sutured and dressed wounds, did neurologic exams and triaged till I could barely stand. Finally, every patient had been discharged, admitted to a bed or helicoptered to a bigger hospital. I'd finally sat down for a cold sandwich and a cup of coffee, thinking only of getting to bed when I felt a tap on my shoulder. I turned to see an equally exhausted Doctor Sparks. "Can I join you?" she said.

"Of course." I pushed out the chair opposite me with my foot. That was as gentlemanly a gesture as I had left in me. She set her meager meal down on the table and collapsed into the chair.

"I really need this," she said and then extended her hand. "Sorry, I've been so brusque. I'm Ellie Sparks."

I took her hand. "I'm Hank Pressman. And don't worry. I wasn't offended, just glad to be of some help."

"You were a Godsend," she said. "I don't know how I can thank you enough."

"Well, you could let me eat my sandwich," I smiled. "I'm starved".

She chuckled, in a surprisingly sweet tone and dug into her own meal.

Between bites, she said, "So where the heck did you come from?"

"Sounds corny, but I was just passing through."

"Cowboy Hank, huh?"

"Sort of."

"You said something about your particular skills. What are they exactly?"

"I'm a shrink," I said. "Or technically, I was one."

"Retired," she said, taking another bite.

"Not...exactly," I said, focusing my attention on my coffee cup.

"Oh," she said, drawing the word out. "I remember. You're that guy in the murder case, the other side of the state."

"Guilty," I said, holding my hands up. "I had nothing to do with the murder. I was what you might call a pawn, a dupe. But I lost my license over it so technically I'm not a doctor anymore,"

"Oh, well. You were a doctor today and I thank you for that," she said more guardedly than before. I was familiar with the change that came over people when they figured out who I was. I just forced a grin in response and we both finished our meals silently.

Meal completed, Ellie rose and dropped her paper cup and sandwich wrapper in the trash. She turned back to me and thanked me again.

"Wait," I said, pulling the walkie-talkie from my pocket. "Do you know how to use this? I've got to call for my ride."

"Sorry but I suppose you push one of those buttons and hope for the best." She smiled and started to leave but turned back. "Or maybe I can give you a lift, after I've cleaned up and changed."

"That would be great. I could use a shower myself."

She smiled stiffly and led me back to the locker room. "The men's shower is on the left,' she said then, after grabbing a change of clothes out of her locker, she headed to the right. I got my own clothes and headed to the left. I took the most welcome shower in history, knowing what waited for me in the RV. I could have stood in the warm downpour for an hour, but I knew Ellie would be waiting for me. I dried and dressed and met her at the lockers. She led me out of a back door to her car and drove me silently back to the town square so I could return my walkie-talkie. I climbed out of the car and thanked her. As I walked away, she called back to me.

"Hey, Hank. I'm sorry if I've been...aloof. I do appreciate what you've done. Maybe we can get together tomorrow at the hospital and talk. That is if you plan to hang around. License or no, I could use your help."

"Sure," I said. She showed me a minimalist smile and I watched her drive away, thinking about a woman in ways I hadn't thought about any woman in a long time. Eventually, I turned and walked to the gazebo.

CHAPTER THREE

I met Dan Gilmore back at the Gazebo, which was now enclosed in a clear tarp and furnished with picnic tables on which were lamps and computers powered by a gas generator on the lawn outside. This had become the base of operations as the city hall and police station, both on the west side of the town square, had been irreparably damaged in the storm. Trucks and tractor trailers with state logos were parked around the perimeter of the gazebo. It was apparent that, while I was working at the hospital, a legitimate disaster relief effort had been pulled together here in the town square. Amber Creek was on the mend but there was obviously a long way to go.

Dan looked like he'd gotten as little sleep since the storm as I had but he was able to give me a quick rundown on the recovery efforts. He was relieved that only three fatalities had been confirmed thus far. An elderly man who'd lost his way getting to the storm shelter behind his house. A young mother who had been rushing home to her children. Fortunately, they had already been safely ushered into the basement by their terrified father. And third was a young woman who had yet to be identified. She'd been found face down under several loose pieces of debris. As sad as these deaths were, Dan reminded me that things could have been so much worse. He again thanked me for my help and had a cop drive me to Charlotte's mother's house where I found my RV carefully parked. I debated just getting in the RV and collapsing in bed but decided to check on Bob's family first. I walked around the house, past a rumbling generator to the front porch, knocked on his mother-in-law's door and was answered by Bob's 6-year-old daughter, Sara. She greeted me with a smile too big for her face and a bear hug that wrapped around my thighs. She seemed little traumatized by the tornado. I had never worked with kids, never wanted 'em. Cramped my style, I guess. Besides, I was never very comfortable around them, but there was something about her ease and innocent delight that warmed me.

Sara kept hold of me even when Charlotte came to the door and took me into her arms as well. I was surprised at the tears that formed in the corner of my eyes. I assumed it was a symptom of my tiredness. After the embrace broke up, Sara led me into the living room and Charlotte called into the kitchen. The gray-haired lady I'd seen two days before appeared at the door and there was another hug before Charlotte could even introduce me.

"This is my mom, Irene," Charlotte said. "And Mom, this is Hank Pressman our savior."

Irene was barely five feet tall, just a little full in the waist but looked otherwise fit. She stepped back. "I know who he is, silly." She looked deeply into my eyes, hers moist and wide. "How can I ever thank you? You're my savior too. You don't know how much I worried until you brought them home to me."

"Thanks," I said. "But it was no big deal, really. I did what anyone would do. "

Irene just smiled knowingly. "Let me get you something to eat."

"No thanks, I ate at the hospital. All I want is to get to bed. Do you know where the keys to the RV are?"

Charlotte jumped in. "In the ignition. You're in the country now, Hank."

Irene grabbed my hands in hers. "And you're not sleeping in that bus out there. I've got a soft, warm bed for you right here."

"Oh thanks," I said. "But all my stuff is in the RV. I'll be just fine there."

"Are you sure," Charlotte said. "There's plenty of room."

"No, but thanks. By the way, where are Bob and the boy?"

Charlotte's smile melted. "They're up at the farm. Checking on the animals, if there are any left, and ...well seeing what survived. We think the house is a total loss but who knows."

"I'm so sorry," I said.

"Don't be," Charlotte said, forcing the corners of her mouth up again. "Like Bob said, we're all alive. The rest is just stuff."

"And they can all stay with me as long as they need to," Irene said. "I love havin' 'em around."

"You're lucky to have each other," I said, with a touch of longing. "Now, I better get to bed before I fall over."

Irene called after me as I walked out of the door. "When you wake up, I want you at my kitchen table for breakfast, no matter what time it is. Got it?"

"Yes ma'am," I smiled and headed to my vehicle. Once inside, I stepped into the cab to check on my keys. They were there, as promised. Marie's angel caught my eye again. I wondered if she would be proud of me for what I'd accomplished in the last two days. I wondered if I had started making up for my past. I hoped so and felt a little proud that I had. I pulled the shades, stripped to my underwear and dropped onto the bed falling asleep almost instantly.

I woke up sometime later and peeked under the blinds beside the bed. It was dark outside, and no lights were visible in Irene's house. Checking my watch showed that I had slept for nearly twelve hours. It was four AM. I got out of bed and started a pot of coffee. While it brewed, I washed up and shaved for the first time in nearly three days. I dressed, poured myself a mug of coffee and stepped outside. The sky above was clear and for the first time in my life I could actually see the swath of whitewash crossing from the horizon in the east and fading into the western sky high above. The Milky Way. Thousands of points of light sparkled above and below it like frozen fireworks. In the city, only a few hundred stars were visible. This was magic to me, and I sat on my doorstep for nearly an hour, sipping my coffee and drinking in the wonder of the universe.

When my stomach started to rumble, I stepped back inside and dug a box of pop tarts out of the cabinet. I only allowed myself to eat one pastry as I knew that Irene would be up and preparing that promised breakfast very soon. I'd only just met her, but I knew that breakfast would not be a bowl of cold cereal and an orange juice. I stepped outside again with my tart and a refill of the coffee. A vague glow was just starting over the hills to the east and one light had come on in the house. I decided to take a stroll before breakfast. The neighborhood around was made up of simple frame homes like Irene's, all at least seventy-five years old. Yards were well maintained and houses in good repair, as far as I could tell in the dim light. I wandered into the path the tornado had taken, and everything changed. I could see clear to the town square several blocks away. My view should have been obstructed by more homes and possibly businesses. Unfortunately, nothing blocked my view now. The gazebo in the town square was brightly lit . With no street lights, I could easily discern smaller pools of light where desperate searching continued. Dan Gilmore had told me about the three known casualties. Could there be more yet to be discovered? I certainly hoped not. I resolved to make my way back to the hospital after breakfast and lend a hand in any way I could. As long as Ellie Sparks was willing to overlook my history.

I made my way back to Irene's place, a little circuitously, considering my lack of familiarity with the town. Fortunately, I'd left a light on in my RV making it easier to recognize. I stepped into the vehicle, flipped the light off to save my battery and walked to the house. What I suspected to be the kitchen light was on and I walked to the door on that side and knocked. Irene showed up almost instantly and welcomed me in. "Did you sleep well?" she asked.

"You bet, and I had a little walk around the neighborhood. It's nice around here, or at least it must have been."

"We think so," she said. "Now pour yourself some coffee or juice and plant yourself at the table. How do you like your eggs?"

"However, you make 'em will be great," I responded, taking a chair.

As Irene worked at the stove, I took a good look at her. She was dressed in snug-fitting slacks and a floral blouse. Her limbs were firm and her back straight. Except for the gray hair, she certainly didn't look like a grandmother. While she worked, she talked about her family with obvious pride and affection. When she asked about my family, she was disappointed to hear that I had none. Then she said, "Well, you have one now."

Irene fed me like a king, bacon, eggs, toast and hash browns. And I mean real hash browns, not those pasty things you get at restaurants. These were brown and crispy on both sides, onions scattered throughout and a slice of American cheese on top. As I dug in, other members of the family wandered into the kitchen, said their good mornings and started into their own breakfasts. Bob was the last to arrive, wrapped in an oversized robe, unshaven and looking like he should be going to bed instead of waking up. I rose to greet him and shake his hand. "Your mother-in-law puts on a good feed," I said.

"Like always," he sat down at the table. "How were things at the hospital?"

"Hectic, but I felt really great about being there. We did some real good."

"Well, thanks for that," he said, staring in on the plate of food Irene had placed before him.

"And the farm," I inquired cautiously. "How did it look?"

He sighed and put his fork down. "It's a total loss. I found the cattle or at least parts of them. Not a single survivor. An equipment shed is all that's left so at least I still have a tractor, and equipment for planting."

"What about that thing that came through the kitchen?" I asked.

"Oh, that. A manure spreader I'd left out by the barn. It wasn't in very good shape to start with so it's not much of a loss."

"I'm sorry about everything else. Are you insured?"

"Yeah, but that never covers everything. We'll get by, though. We got each other." He smiled half-heartedly and wrapped his arm around Charlotte, who sat beside him. I envied the warmth and hope they shared. I could have had that with my wife if only I had made the effort.

Finished cooking, Irene brought her plate to the table and sat down. "You all are half done with your food, but I didn't hear Grace from any of you. Put your forks down right now." We all followed orders, and Irene nodded to Bobbie, the ten-year-old who led a prayer of thanks. I just lowered my head and thought of other things. Prayer has never been my cup of tea. Besides, I would have had trouble coming up with much gratitude, considering the circumstances.

After breakfast, I insisted on helping Irene with the clean-up while Bob ran upstairs to shave, shower, and change his clothes and Charlotte herded the children upstairs to brush their teeth.

Irene filled the sink with soapy water and handed me a dish towel. As she washed and rinsed the dishes, she handed each one to me. I dried and stacked them on the counter, having no idea where they belonged. After more moments of silence than I suspected Irene capable of, she cleared her throat. Without looking at me she said, "Hank, I want you to know that I know who you are."

I responded with a vague "Oh?"

"I read the papers, Bob and Charlotte don't have time or interest for that matter but I do. What happened was terrible. But from my reading, you weren't completely to blame."

"Completely?" I inquired.

Irene set her skillet into the hot water and turned to me. "From the way I read it, you were sort of duped. I was a little surprised that a man with your training could have been fooled but I guess you're only human."

"Well, thanks for that, anyway," I said uncomfortably.

Irene picked the skillet back out of the water and started scouring it with a soap pad. "I don't mean anything by that. You seem like a decent guy, Hank. I know that papers can be pretty biased. I just wanted you to know that I wasn't going to hold anything against you. What you did for my family outweighs whatever else you've done in the past." She turned to me and smiled with pinched lips. For once, I was at a loss for words.

Bob came downstairs, dressed in jeans and a plaid shirt looking more alive than he had at breakfast. "Ready to go?" he asked.

I looked at Irene, my eyebrows at full staff. "Go ahead," she said. "I'll finish up." She took the towel from me, dried her hands, and placed them on my shoulders. "And thanks again." Uncharacteristically, I leaned down and gave her a gentle kiss on the cheek. "No," I said. "Thank you."

Bob drove me to the hospital. He didn't have a lot to say on the way. I'm sure that thoughts of what the future held for him and his family weighed heavily on him. I couldn't imagine having to start all over. Then again, maybe I could.

.

CHAPTER FOUR

A police car was out front of the hospital when we arrived. I said goodbye to Bob and walked in the front door this time. The woman at the reception desk directed me to Dr. Sparks' office. There I found Ellie and Dan Gilmore. I tapped on the door frame and Ellie invited me in. Dan stood and grasped my hand again. "Hey, Doc, great to see ya' and thanks again for pitching in." Ellie remained seated, her expression unreadable.

"It was my pleasure," I said. "I came back to see what else I might be able to help with."

Dan turned to Ellie. "What do ya' think?"

She forced a smile. "Hank and I will need to discuss it later. Let's get back to the matter at hand, shall we."

"Sure," he said and pulled out the chair beside him, gesturing to me. "Take a seat Doc. Three heads have got to be better than two." Ellie nodded so I took a seat.

"We were discussing how lucky we were," continued Dan. "Only three casualties. Out of over six hundred residents. That's got to be a miracle."

"I'm not much for miracles, but it is incredible for sure," I said. "What do ya suppose explains it?"

"We had a near-miss tornado 'bout seven years ago. Scared folks and everybody started building storm shelters. And then there's the new warning siren. It was on top of city hall. Went off just a few minutes before the storm hit but that was enough, I guess."

"And the casualties?" I inquired.

"Like I told you before, two were local. Families already claimed them. The third is a mystery. That's why I'm here. I was hoping that I could get some pictures of the remains and show 'em around town."

"I can help you with that, Chief," Elie said, pushing a folder across her desk. "We got several pictures, some x-rays and a few lab tests. You're welcome to these copies."

Dan thanked her and opened the file. I looked with him at a picture of a thin blond woman who couldn't have been more than twenty. She was dressed in jeans and a T-shirt that were dirty and ill-fitting but otherwise intact, with no rips or embedded debris. Her arms were thin and bruised. Her face gaunt. Dan flipped to the next picture and shook his head pensively. The same woman was shown naked with small towels covering her groin and breasts. The image was arresting. Her prominent ribs and hips suggested starvation, perhaps anorexia. Dan flipped to the next picture, a whole body x-ray. Obviously, the hospital didn't have the best equipment for such a shot, so the image was fuzzy, being pieced together from several separate shots. Even so, I could see apparent fractures of both upper arms that appeared fresh. Several other partially healed fractures were suggested, including injuries to several ribs, the left wrist and the right leg just above the ankle. In addition, the large bones appeared faded inside darker edges. It looked like Osteopenia, loss of bone mass.

"She looks like a concentration camp victim," Dan said, closing the file.

"Or maybe an anorectic," I said. I'd treated many anorectic patients in my career but something about this image was different. "Is the body still here?"

'Yes," Ellie said. "We have a small morgue downstairs. She's there in a refrigerated room."

"Could I see her," I asked. Ellie displayed obvious reluctance until Dan said, "Yeah. Let's take a look. This one's a head scratcher and I bet there's a family out there wondering about the poor thing. I know I would be if it was my daughter."

Ellie nodded and rose from her chair. "This way." She led us out of her office to a stairwell and down one flight. We stepped out into a high-ceilinged, unfinished hall with pipes and wire conduits overhead. At the end of the hall was a metal door with a keypad beside it. Dr. Sparks keyed a code and the door popped open. We followed her inside. There were several lab tables with glassware, computer terminals and white boxy lab machines on them. To the back of the room was another door with another keypad. Ellie entered the code and we stepped into a narrow, very cold room with two metal shelves, one on each side. On the right shelf was a figure covered in a heavy white sheet. Dr. Sparks pulled the sheet back. "This is her,"

Dave stepped back suddenly, bumping the shelf on the opposite side of the room. "Looks different, in person," he said.

The body looked worse than it had in the picture. More drawn, more gaunt. Pale except for prominent bruises on her upper arms, legs and abdomen. The arm bruises were fainter and bluer while the others had started to yellow. She appeared wasted with her flesh pulled tightly over her bones. I stepped to the shelf and looked to Ellie. "May I?"

"So, you're a pathologist now?" she said, sarcastically handing me a pair of latex gloves. "Ok, but be careful. The BCI people don't want her messed with. They plan to pick her up later today." BCI, the Bureau of Criminal Investigation, was our state's version of the FBI. I'd dealt with them once or twice before. They were thorough and conscientious.

"I'll be careful," I said, slipping the gloves on. "Just wanted to check a few things. I lifted the dead girl's right hand and examined it carefully. Next, I checked the left. Her fingernails were broken. There was either dirt or dried blood under what was left of them. Her palms were scratched and her finger tips badly abraded. Interestingly, the backs of her fingers were pretty normal looking. I laid her hand gently beside her. And stepped toward her head, opening her mouth and peering inside. Her mouth was a mess, dry and crusted. Small red spots were scattered inside. Her gums were red and swollen. Her teeth were stained but otherwise intact. I moved to her eyes, opening one at a time. The sclera and conjunctiva were red-speckled like her mouth. Finally, I looked at her scalp. Again, the red spots that I now realized were thinly scattered on much of her face. Her hair was brittle and sparse, with dimpled pores where follicles should have been. I stepped back and looked at Ellie again.

"I'm sure you've examined her. Any ideas?"

"Well, obviously, she's cachectic. Maybe cancer. I considered anorexia nervosa, too."

"English, please," Dan interjected.

"I mean, she looks starved, wasted away. Cancer can do that."

"Anorexia nervosa is a mental disorder," I added. "Basically, self-starving for psychological reasons. Her knuckles aren't scarred though and her teeth are intact. Damage there is often a sign of purging, that's forcing oneself to vomit. There is also a restrictive version of the illness where people limit their food intake to very small portions of often unusual or monotonous foods."

"If she was seeing a shrink about that, it had to have been out of town," Dan said.

"I don't remember treating anyone with those symptoms myself," Ellie said. "And, at present, I'm the only doctor in town." She'd inserted a touch of sarcasm in that last bit.

"Sometimes anorectic patients can't or won't recognize their need for help. It's usually the family that ends up bringing them in," I said. "Did you notice the bruises and the petechiae?"

"P what?" Dan asked.

"Small points of bleeding in the tissues," Ellie said. "And yes, they did bother me. That's part of why I asked Dan to call BCI. I'm no expert, but this looks like an abused woman to me."

"A runaway, maybe," Dan said. "That would explain why no one recognized her."

Ellie covered the body again. "Well, there's nothing we can do to help this poor soul anymore but I have a lot of live patients that could use some attention upstairs. Unless there's something else you want to look at." Dan and I shook our heads and followed Ellie out of the basement. Dan said goodbye and headed to his squad car. Ellie led me back to her office.

"Pretty observant," she said, taking a seat behind her desk.

"Thanks, but I *am* a physician," I said.

"You were a physician," she said.

"They took my license, not my MD."

"Be that as it may, I'm not sure what role you can play here at the hospital."

"That didn't seem to be an issue yesterday," I said with an edge.

"Don't go there," she snapped. "You should have been up front with me. You could have put my license on the line. And that of the hospital. We are all this town has."

I felt a twinge of guilt. "Okay, you're right. I should have been up front. But honestly, I didn't even think of it at the time. There was a crisis and you needed help."

"You're right, too." she admitted. "The question now is whether I can allow you to help out."

"You still need the help, right?"

"God, yes," she said.

"So let me talk to your hospital big wigs and we can work something out."

"Can't. None of them are around since the storm. They're no help in an emergency around here but they all wanted to volunteer in town."

"So, if I help out while they're gone and you don't admit to knowing about my record once they get back, I'll be the only one with his nuts on the grill."

Her eyebrows went up over a wry smile.

"Oops," I said. "I've got a potty mouth when I'm worked up."

"Don't worry, I am too," she said. "So, we have nearly thirty patients in a ten bed hospital. Let's get to work." We walked out of her office and into a full day of follow up visits. There were two nurses and several aides so Ellie divided us into teams and we visited every patient, at least once. Several times, I had to ask for Ellie's expertise but all in all I was pretty pleased with how doctory I could be. I hadn't done primary care in years but it had come back and was surprisingly satisfying. At lunch the teams gathered in the nurse's station, sharing reports and gossip and eating what was left of the previously cold sandwiches and soda from machines by the break room. Due to the power outage, only essential equipment was operating and that didn't include vending machines. The cafeteria staff, what there was of it, was too busy feeding the patients and making meals for the community to indulge us.

Ellie and I sat at a desk at the back of the nurse's station, working on charts while eating. I watched her while her attention was focused on the records. She was pretty in the way that they used to say a woman was handsome. Her blond hair was just starting to show random strands of gray. Tiny wrinkles collected under her eyes. Her skin was tight and clear across the rest of her face and reflected the fluorescent ceiling lights. A few faint freckles dotted the bridge of her nose. It was a good face. When Ellie turned to me and smiled, I felt my own face flush. Was I embarrassed, like a school kid caught admiring a pretty teacher? I took a bite of my sandwich by way of cover and got back to work on the chart in front of me.

After lunch we finished hospital rounds, a few minor ER visits and reams of paperwork. Dan had popped in about three in the afternoon to let us know that the BCI people had come to take the body from the morgue. Ellie printed up a set of records for them and ran through her impressions before they left. Afterwards, I dictated my hospital notes to Ellie so she could enter them in the chart under her name. A little unethical but I doubted anyone would call us on it. By the time we were done it was nearly six o: clock. As we left the hospital, Ellie turned to me. "I should thank you. You were a great help."

"My pleasure," I said. "Really, I enjoyed it."

"I was a little surprised that a psychiatrist could act like a *real doctor*," she said with a sly grin.

"Like riding a bike. It all comes back, more or less."

"So let me feed you, as my way of saying thanks," she said.

"Sure, I could use a good meal. Got any five-star restaurants in town?"

"The closest we have to that was Andy's Bar on the square. It's taking a little time off right now." Her wry laugh warmed me. "There's a bar up on the highway and the nearest restaurant guaranteed to not give you food poisoning is at least twenty miles away."

"I'm pretty sure Irene is making a pot of chili and some cornbread tonight. I'm invited and I doubt she'd turn you away."

"Better not, unless she wants to find a new doctor," she said. "Let's stop off at my place for a six pack of beer to add to the repast."

"Okay," I said. "But I'll stick with soda. I'm a friend of Bill's."

"A what?"

"Oh, that, ah, means I'm an alcoholic," I said sheepishly.

"Oh, sorry," she said. "I guess I should have known. My husband was one too. I'll skip the beer." After an uncomfortable pause she pointed to a blue, aging Toyota Corolla. "That's my car. I'll give you a lift."

We got in and drove wordlessly west through the debris zone to Irene's house. The tension had broken and I was glad of it. I was starting to like this lady.

CHAPTER FIVE

Irene welcomed Ellie with open arms. That was her way, but especially with a guest she already knew and admired so well. Then she put us to work setting the table as she stirred an aromatic pot on the stove and removed a cast iron skillet of cornbread from the oven. She called the family with a surprisingly forceful "Come and get it!" through the open window over the sink. Bobbie and Sara burst through the door, doffed their shoes and headed to the bathroom to wash their hands. Well trained, I thought, at least at Grandma's house. Bob and Charlotte strolled in from the living room. Charlotte pulled a pitcher of lemonade from the fridge and filled glasses around the table. Under Irene's supervision, Bob set the soup pot in the center of the table. Then the kids returned, displaying their damp palms and everyone took seats, Irene last, having delivered the cornbread to the table with accompanying honey and butter. Irene stood to ladle chili into everyone's bowl while Charlotte cut the bread and passed warm wedges around the table. We all prepared to dig in but were again stopped by Irene's insistence on a prayer. Sara recited Grace with a surprisingly good rendition for a six-year-old. Irene finally signaled us to dig in and we complied.

The chili was hot and spicy and Bob forgot to blow on it, burning his mouth. He grabbed the lemonade and took a swig to douse the burning sensation. Relieved he set the glass down. "The lemonade is great," he said," but I could use something a little more potent. How 'bout you, Hank?"

I looked at him blankly for a second then said a reserved "No... thanks, I'm fine." My expression must have communicated more than I realized, judging by Irene's. She cocked her head slightly then turned to Bob. "How about after supper," she said. "It's your turn to help with clean up and I don't want you breaking any of my nice dishes again." Bob lifted his glass to Irene and took another sip, obviously chastened.

Sara, looking across the table at Ellie and I, changed the topic in typical six-year-old fashion. "Hey, are you two married now?"

"No," Ellie said. "Just friends."

"Well, you should get married," Sara went on. "Then you could have a baby and I could help take care of it."

I looked at Ellie and smiled. "Well, she has a point."

Charlotte, obviously embarrassed, admonished her daughter, "Sara, mind your own business and eat your chili."

After an uncomfortable pause, Irene turned to Ellie. "How are things up at the hospital?"

"Oh, coming along," Ellie said. "With Hank's help, we've been able to take care of everyone pretty well. Of course, the worst injuries were helicoptered out."

"Any idea how those folks are doing," Charlotte asked.

"Yeah," Ellie responded. "I got an update from the university hospital this afternoon. There are still a few folks in critical condition but everyone is at least stable. No more casualties, fortunately,"

"Well thank the Lord for that," Irene chimed in.

"I guess that gives us another reason to thank Hank," Bob said solemnly raising his glass to me this time. "And, of course, you too, Doc," he added, swinging his toast her way.

"And how about the farm," I asked Bob while all of us dug into our meals.

Bob's gaze dropped to his bowl. "Not good," he said. "I called my insurance man. We have to get in line to meet with him. I'm hoping he can help, otherwise, we're pretty much screwed,"

"Language, Bob!" Irene and Charlotte said in unison.

"Don't worry," 10-year-old Bobbie said. "I've heard worse."

"Well, I'm sorry about your loss," I said. "I don't know you very well, but you seem like the kind of guy who lands on his feet."

"Hope you're right," he said.

"We don't know much about you either, Hank," Charlotte said. Irene looked my way and smiled conspiratorially.

"Not much to tell," I said. "I'm a retired psychiatrist from the other side of the state. I've got no family, so I decided it was time to explore a little while I still could."

"Single," Charlotte said, her eyes darting between me and Ellie.

"No," I cleared my throat. "Well technically yes. My wife passed away."

"Oh, I'm sorry," Charlotte said.

"No, don't be," I said. "You didn't know."

There was another uncomfortable silence before Ellie broke it. "Charlotte, you never told me how you and Bob met."

"We met at community college. He was a big city boy."

"Big city compared to Amber Creek," Bob interjected. "I'm from a town of about thirty-thousand, fifty miles south of here. That's where the college is. I was studying criminal justice and Charlotte was in accounting."

"So, how did you end up here," I asked. "And farmers no less."

"I found I really didn't like criminal justice much. Part of me always liked the idea of farming. And then, to make a long story short," Bob said, reaching for Charlotte's hand, "this lady won my heart and changed all my plans on me. She wanted to come home to help out while her dad was sick, so we moved here to take over the farm. Eddie and Irene moved into town after a few years. So here I am, a farmer."

"You poor baby, " Charlotte soothed him mockingly. "You've had it so hard."

"Well," he said changing the tone, "Not until lately, I haven't."

Charlotte gave his hand a squeeze and leaned in to kiss him lightly on the cheek. "We'll get through this", she said. He smiled stiffly back at her but said nothing.

"The chili is great," Ellie said, redirecting the conversation. "And I've got to learn how to make cornbread like this."

"Old family recipe," Irene laughed. "Right off the cornmeal box." The tension broke and the conversation was diverted to old family stories, what the kids were doing and the plans for getting the town back on its feet.

Once we'd finished second helpings of chili, Ellie said "Well this has been great but I've got to get home to bed or I'll fall asleep right here."

"I'd better go too," I said, coming to my feet beside Ellie. "But this has been great."

Irene smiled suggestively. "Well, if you must go then go. But I'm glad you both could come."

"I could stay and help with the clean up," I added, hoping I wouldn't have to.

"No," Irene said, "Bob was looking forward to helping me." Bob rolled his eyes and shook his head but did not contradict her.

Irene, her eyes moistening, stood and took my hand in one of hers and Ellie's in the other. "And thanks again, to both of you...for everything,"

"Our pleasure," I said and bid everyone goodnight.

I walked Ellie to her car and, standing there beside her, felt a brief urge to kiss her goodnight. I fought it off. In the past I might have jumped at the chance for a little...romance. But I was trying to be a new man, a better man. Instead, I promised to meet her around eight at her office and watched her drive off again. Then, I found my way back to the RV where I dropped into my recliner and contemplated where fate had led me. I had enjoyed the feeling of belonging while sitting around the dinner table with the Owens family...and Ellie, of course. I enjoyed the feeling of being needed and of helping out without compensation or at least the monetary kind. These were unfamiliar sensations for me. And like all new sensations, there was a mix of pleasure and unease in them. My reverie was interrupted by a tap on the door. I rose to answer it and found Irene standing outside, a covered tray in her hands. I opened the door.

"You left without dessert," she said. "Besides, I needed to get away from Bob's whining."

I stepped aside for her. "Come on in."

She climbed the few steps into my home on wheels and offered the tray, removing its cover to reveal two plates with generous slices of pie on each. "I thought we could share the last two pieces."

"Sure," I said and took the tray from her, setting it on the little banquette table. "I could make a little coffee."

"Not for me," she said. "I'd never sleep. Let's just dig in."

We sat facing each other across the table, though Irene resisted eye contact. After my first forkful of pie, I complimented her baking and she responded with a pinched smile. I put my fork down. "Is there something wrong?"

She finally looked at me, and after a pause, said, "No, not wrong. I just wanted to talk about something."

"Of course," I responded. "What is it?"

She paused again and played her fork through the crumbs on her plate. "My husband, Ed died. He was a good man, really. But he had a problem. He drank...too much. He fought it but it always won. I guess that's what killed him."

"I'm sorry," I said, "but what brought that up now?"

She looked up from her plate again. "I saw it on your face tonight. When Bob offered you a drink. That same look my husband would have when he was trying not to drink, even though he really wanted to."

"Irene, I... I don't know what to say."

"Don't say anything," she said. "Just know that I like you and I want to help if I can. I know how hard it was for Eddie and for all of us. I owe a lot to you. You saved my family and you're helping to save my town. If I can help you save yourself, I would be glad to do it."

Now it was my turn to play with my food as I avoided returning her gaze. "You're pretty perceptive. I did have a drinking problem. I guess I still do if I'm honest with myself. But I think I've got it under control now." I brought my eyes up to meet hers. "I do appreciate your offer though."

She smiled. "Let's finish our desserts, shall we. I don't want to be out here so long. Bob and Charlotte will start suspecting my motives." Her eyebrows bounced up and down slyly. I had to laugh. Irene wasn't an unattractive woman, but I knew that wasn't the kind of relationship either of us expected.

When we finished the dessert, Irene put the plates back on her tray and stood. I got up too. "Can I carry those for you?" I asked.

"Sure," she replied. "And you can be a gentleman and escort me home if you're up to it."

"It's the least I can do." I took the tray and led Irene down the steps out of my RV and walked her to her kitchen door. She took the tray back, and surprised me with a motherly peck on the cheek before saying goodnight and going into the house. Irene was probably a little younger than I but I somehow felt like she was older and maybe wiser too. She was someone I thought I should pay attention to.

I walked back to my RV, undressed and climbed into bed feeling good about my decision to come to Amber Creek. I've never been a believer in fate but that tornado may have been a stroke of good luck for me. Admittedly, it had not been great for a hell of a lot of other people and I couldn't imagine any supernatural force that would destroy so many other lives to teach me a lesson. I wasn't that important. But, no matter the reason, I felt I'd found what I may have been looking for all my life.

A home.

CHAPTER SIX

It was still dark outside when I sat bolt-upright in bed. I hustled out of bed and dug through my pants pockets for my phone. The battery was dead and I cursed, putting it in its charger. By then my head had cleared enough to remember that there was no cell phone service here anyway. Besides, I didn't have phone numbers for Ellie or Dan Gilmore. My sudden dream-fueled realization would have to wait til morning. As I was too aroused to go back to sleep anyway, I cleaned myself up, got dressed and brewed a pot of coffee. I stepped outside with a mug in one hand and a pop tart in the other. I sat on the stoop to watch as the sky over the east hills began to lighten. While eating my sparse breakfast, I reviewed my dream.

I had been an observer, watching as a man, vague and shadowy in form, struck a young woman to the ground, and dropped onto her, his knees landing hard on her upper arms, pinning them to the ground. As she screamed in agony, he grabbed a pillow from out of thin air and slammed it onto the woman's face, holding it there with all of his strength until she stopped resisting him. He had finally lifted the pillow to reveal her face. It was the woman in the morgue. And, in my unconscious mind, I had figured out how she had died. I didn't know where or by whom but I knew that that poor girl had been murdered, suffocated. Her body must have been planted in the storm debris in hopes that she would be seen as just another of the tornado's victims. I dumped the dregs of my coffee on the grass, set the mug inside my RV and headed for the town square. I had to tell someone about my suspicions.

The sun was just peeking over the horizon as I approached the square. The gazebo was already brightly lit. I went inside and found one of the police officers talking with several local volunteers and a few official looking people I'd yet to encounter. I listened as they discussed progress so far and the day's assignments. Once they'd finished and scattered, I approached the cop.

"Hi," I said. "I'm Hank Pressman."

"Okay," he said. "I'm Officer Albright. What can I do for you?"

"Is Dan Gilmore around?"

"Not til seven," he said, not offering any further help.

"Well, I need to talk with him as soon as possible. Is there any way I can get hold of him?"

"What's this about?"

"I think I figured out something ...about the body of the young woman that was found after the storm. I'd like to tell him about it. "

"Tell me and I'll pass it along," he said, showing guarded interest.

"No, that's okay," I said. "Maybe I'll just wait around for him."

With obvious reluctance, Officer Albright said, "Okay, I'll try to call him on the walkie-talkie." He picked the device up off the table and spoke into it. I could hear Dan on the other end of a brief conversation. "He's on his way," the officer said. "He planned to relieve me at seven anyway. There's only four of us in the department, so we take shifts just monitoring things from here."

"Well, thanks again. Like I said, I'll just wait here."

"Suit yourself," he said and walked away to light a cigarette outside the gazebo.

I grabbed a cup of coffee and took a seat at a picnic table. I hadn't drained the cup before Dan stepped into the Gazebo, poured his own coffee, and planted himself beside me.

"What's up Doc," he said with a lame attempt at Bugs Bunny.

"Your deputy, or whatever he is, he's a real charmer," I said.

"Jerry," he said. "Sort of a work in progress. He said you had something to tell me."

"Yeah, I've got a theory about that woman in the morgue."

"She's not there anymore. The BCI has her."

"No matter. I think she was murdered. I think she was held down and smothered. Her arms were broken when her killer kneeled on them. The petechiae in her eyes and on her face are signs of suffocation. I'm sure of it."

"I think you're right," he said. "As a matter of fact, I came to a similar conclusion. She was dumped after the storm to cover the murder."

"Yes," I said. "But I bet she was held captive for a while before that. It would explain her cachexia. She was probably abused too. That would explain her other injuries."

"Well, right now we're going to let the BCI figure this one out."

"But aren't you concerned that you have a murderer in your midst."

"Sure, but I have other fish to fry and, anyhow, I haven't got the expertise of the BCI. Let them sort things through. They'll get back to us in a couple days and meanwhile, we'll keep our eyes open."

"Well, I guess you know what you're doing."

"But thanks for your help."

I got up, dropped my paper cup in the garbage and headed across the square toward the hospital. I'd hoped that Dan would take my concerns more seriously but I guess there really wasn't a lot he could do at the moment. Meanwhile, like Dan, I was going to keep my eyes wide open.

A brisk walk later, I was at Ellie's office. Someone was already sitting across the desk from her. He had a balding head and wore a black, simply cut jacket. Ellie noticed me lingering outside the door and motioned me in.

"Hank," she said. "I'd like you to meet Sam Cannon." Sam turned to me and extended his hand. He was about 20 years my junior, trim, and wore a clerical collar.

"Father Cannon?" I inquired, taking his hand.

"Well, officially," He said. "But most people just call me Sam." He motioned me to the chair beside his. "Ellie told me about you. Amber Creek was lucky you were passing by when the storm hit. I want to thank you."

"It was the least I could do," I said. "Is that church on the square yours?"

"What's left of it. I've been the pastor at St Michaels for fifteen or so years. I actually have a circuit of three churches, within a thirty-mile radius. St. Michaels was my base."

"Was?"

"Yeah, now I've taken up at Immaculate Conception in Halston, 'bout 30 miles west of here. I'm back to check on my flock, and the church, of course."

"Are any of the hospital patients in your *flock*?"

"Hank," Ellie interrupted. "Just about everyone in town attends St. Michaels. Sam's like me, one of a kind in this town."

"I'd welcome you to join us at Mass this Sunday, in Halston of course. Won't be much going on at St. Michaels for quite a while."

"Thanks," I said, "but I'm not much for church."

"Well, it's a standing invitation if you change your mind." Sam smiled broadly and the genuineness of his expression made me like him in spite of my divergent opinion about his career.

Ellie stepped in, maybe sensing my tension. "We were just talking about arranging a funeral here at the hospital chapel for Mr. Anderson, the older gentleman who died in the storm. His family wants his service here, close to home."

"And that won't be a problem for me," Sam said. "I'll talk with the funeral parlor today. By the way, how about the young woman? Has her body been identified?"

"Not yet," Ellie said. "She's at the state lab. We won't know a thing for several days."

"Ellie, I wanted to speak with you about that," I said. "Maybe when you're done talking with Father Sam."

"Go ahead," Ellie said. "Sam's a priest. You can't shock him."

Sam grinned and shook his head at her. If he hadn't been a priest, I might have suspected that there was something going on between them. The ease and affection they shared was obvious. And was that a tinge of jealousy I was feeling?

"Well, I have a theory about her, the girl. I think she was tortured and murdered." I gave them a rundown of my ideas and how they meshed with what evidence we had."

"Well, as ugly as that sounds, I think you're probably right," Ellie said.

"I know everyone in town," Sam interjected. "I can't believe that there could be a murderer among them."

"I don't want to think so either," Ellie said, "but it seems there might be a wolf mixed in with your flock, Sam."

"I guess I better give that some thought," He responded. "Did you talk with the police?"

"Yeah, I met with Dan this morning. He was already thinking along the same lines. Not much he can do til he hears from the BCI."

"Well, in the meantime, I'll say a few extra prayers for the poor girl." He rose from his chair. "I guess I'd better get going. The state building inspector wants to meet me at the church this morning. I don't think I'm going to like what he has to say."

I stood too. "Well good luck and it was nice to meet you."

"Same here," he said. He shook my hand again and gave Ellie a not so fatherly hug before leaving the office.

"Nice guy," I commented. "Not as stuffy as most priests."

"Judgmental much?' Ellie said. "Actually, he's a really good guy. One of the pillars of the community and a good friend."

"Well, I suspect we have a lot to do this morning. Point me in the right direction." Ellie laughed and led me to the inpatient wing and another day of playing real doctor began.

The sun was settling by the time we were done. The patients were doing well overall. Several could have been discharged to home, had there been homes to go to. A few were picked up by out-of-town relatives. I suspected that our workload would lessen with each passing day. Of course, I was glad of that for the patients' sakes but I knew I would miss having my hands in things again. And I had to admit working with Ellie had been a joy. She was warm and loving with her charges but still professional and thorough. She could share a funny story with one patient and explain an unfortunate prognosis to the next, without losing her warmth or concern. She was an excellent physician and a wonderful person. And I was starting to feel very fond of her.

We walked out of the hospital together, me heading across town on foot back to my RV and her to her car. She called back to me. "Hey, what are you doing for supper?"

I turned back. "Don't know. Maybe Irene has some left-over chili. If not, I can open a can of something myself."

"Doesn't sound too exciting. How 'bout coming to my place and I'll fry you up a steak."

"Oh, I don't want to put you out."

"Come on. I need a little company."

"You've convinced me." I walked with her to her car and we headed out of the parking lot up into the hills to the northeast, leaving the town behind.

"Where the hell do you live?" I asked as we passed a plowed field and entered a wooded area.

"I live in what you might call the boonies," she said. "It was my husband's idea. I mean my ex-husband's."

"Oh yeah. Was he a woodsman or something?"

"No, just paranoid. He didn't like having neighbors and he wanted to live off the grid. We have a propane powered generator and solar panels. That's why I can offer you a steak. Take your blessings where you can find them, I guess."

"If you don't mind me asking, what happened to him?"

Ellie turned in at a narrow unpaved driveway and up a small rise to a very modern looking home in a small clearing. "According to him, he fell in love." She parked the car beside the house and climbed out.

I got out of my side and followed her. "Pardon?"

"It was sort of messy," she said. "Come on inside, I'll need a beer if I'm to tell you my life story." She led me into the house. We left our shoes and jackets just inside the door and walked to the tiled and stainless-steel kitchen. She directed me to sit at the island bar, opened the refrigerator and pulled out a beer, offering it to me. I just smiled at her, unsure if I really wanted to refuse her offer. "Oh, yeah. I forgot."

"It's fine if you want to have one though. I'll take a soda."

She took a Coke out of the fridge and closed the door. Sitting on the stool beside me, she slid the coke over and popped the lid of the beer. A long swig later, she started to talk, not looking at me. "My husband and I met in residency in Chicago. He'd been mugged once and hated the city ever after. He wanted to get away to someplace he could feel safe. He found Amber Creek. The local doctor was retiring and sold us his practice. I wasn't real excited about it. I mean, I had nothing against the place but I would have preferred a bigger town."

"But you came here to appease your husband?"

"Not so much that. I thought we were a team and we could build something here. We lived in town for a few years then he started getting antsy and wanted to build this place. I thought it was just his paranoia again but apparently there were other motivations, too."

"Such as?"

"He got involved with another woman at the hospital. They couldn't be seen together in town. This place could be a love nest when I wasn't around. We alternated days in the office being, as there wasn't enough work there for both of us. The day we weren't in the office we were supposed to take call and do the hospital rounds. So, when I was in the office, he and she could sneak up here."

"It must have been horrible when you found out."

"I was so naive. I suspect everyone in town had it figured out before I did. When I finally put two and two together, a few years later, I confronted him. His solution was to pack his bags and skip town with his girlfriend. She left a husband and two kids behind."

"But that must have been, what, five-ten years ago and you're still here."

"By that point I had started to feel responsible for the town. If I'd left, they would have had no one. The hospital would have had to close. There are no other medical services for over thirty miles. We tried for a while to recruit another doctor, but there were no takers. The previous doctor had tried to recruit for years before we came."

"So, you stayed."

"Yup."

"Ellie, you're a good person."

"Or maybe just a sucker," she smiled. "I'm starving. I'll start on the steaks. You think you can make a salad?"

"Show me the veggies and the equipment." The topic changed, we dove into meal preparation.

We enjoyed medium rare steaks, slightly wilted salads, oversized bowls of chocolate almond fudge ice cream...and conversation. I told some of my story - marriage, loss and my legal disasters. She talked about her childhood in New York, her family that sounded as screwed up as mine had been and her failed marriage. It seemed that we had a lot in common. Of course, there were some pretty big differences. For example, she had been a faithful spouse. She had never been involved in a murder trial. And she hadn't run away when things got tough. So, there's that. But all in all, the evening went well.

After cleaning up and finishing a last cup of decaf, I suggested Ellie drive me home. She said sure but her expression was sort of hard to read. Part agreement, part regret. We stood smiling at each other uncomfortably until Ellie broke the tension by retrieving her keys from her purse. She offered them to me. "How about you drive yourself home and pick me up in the morning? It's getting late and I'd better get to bed."

"What if you get an emergency call in the night?"

"I rarely do, barring tornados," she said. "Besides, the phones are still out. If they need me at the hospital, they have to come up to tell me anyway. They can give me a lift back."

"You're sure you're okay with that?" I said.

She opened the door for me and said, "See you in the morning and ...thanks for a really nice evening."

Of course, my instinct from past experience would have been to take her in my arms and, using my undeniable charm, coax her to bed. I admit, it crossed my mind. Instead, I thanked her for dinner and headed for the car with my own mix of agreement and regret.

CHAPTER SEVEN

The next morning, as I was getting ready for the day when there was a tap on my door. I opened it to Sarah. "Grandma says you'd better come to breakfast now or you won't get none."

"On my way," I said and quickly finished dressing. I headed over to Irene's and let myself into the kitchen.

"There you are," Irene said. "You know, out in the country the morning starts at sunrise. Everybody else has finished their breakfasts. I was about to clean up."

"Sorry," I said. "Late night."

"Oh," she said, while setting a stack of pancakes and a cup of coffee in front of me. She made no effort to disguise the curiosity in her tone.

I couldn't help but smile. "Ellie had me over for dinner last night."

"I did notice her car parked on the street. Was she coming to breakfast, too?" she said, cocking her head to the side and raising her eyebrows to full mast.

"Irene," I said in mocked disgust. "I barely know the woman. She loaned me her car and I'm going to pick her up before work this morning."

"Oh, I see. Well, to be honest, it wouldn't do either of you any harm to trip the light fantastic."

I started into my breakfast. "What are you, the local matchmaker?"

"No," Irene said, sitting across the table from me with a cup of coffee in hand. "Ellie's a wonderful woman but awfully alone. I feel sad for her. And you and she have a lot in common."

"I suppose we do."

"The other night, I got the impression that the two of you hit it off pretty good."

"I like her and working with her makes me feel good about myself. It's really nothing more than that."

"Okay, if you say so," she said, smirking over the rim of her coffee cup. "Will you be here for supper tonight or do you have other plans?"

"Don't count on me," I said. "If necessary, I can whip up a little something in my own mini kitchen."

"You forget, I've seen your kitchen. You'd be lucky if you could make toast in that space."

"We'll see," I said.

Irene took a long sip of her coffee then set the cup down. "Hank, I just want you to promise that if you and Ellie do get, I don't know, involved that you'll be careful. She's a special lady and she's been hurt...bad."

"Irene, I don't have any designs of Ellie but if I did it would be because I respect her and like her. And I would never want to hurt her in any way."

"Good," Irene said, standing, taking her cup to the sink, and washing it in the soapy water. "Now eat your breakfast and bring your dirty dishes over here so I can finish cleaning up."

"Yes ma'am," I said and followed orders.

I thanked Irene, left the house and climbed into Ellie's car. I hadn't noticed that the car smelled of her. A slightly sweet and musky aroma blended with the antiseptic tang of the hospital. I smiled, remembering what Irene had implied. I had to admit though, that exploring a relationship with Elie had crossed my mind, more than once. She was smart and pretty and would likely be able to counter my natural bullshit. I needed someone like that. Then again, I had had several someones like that over the years. I had expertly botched every one of those relationships. I began to wonder if I was even ready for a relationship, were I lucky enough to be Ellie's type. Or would it be better if I just swore off women entirely until I could make a better man of myself. Of course, I was no spring chicken and didn't know how many chances I might have in my future. I forced myself to put all thoughts of romance on the back burner and started the engine.

Driving Ellie's car back through town to pick her up. I noticed a police car parked near one of the storm-ravaged houses. Dan was walking the perimeter of the rubble, stretching a yellow police tape around tall stakes he'd already driven into the ground. I pulled over and got out, calling out to Dan. "What's going on?"

He tied the end of his tape around a stake and turned to me. "BCI asked me to mark the spot where we found the girl's body. They're coming by later today to search it."

"Didn't you already do that?"

"Yeah, but they're the experts," he said, making air quotes. "I told them that there had been a lot of people searching around town after the storm. I'm sure the evidence, if there was any, has been disturbed."

"Whose house was this anyway?"

"The Cartland's. An older couple. They were in Florida all winter and just about to come home."

"Shame," I said. "But it's just as well they weren't in the house. Say, did the BCI give you any report."

"Yeah," Dan said. "I was planning on stopping up at the hospital when I was done here to talk with you and Ellie about it. I asked Sam - ah- Father Cannon, to join us there. I'll be done here pretty soon."

"Ok, well I was just heading up to Ellie's to get her and then to the hospital."

"I noticed you had her car," he said. "You and her hitting it off pretty good?"

"Nothing like that. I just had supper with her last night and she loaned me her car to get home."

"I see. You be nice to her, Hank. She's kind of a favorite around here."

"Don't worry, Dan. I'm a gentleman and a scholar." I waved and got in the car.

"I'll see you at the hospital," he said. "I'm heading there as soon as I'm done here."

"There seem to be a lot of favorites in this town," I replied. He just shrugged and turned back to his task.

Ellie was ready to go when I got to her house. She jumped in beside me, greeting me with none of the tension we'd experienced the night before. We headed back toward the hospital where Dan and Sam were already waiting for us. Ellie led us all to a small conference room, offered us coffee and, hearing no takers, sat down.

She started. "So, Dan, give us the scoop." I had already told her about my meeting with Dan on the way to the hospital.

"Well, as I told Hank, the BCI sent a report, and they plan a further investigation. They agree with us that the girl was murdered."

"Did they identify her?" Sam asked.

"Yeah," Dan said, a heaviness in his tone. "Her name was Sally Franklin. She was nineteen, a... a prostitute. From Omaha. Went missing about three months ago. 'Course there weren't a lot of people out looking for her. She had no family contact for a couple years. Seems everyone just kinda gave up on her."

"Poor thing," Ellie said. "Did they find any DNA evidence to link her with her killer."

"They looked. She's been raped multiple times. He either used condoms or something else, like a broom handle." Ellie cringed.

"Any idea how she got here?" I said.

"No, but the BCI is looking into it. They'll be here this afternoon. They suspect she was held captive for some time, several weeks or more. There were signs of multiple injuries. And sexual assault, of course." He sighed. "They may want to talk to you, Ellie. And I thought you might be able to give some insight, Hank."

"I wasn't a forensic psychiatrist, Dan, but I'll do anything I can to help."

Any suspects?" Sam asked.

"Your guess is as good as mine at this point," Dan said. "Maybe better. Any word from the confessional?"

"You know I couldn't say if there was," Sam said.

"I don't know," Dan said. "I just thought that a little of God's influence wouldn't hurt right now."

"Let's say a little prayer for the poor girl, shall we." Dan, Ellie and Sam bowed their heads while I sat and squirmed. "May the Lord accept Sally's soul into his arms, forgive her shortcomings and bless her with eternal life. And may he guide us all in finding those responsible for her death and bringing them to justice and peace."

All three said "Amen."

"Was there anything else we needed to discuss?" Ellie asked.

"There is one thing," Sam said. "I could use a little help from your department, Dan. The building inspector says the church is a total loss and they suggest we put up some kind of barrier to keep people away, especially west of the steeple. They're afraid it could come down with the next good wind."

"That's around your old graveyard, isn't it?" Dan asked.

"Yeah, but it's not so old. We had our last burial there only a few months ago. People still stop by to pay their respects. We don't want the steeple falling on them while they're grieving someone else's death."

"You've got a point," Dan said. "I'll send one of the deputies over to set something up this morning."

Sam thanked him and rose to leave. "I'd better get going, I've got a service in Halston today. No rest for the wicked, I guess." He left and Dan followed him out.

I started to get up, but Ellie grabbed my hand. "Hank, what do you think about all this?"

"Like I said, I'm not a forensic expert."

"But you must have some ideas."

"Well, whoever did this was obviously a sexual sadist. And a planner. He was able to hold that girl captive without anyone knowing. He must have held her in town somewhere or he wouldn't have been able to plant her body so quickly. He must also know people around here, at least enough to know that the Cartlands would be out of town. My guess would be that he lives alone. Easier to keep a secret that way. That's as much as I can think of, except..."

"Except what?" Ellie asked.

"Except," I cleared my throat. "He seems to have known what he was doing. This may not have been the first woman he abused or killed."

"I was afraid you might say that," she said. "I can't imagine anyone like that living in this town, right under our noses."

"Sociopaths can be very clever and smooth. They've got no scruples so they can be anyone they need to be. Even us professionals can be fooled. Trust me, I know." I had been the victim, if you can call it that, of a sociopath. She had tricked me and used me and she was why I no longer had a medical license. Thankfully, she was now behind bars for life.

"Well, let's hope the BCI finds the killer soon," Ellie said. "Meanwhile, we have our own work to do." We got up and headed to the patient wing.

Four hours later we'd finished. Most of the patients had finally been discharged. Ellie made plans to get back to her outpatient practice that she had moved into another wing of the hospital after her divorce. She and I sat down to a bag lunch that Irene had supplied us. We ate slowly and quietly. Finally, Ellie broke the silence.

"Hank, you know that there won't be much more for you to do around here, after today."

I smiled. "Are you asking me to leave?"

"No, of course not," she said. "But, now that the crisis has calmed down, I don't think I can continue to justify working with an unlicensed physician. Nothing personal."

"I get it, don't worry. I've really enjoyed working with you but I knew it couldn't last. Besides, I thought about my options. And decided to stick around and help with the cleanup around town."

"That's great," she said. "I'd hate to see you leave."

"Really?" I said, trying to disguise the hope in my tone.

"Sure. You've been a big help and the town could use you."

"The town?" I raised my eyebrows.

"Alright. I'll admit, I'd like to see you stay around too. I don't have a lot of colleagues, defrocked or otherwise."

"Well in that case," I said, standing, "I better get out there and make myself useful." I crumpled my lunch bag, took a last drag from my soda can and threw them both in the trash.

I headed for the door but turned back. "Ya' know, with this murder and all, if you'd like me to come out to stay with you at your house, I wouldn't mind. It's pretty isolated."

She gave me an indulgent smile. "Thanks. I think I'll be okay but can I give you a call when I need help crossing the street."

"Listen, I'm no boy scout and you are certainly no little old lady."

"Thanks for that, I guess," she said. "I would like to do dinner again one of these nights. That was nice."

"Say when and where." I waved and headed out of the door. I couldn't help it that my mind had already started to wander where it shouldn't. Ellie was beautiful, smart and, once she let you get to know her, a lot of fun to be with. But I wasn't sure if either of us was ready to take the relationship further and I had made enough mistakes in the past that I didn't want to rely on my instincts.

CHAPTER EIGHT

The next several days, I worked with Dan Gilmore, Bob Owens and a group of other locals to clear rubble, help folks find their personal belongings and dispose of what couldn't be saved. Several times I noticed Sam digging in with the rest of us. My prejudice had led me to believe that the clergy was above such menial tasks but there he was, in jeans and a t-shirt, digging through rubble and mud to rescue what he could of his flock's possessions. Bob had told me that Sam was working night and day since the storm with his clerical tasks, support of his parishioners and, with what little time he had left, the messy work of community clean up. I found myself developing a healthy respect for him, in spite of our philosophical differences.

The state had sent in plenty of heavy equipment and, after a week, FEMA finally showed up. They brought temporary housing, food and water and a handful of clerks to process relief claims. They relied on community members to provide most of the elbow grease. There was plenty to do. It was hard work. Every night I fell into bed usually after one of Irene's generous suppers. I slept like I hadn't in years. Ellie and I did bag lunches on the square most days and supper when we could both get away. I was proud of the work I was doing and I had really started to feel at home in Amber Creek.

One evening, Bob and I headed back to Irene's house after a day that had been particularly difficult, both physically and emotionally. We'd helped several townspeople load what little they had found worth saving from the rubble that had been their homes. We piled boxes and bags of belongings, memories and aspirations into pickup trucks, car trunks and back seats and waved as tearful families drove away. It was particularly hard for Bob. These people were his neighbors and his friends. People who had accepted him in Amber Creek and allowed him to be one of them. To see them leave, some probably never to return, ripped him apart. Somehow, he had been able to put his own losses on the shelf long enough to be of help to others. But seeing their losses had nearly broken him. We walked back to Irene's house and without a word Bob had disappeared into the house, passing his son who had been waiting on the stoop.

When I approached Bobbie, he looked up at me, tears in his eyes. I recognized his pain as the same I had experienced with my own father, who had so often been too busy, too drunk or too angry to notice me. My heart went out to him and I took a seat beside him on the stoop.

"How's it going," I said, knowing how lame it sounded.

He sniffed a few times. "Okay, I guess."

"Really?" I asked. "You look kind of upset."

"No, but," he said, examining a baseball he'd been rolling in his hands. "I know that Dad and Mom are bummed about the farm and all but..."

"But?" I prodded.

He looked up at me. "But it's like they're mad at me about it."

"Why do you say that?"

"They barely talk to me anymore." He flipped the ball from one hand to the other. "Dad and I used to play catch almost every night before supper."

I rested my hand on Bobbie's shoulder. "They've got a lot on their minds, since the storm."

"I know, but it ain't my fault."

"Of course, not Bobbie," I said. "Listen, I know they still love you and Sara very much. Your dad told me so. That's why he's so preoccupied. He's trying to figure out how to make sure you guys are taken care of. It'll work out. You wait and see,"

He gave me a feeble smile and nodded.

"Meanwhile," I said, "how 'bout you and I play catch."

"Sure," he said and stood, revealing two baseball gloves he'd kept beside him. He handed the larger one to me. "That's Dad's but you can use it." I took it and slipped my left hand into the glove. It was a little snug but the leather was soft and well-oiled. This glove had been used often.

"Does your dad play a lot of baseball?' I asked as I backed away from Bobbie and held my glove up, inviting him to throw the ball.

"Not anymore," he replied, chucking me the ball and struggling into his own glove. "He used to, in high school. He says he was the star on the team. He was a pitcher."

"Wow," I said, lobbing the ball back. "You must be pretty proud."

"Yeah, but now he only plays catch with me. I mean he used to."

"He will again," I said. "I'm sure of it."

We tossed the ball back and forth for at least half an hour, talking little. Bobbie's face slowly brightened and we shared a few laughs over missed catches and flubbed pitches. We finally stopped when Charlotte opened the kitchen door and called us in for supper. I followed Bobbie past his mother and at the kitchen door Charlotte stopped me with a hand on my arm. "Thank you," she said, smiling sadly.

We all sat around the table and after Irene led us in grace, we dug in. I don't remember what we ate. I do remember watching the family. Bob's heaviness gradually lifted and he and the kids began to engage in pleasant banter. I wondered if Charlotte had overheard me talking with Bobbie and brought it up with Bob. Now, I saw Bobbie light up at the attention from his father. It was like magic. I saw how easy and loving everyone was with each other. I'd never really known this kind of family. And, I'm ashamed to admit, I was a little jealous. My own family had been nothing like this.

My father had been an alcoholic and my mother was the classic depressed enabler until she couldn't take it anymore. Their divorce had been acrimonious and once or twice even violent. My brother and I had been sort of lost in the chaos. He had become the caretaker, the good boy who was there for everyone. I had been the problem child who got in trouble in school and out. I learned to play my parents against each other to avoid consequences of my own misbehavior. Maybe that was why I grew up to be the cad I had become.

After supper, Irene and I cleaned up, while Bob and Charlotte helped the kids with homework and got them ready for bed. It was pleasant doing such a simple task and feeling useful. The last few days had taught me to appreciate such things.

Offhandedly, Irene said "It was a nice thing you did for Bobby tonight." Then, not breaking her stride, she handed me a soapy dish.

"Bobbie's a nice kid," I said.

"Okay then, I guess I'd have to say, you're a nice man, Hank Pressman."

I took another dish from her foamy hand. "Thanks, that means a lot more than you probably realize."

When the dishes were done, I shared a warm embrace with Irene and headed back to my RV, exhausted and ready for bed. I took a quick shower and slipped under the covers but struggled to get to sleep. I kept seeing Bobbie sitting there on the stoop. It reminded me of myself at his age but it also reminded me of lost opportunities. I had no children. Marie, my wife, had had a miscarriage shortly before we married. I'd actually proposed to her because of the pregnancy. Sure I'd loved her but, after we lost the baby, I'd felt somehow trapped even though I knew that Marie wasn't the kind to trick me into marrying her. We'd never had children after that. Marie had wanted them. I pretended I did too but, I don't think I really did. Maybe I was afraid they would tie me down too much. Or maybe I was afraid I would be the kind of father mine had been. Besides, I had a lot of extracurricular activities that were most decidedly not family oriented. But lately, since Marie's death, I had struggled with lots of missed opportunities, having children being only one of them. Now watching Bob and Charlotte, I could see what I'd missed. Even with the terrible loss they had suffered, they had each other and could rely on each other. They had the kids and Irene. They had a sense of belonging, something I'd never really had or let myself have. I wasn't sure which. Now, of course, it was too late. I'd never be a father. I'd never play catch with my own son. But maybe, I could be part of Bob's family. Maybe I could find someone to be with. Maybe Ellie. I knew that I was being presumptuous, but belonging appealed to me now.

CHAPTER NINE

Anyone who has ever lived in the Midwest knows about the weather. Summers are hot, humid and buggy. Falls are brisk, breezy and too short. Winters are frigid, icy and too long. And Spring is a crapshoot. Chilly one day, baking the next. And storms. Lots of storms. Two weeks after the tornado, Spring did its thing again. I was asleep in my RV when a clap of thunder yanked me out of a pleasant dream and into a light show. Lightning flashed almost continuously at my window and the RV rocked in the wind. Rain started to pelt my aluminum roof, blotting out any other possibility of sound. I thought about running to Irene's house but chose to curl up instead and wait it out. I must have fallen asleep again, because the next time I looked out the little bedside window, the sun had come up, the sky was clear and other than a few downed branches, everything looked as it had when I'd gone to bed. I rolled to my feet, cleaned myself up and headed to Irene's for breakfast.

Bob and the kids had already started to dig into bacon and French toast. Irene and Charlotte were cooking and serving up. On command, I took a seat and an overly generous plateful was planted in front of me. The kids griped about going back to school, now that the bus was able to pick them up to take them to school in the next town over. I suspected that they were actually relieved though. The previous two weeks must have been hard for them too, though they'd never have admitted it. Irene and Charlotte exchanged opinions about what the ladies in town were doing to feed the folks who'd been left homeless. Bob and I talked about the cleanup efforts so far and what was left to do. He admitted that he wanted to get back out to the farm soon and I offered to pitch in when he did.

Then the walkie-talkie beeped in its charger. Six-year-old Sara jumped to answer it before her brother could. She spoke politely and then handed it to her father.

"Owens here, what can I do for ya', Over."

"We need you and Hank down here ASAP. Most of my guys are on another run right now." It sounded like Dan's voice. "The storm took out the church steeple. It landed in the graveyard and when folks find out, they'll be down here checking on family plots. Over"

"Hank and I are just finishing breakfast. Be there soon. Over"

"Breakfast? What's that?' Dan said with his usual sarcasm. He'd been working day and night since the first storm. "See ya' soon. Out."

We cleaned our plates quickly and headed to Bob's truck. As we neared the town square it became obvious that word had gotten out. People were headed to the church yard in multiple small groups. Somehow, Dan had kept them at bay near the yellow police tape. Allowing only a few at a time to enter. We parked and walked to the churchyard where a disorganized pile of bricks and stone stretched from the church foundation across the grass forming a wall of sorts. Some parts still resembled the tower that it had been. The falling structure had buried maybe twenty headstones and the graves beneath. Part of the church wall had come down with the steeple leaving a gaping hole that exposed the sanctuary within. We had been standing for a moment, scanning the scene, when a piercing scream sounded. We bolted through the crowd and took Dan's place while he responded to the scream. The crowd had grown very restless but were still cooperating with staying behind the police tape.

Moments later I heard my name called and I went into the graveyard to join Dan. "Doc," he said. "Can you take a look at something?"

"Sure, "I said and he led me to a toppled headstone half buried in bricks. A woman stood, her arms wrapped around what must have been her husband's shoulders, sobbing. I stooped down beside Dan and he pointed to the broken, rain-soaked soil. A large clod of dirt had been pulled out when the headstone fell. There was an oval of dirty white in the muddy hole that looked familiar. I reached to brush more of the soil away but Dan pushed my hand aside. He pulled a pair of blue plastic gloves from his pocket, like the ones he'd already donned. I slipped them on the cleared a few inches of mud aside and immediately drew back. There, in the hole, was a bony eye socket and a skull sloping away from it.

Dan pulled my hand back. "Shit," he said. "I gotta call the BCI again."

Another squeal sounded from behind us as the woman pulled from her husband and shouted, "Momma."

Dan jumped to his feet. "Now, Thelma, wait a minute. That can't be your mother."

"That's her grave, isn't it," Thelma whimpered.

"Yes, but she's in a concrete vault six feet down," he said. "This has got to be someone else." Thelma started into another crying jag and Dan asked her husband to take her away. Once they were gone, Dan called his deputies pm the walkie-talkie and ordered them to get back as soon as possible to close the graveyard again and to then stand guard. He walked to the yellow tape. "Folks," he shouted, "I know you want to check on your loved ones but this has just become a crime scene. I can't let anyone else in so please go home and we'll keep you informed."

After a rumble of murmuring, some shouted complaints and a few epithets, the crowd began to clear. A few gawkers stayed nearby, craning their necks to get a better look. Dan went to his car and used his police radio to contact BCI. They had cleared out of town within a day of their last visit but the case of the dead girl in the debris was not closed. They assured Dan that a forensic team would arrive before noon.

I took Dan's arm and walked him back to the damaged grave. "What do you think?"

"I don't know what to think," he said. "We've never had anything like this before in Amber Creek but it looks like there was another body buried over Thelma's mother."

"But why?" I implored.

"My guess is someone wanted to get rid of a body without anyone knowing," he said.

I scanned the area around. "Isn't it kind of a public place for a surreptitious burial?"

"Not before the tornado." Dan said. "The church here on the east, the abandoned convent and school were on the west side and the school gym was to the north. There used to be a playground there too but, after the school closed, it was dug up to make more room for graves. Those buildings are pretty much gone now but they would have provided good cover, especially at night. Till last night, there was surprisingly little debris here."

"I hate to think this," I said," but maybe this is another murder victim."

"That's why I called the BCI again. We've just got to keep this area secure until they get here." He said. "The rest of my squad will be here soon, so it looks like we'll have enough guys to do that. Once they're here, you and Bob can head home if you like." I agreed and within a few minutes a police car pulled up and two cops climbed out. I started out of the cemetery, just then noticing a stocky balding man in a tan overcoat and wearing oversized glasses. He'd been standing away from the others outside the graveyard, near the corner of the church. When he realized I was looking at him, he nodded, turned and walked around the front of the church. Not another grieving family member, I thought. Probably just a gawker.

I walked back out to the street where Bob was waiting. "They don't really need us anymore," I said. He didn't seem to hear me. He was staring off along the line of the cemetery wall. I turned and saw that Irene was standing alone near the wall, looking into the graveyard silently. I watched as she pulled a tissue from her pocket and dabbed at her eyes. I started to call for her but Bob stopped me.

"No," he said. "She's checking on Eddie's grave. I know her and this is something she would want to do alone."

"Why do you say that?"

"She and Eddie had a... a different kind of relationship. His drinking made things hard on her. Last night I said we'd come to town because of his illness. It was actually because he was failing on the farm. With all the booze, he just couldn't keep up. I suspect that Irene has a lot of resentments but she stood by him through everything, right up 'til the end. She's not a quitter but she keeps things about their marriage pretty close to the chest. She wouldn't even want us to mention she was here."

"What a shame," I said, observing her quiet grief. "She's such a wonderful person."

"Yeah, well..." His face was painted with sympathy for a woman he obviously loved and admired.

Uncomfortable with the situation, I said, "I suppose we'd better get going, though I don't have much else planned for the rest of the day."

"Then maybe you wouldn't mind driving out to the farm with me. I'd like to check it out though there's probably very little additional damage the storm could have caused."

I agreed but lingered for a minute watching Irene. Her sadness was so apparent and so familiar. I was reminded of the day I knelt in the snow at my wife's grave, crying with guilt and regret. Irene could at least say that she had been there for her husband when he needed her. I wasn't there for Marie when the drunk driver ran into her car. I wasn't there when she died in the hospital emergency room. Of course, I had never really been there for her through most of our marriage. Not like she had been for me. I almost envied Irene because she at least knew she had done her best.

Bob roused me out of my self-pitying reverie with a tap on the shoulder. I wiped my eyes and followed him. Then we hopped in his truck and headed back toward the river. As we retraced the route the twister had taken through town, I was surprised at how much had changed. Piles of debris had been cleared and collected in a flat area beside the river. Concrete foundations showed on both sides of the once tree-lined streets. Of course, Bob and I had done what we could to help in the cleanup but there had obviously been a lot of other busy hands at work here too. Now, there weren't many people around anymore. I guessed most people had salvaged all they could and found new places to stay.

We crossed the river, passing the demolished grain elevators where trucks were being loaded with what grain could be saved. We turned south toward the highway and Bob's farm. On the hill just past the highway, utility trucks were crowded around a partially reconstructed cell phone tower. "They say we'll have phone service by the end of the week," Bob said. "Hope last night's storm didn't slow 'em down." He turned into his driveway but slammed on his breaks within a hundred feet of the little mound where his house had been. Now, a pile of broken lumber and twisted siding was all there was left. Tracks of debris lead east along the tornado's route and south where last night's storm had thrown them.

Bob's head settled on the steering wheel and his shoulders began to heave. This was the first time I'd seen him cry. He'd lost so much. Charlotte and the kids had been able to retrieve some belongings scattered around the property while Bob and I were helping out in town but no one had been in the house for fear that it would collapse on them. Now whatever had been left was gone for good. I reached a helpless hand to Bob's shoulder and just laid it there, wordlessly. He lifted his head and looked at me, forcing a smile. "It's only stuff," he said, wiping tears away. "I still have my family. And the land."

"How about I help you look around and see if there's anything else we can salvage," I said. He nodded and we climbed out of the truck to start searching. By noon, we'd loaded the truck bed with sodden clothes, furniture that was worth repairing and family heirlooms, some intact but most broken. We climbed in the truck and drove back to town. I asked Bob to drop me off at the hospital so I could check on Ellie. As he drove away, I thought about the things I had lost in my life, mostly through my own fault. But this poor man had lost almost everything through bad luck alone. I felt sorry for him and ashamed of myself.

Ellie was in her office having seen hospital patients in the morning. She told me she had a few patients scheduled in the afternoon but had time for lunch. "Let's skip the cafeteria," she said. "I need a change of scenery." So, we took her car to the only place around that served food and that was still open, a country bar a few miles up the highway.

"It's okay that it's a bar, isn't it," she asked.

"Sure," I said. "Though I've gotta admit that what I've seen today could drive almost anyone to drink." I scanned the room where scattered patrons were eating and drinking...beer mostly. My mouth still watered at the sight of people enjoying booze. I didn't feel a conscious urge to drink but I feared what would happen if I let my guard down.

We went in, took a table as far from the bar as possible and ordered burgers and soft drinks. While we waited for them to come, I filled Ellie in on my morning. She listened intently. I liked that about her. She was a great listener. She said nothing until I had concluded my tale.

"So, does Dan think he's got another murder on his hands?" she said.

"Don't know but it's a possibility," I replied.

"And poor Bob. I can't imagine how he's dealing with his loss."

"He's a tough guy and Charlotte and the kids are there for him. It'll be a long row to hoe but I think they'll do fine." Our food came and we dug in.

As we walked back to the car, I realized I hadn't asked if the storm had hit Ellie's property. "Any storm damage at your place?"

"Minimal,' she said. "A lot of branches down, some siding twisted around. Nothing major."

"Listen, I've got nothing pressing this afternoon. How about you drop me off at your place and I'll do some clean up while you're working at the hospital?"

"Oh, that's not really necessary"

"It would be my pleasure," I said. "Besides, I don't want to go back to Irene's place just now. Bob and Charlotte have a lot to deal with and they don't need me around."

"Okay, but I'll plan on making you supper again by way of payment," she said.

"You're on."

She dropped me off and handed me the key to her house. As she drove away, she shouted out of the car window. "Don't overdo it, old man."

I flipped her the bird and headed to the house.

CHAPTER TEN

I worked in the heat for three hours, cutting and piling fallen branches. I collected a small heap of asphalt shingles though I wasn't sure where they came from as Ellie's roof was copper, green with verdigris. I raked what little lawn she had and pulled weeds in her vegetable garden for good measure. I declared myself done a little after four and headed into the house. I didn't expect Ellie 'til after five so I stripped out of my grimy, sweat-soaked clothes and popped them in the washer. Then I found my way down the hall to the master bath and helped myself to a long hot shower. I climbed out, dried off and suddenly realized how beat I was. I wrapped the towel around myself and walked to the nearest bed, not caring that it was Ellie's or the message I may be giving, and collapsed.

I woke up with a start to the sound of a woman's voice. I looked up and Ellie was standing over me. "Comfortable? " She asked with a wide grin plastered on her face.

I sat up and swung my legs over the side of the bed, pulling my towel tight around me as I did. "I'm sorry," I said. "I was a mess after working in the yard and..."

"Don't worry," she said. "You did a great job out there. You deserved a break."

"Let me just get my clothes."

"Not yet,' she said. "I only just threw them in the dryer for you. Meanwhile," she walked to the closet and pulled out a pink, terrycloth robe, handing it to me. "You might feel more comfortable in this. It may not be the best fit or color, but you'll have to take it or leave it."

Standing, I took the robe and slipped into it. Turning my back to her I dropped the still damp towel and tied the sash. The robe hung well above my knees and barely closed around my waist. I picked up the towel. "Where should I put this?"

"Just drape it over the hamper in the bathroom," she said.

I followed her directions and glanced at her bed as I came out of the bathroom. "Sorry, it seems there's a wet spot on your bed."

She shook her head. "Just like a man to notice. I'll turn the ceiling fan on. That should take care of it. Meanwhile, I'm starved. The steaks are thawing. Let's get supper started."

"I'll make the salad again," I volunteered, following her out to the kitchen.

While preparing the meal we reviewed our day's activities. Then we sat down to medium rare steaks, slightly freezer-burned hashbrowns and canned corn. Fresh vegetables had run low so the salad was basically limp lettuce, sliced carrots and stale croutons. Ellie had already started an extensive and well-thought-out grocery list, knowing it would be a half-hour's drive to and from the store. I offered to go for her the next day but she decided that it would be a better joint mission. She claimed that she didn't know me well enough to trust me with an empty shopping cart.

When the meal was over and a hot cup of coffee sat before each of us, Ellie's tone changed. "Dan came to see me just before I left the office," she said. "The BCI gave him a preliminary report. They scanned the whole church yard with some kind of sonar device. They think that there may be two more bodies out there."

"Well, it is a cemetery," I said, cocking my head.

"You know what I mean. That makes three with the one you found this morning. And, of course, four...if you include the girl in the rubble."

"So, they think there's a connection?"

"Dan didn't say that, but it stands to reason, doesn't it. You said there would likely be more.'

"That was only speculation," I said.

"Be that as it may, It's getting pretty disturbing. To think that there might be a serial killer in a flyspeck of a town like this." Her voice cracked. "I can't imagine what's next."

I reached across the table and put my hand on hers. "Don't get ahead of yourself. This may not be what it seems," I demurred, suspecting that it was exactly what it seemed. "Do you know where the investigation goes from here?"

"Not really. Dan says they've begun recovering the body from this morning. They have tents over several of the graves and barriers at all the entrances to the graveyard. They asked Dan to post a twenty-four-hour guard."

"So, this is going to take a while," I speculated. "Have they started screening suspects?"

"You'll have to ask Dan about that." she said, getting to her feet and collecting dirty dishes from the table. "In the meantime, do you want to wash or dry?"

"I better wash. I don't know where anything goes after it's dried." I picked up my dishes and took them to the sink. I started the water, filled the basin and added dish soap. It wasn't until we were nearly done with the dishes that I noticed that Ellie had a perfectly good dishwasher under the counter. I pretended not to see. Had she wanted me to linger? Was she more afraid than she wanted to let on? I didn't ask. I wasn't sure I wanted to know.

The last dish washed and put away. I turned to Ellie. "Well, I'd better get dressed so you can drive me home."

She smiled, averting her gaze. "We don't need to hurry, do we?"

At one point in my life, I would have seen this as the starting gun and I would have been off to the races. But I had convinced myself that I wasn't that guy anymore. "Well...I don't want to overstay my welcome."

She took on a serious tone. "Listen, Hank. Not to toot my own horn, but in this town, I'm sort of a, I don't know, a saint, a hero. Unfortunately, that also makes me an untouchable for some men and a challenge for others. You're the first person in a long time who has treated me like just another person. I supposed it's because you're a doctor too, but whatever the reason, I like it. I like having a friend who understands what it means to practice medicine, both the good and the bad sides."

"Well, it's been sort of like that for me too," I said. "I miss the collegiality. The inside jokes. The support. It's been a long time for me."

"Me too," she said softly. "But that's not all. Maybe I've grown tired of being alone. I could never leave Amber Creek but sometimes I resent the life I've had to live here. I'd like more."

"More?" I asked.

"I like you, Hank."

"I'm old enough to be your father."

"But you're not my father," she said, approaching me.

I put my hand up, palm out. "Don't get me wrong, Ellie, but I'm not sure you know what

you'd be in for."

"I'm a grown woman," she said. 'And I've got my eyes wide open."

"We need to talk first," I said, taking her hand and leading her to the sofa in the living room. We both sat. "You know a little about me, from the murder case. The newspapers didn't miss a beat. But there are things they didn't get into."

"Such as?" she asked, her eyebrows tightening.

"I was married, for a long time, to a wonderful woman." She tried to interrupt but I held my hand up again. "But I was a shitty husband."

"You couldn't have been as shitty as mine was."

"I don't know about that," I said. "But even so, you don't deserve to be hurt again."

"I think I should be the judge of that," she said, pulling back from me a little.

"I wasn't faithful. I had multiple affairs behind her back. Hell, I was in bed with another woman the night she died."

"The papers said you had sex with a patient."

"Yes but only the one time and there were extenuating circumstances."

"I know all about the case. It was in the paper for weeks, months. I know that she tricked you and then drugged you. I don't like it but I understand. And you've changed, haven't you?"

"I can only hope so," I sighed. "I just don't want you and I to start anything without being totally honest. I don't want to hurt you."

"I told you before. I can take care of myself." She reached her hand out to me. "But I don't want to be alone again tonight."

"Is it the murders?" I asked.

"Yes and no," she said. "But either way, I still would like to see if you and I have the possibility of something together. I've been alone a long time."

I leaned into her. "So have I." I took her face in my hands and kissed her. Her tongue responded, parting my lips and exploring beyond. We slid closer across the leather sofa until we were able to wrap ourselves around each other. My robe parted, no longer able to contain my interest. Ellie lay back against the arm of the sofa and reached into her pocket. She took a square packet from it and peeled it open. "This is the last one my husband left behind. He wouldn't like me using it like this."

"Screw him," I said.

"No, not him." She skillfully unrolled the latex onto my very excited penis then reached down to loosen her pants. I pushed her hands away and worked the buttons myself before lowering the top of her jeans and revealing white cotton underpants. I stroked her gently and

she reached down to caress me. Soon we were both naked and wrapped around each other, her on top of me and kissing me deeply. I flipped us around rather adroitly, I think, and was atop her. I kissed her lips then worked my way down along the line of her neck to her nipples that stood erect. I closed my teeth around one, tenderly nipped at it. Ellie moaned and pushed my head away, guiding me downward. I explored her with my tongue and then rose up and looked into her eyes. "Are you sure?" I asked. She said nothing but took me in her hand and directed me into her moist warmth. I was a little out of practice and came after only a few thrusts but she matched my enthusiasm. I heard her gasp and felt a wave of pressure on the shaft of my penis. Afterwards, I lay atop her breathing heavily and feeling the last throbs of passion. Our eyes met and we smiled knowing smiles. It had been better than good, for both of us.

Ellie whispered into my ear. "I think it's time for bed." I rolled off of her and she led me to the bedroom. I'd like to say we made love again but, in truth, we fell asleep in each other's arms almost immediately.

We woke still in each other's arms. It felt good. I offered to take it further but Ellie reminded me that she had to get to work. She climbed out of bed and walked into the bathroom, closing the door firmly behind her. I got up, went to the laundry room and retrieved my fresh but very wrinkled clothes. I slipped into them anyway and went to the kitchen to chase up a little breakfast for the both of us. Ellie hadn't been kidding about the need for a grocery run. There was one egg, a little milk that was past its prime, some instant oatmeal packets and an unopened can of apricot nectar. Nothing else sounded even vaguely breakfasty. I went back to the bathroom and tapped on the door.

I heard a "Yes" muffled by the shower. Opening the door a crack I shouted, "I'm taking you out to breakfast."

She pulled the shower curtain aside to stick her head out. "Good luck with that, but I'm hungry. Go for it."

I headed back to the kitchen to brew some coffee and Ellie joined me fifteen minutes later. I offered her a cup.

"So, what are these breakfast plans?" she said before taking a sip.

"Irene makes a great breakfast."

"Good, let's go," she said, emptying her cup in the sink. "You make lousy coffee."

I dumped mine, too. I had to admit she was right. We headed to the car and drove to Irene's place. She greeted us at the door with no surprise or ceremony. "Come on in," she said, eyebrows raised. I took a second to look at her more closely. Was this the same woman I had seen at the cemetery? There was no sign of the grief I'd seen then. I wanted to ask her about Eddie's grave but knew it was not a good idea.

"Is Bob around," I inquired to redirect us both.

"No. He and Charlotte went back to the farm. The kids were on the school bus an hour ago. It's just little old me." She led us to the kitchen and poured us each a large mug of fresh coffee.

Ellie took a sip. "Irene, do you give lessons? Hank here needs to learn how to make coffee."

Irene looked over her shoulder with a knowing grin. "Next time. Right now, I can teach him to fry eggs." She did.

Ellie and I sat down to a classic Irene breakfast. Irene herself just nursed her mug of coffee, having had breakfast at what she called 'a decent hour'.

I looked across at Irene. "How are Bob and Charlotte...really?"

She put down her mug and pursed her lips for a second before responding. "They're not as tough as they try to appear. The farm was all they had and the bank owned more of it than they did."

"Any insurance?" Ellie asked.

"Well, yes, but is there ever enough. With everything else going on they hadn't even gotten a chance to meet the insurance man till today. That's why they went to the farm this morning."

"I imagine Andy's pretty busy these days," Ellie said.

"Andy?" I asked, before shoveling more eggs into my face.

"Andy Folger, the insurance guy, " Irene said. "Only one in town. Maybe the only one for forty miles. And yes, he's as busy as an elf on Christmas eve. "

"Do ya' think Bob and Charlotte would mind a little company?" I asked.

"No," Irene said. "I think they would appreciate it."

"Ellie, can I borrow your car again? I'd like to stop by the farm after breakfast."

"Sure," she said, smiling like a proud parent. We finished our meals and Ellie stood, picking dishes up as she did. She walked them to the sink and looked over at me. "On your feet," she said. "KP time."

"Oh, don't bother," Irene said. "I can handle it."

"You sure?" Ellies asked.

"Been doin' it for many a year," Irene winked. "Got it down to a science. You head out."

"Can I use your bathroom for a second," Ellie asked.

Irene nodded and once Ellie was gone, she turned to me. "While she's in there, you can help with clean up."

"But you just said..."

"Pick up your dishes and get over here," she said.

I complied. While she washed and I dried, Irene was silent but then she dropped her dishcloth in the sink and turned to me. "You and Doc Ellie getting pretty close, are you?"

"Yeah,' I said uneasily.

"Well, that's between the two of you," Irene continued, "but you need to remember that she's been hurt. And I don't want to see her hurt again."

"She told me about her husband."

"Then you know what I'm talking about then. So, watch it, Hank. I like you but I like Ellie a whole lot more. I'm keeping my eye on you. '

"Yes, ma'am," I said just as Ellie came back into the kitchen.

"Sorry it took so long," she said.

"You're not the only one," I said.

"Oh, get the hell out of here," Irene said. "I'd rather finish myself than have to listen to Hank's whining anymore."

"I'll take him off your hands," Ellie said as she pushed me to the kitchen door. "But thanks for breakfast. It was wonderful."

"Come by anytime," Irene said as Ellie and I made our exit.

"Once outside, I led Ellie to my RV. "Just gotta clean up and change my clothes. Won't take a minute."

We stepped inside and Ellie surveyed the space. "A bit Spartan, isn't it?.

I looked around with a new perspective. "Yeah, I guess. But what does a single guy need?"

She scanned the room again. "Ya know something's beeping in here Somewhere."

"Oh, it's just my phone," I said, picking it up with sudden recognition. "My phone, the towers must be working. What's Dan's number?" Ellie gave it to me; I punched it in and Dan answered. "The phones are working," I said.

"Duh," Dan replied. "And who might this be?"

"Hank," I replied. "I was just testing the phone."

"Well, apparently it works. Are there any other critical issues I can take care of for you?"

"Well, I was wondering about the investigation."

"BCI is still working on it. I'll let you and Ellie in on the results when they come."

"Great, thanks," I said and disconnected.

I looked at Ellie. "Do you have your phone?"

"Not on me," she said. "No need until now so I left it at home."

"Okay, so after I've cleaned up, I'll take you home to get it then drop you off at the hospital. I still want to get to Bob's farm."

"Sure," she said as I ducked into the bathroom.

CHAPTER ELEVEN

A half-hour later, I pulled into Bob's driveway. His truck was there and another car, a nondescript, tan-colored sedan. I parked and walked to what was left of Bob's house. Behind it, Bob and Charlotte were sitting at a battered picnic table, talking with a balding man with glasses. I recognized him as the man I'd seen the day before by the church. I assume that he was the insurance man and guessed that he had been at the church for the same reason he was here, to assess damage and discuss insurance payouts. I walked around the rubble and up to the table. Charlotte looked up, a little surprised. "Hank, what are you doing here?"

"Just wanted to connect with you guys and see what I could do to help," I said. "If you're busy I can come back."

"No, of course not," Bob said, coming to his feet. "Join us." He pointed to the other man who was already scrutinizing me over his shoulder. "This is Andy Folger, our insurance man." I extended my hand and Folger shook it noncommittally. I took a seat beside him.

"Go ahead with what you were discussing."

For another twenty minutes, the Owens and Folger debated back and forth about property values, contract clauses and what was needed versus what was owed. It was clear to me that a middle ground was not going to be easily found.

Finally, Folger came to his feet. "I'm sorry," he said, not looking particularly sorry. "But these are the figures. Why don't you two talk them over and get back to me." He nodded at me. "Nice to meet you, Doctor. Too bad it wasn't under better circumstances." He turned and headed back to his car. Neither Bob nor Charlotte acknowledged his departure. The three of us sat at the table for several minutes before anyone said a word. That word was "Fuck" coming from Bob, who generally wouldn't have said shit if he's had a mouthful.

"Sounds like a raw deal," I said.

"You could say that," Bob replied. "What the insurance company is willing to pay me won't even cover my mortgage."

Charlotte put an arm around Bob's shoulder. "We'll find a way," she said. "We always do."

"Maybe you should talk with a lawyer," I suggested.

"I've known Andy since I moved to Amber Creek," Bob said. "He ain't cheating us."

"I'm not saying that," I said. "But you should know your rights."

"And who's gonna pay for a lawyer? I sure can't," Bob said.

"How about legal aid?"

"We don't have that around here, that I know of," he said.

"We could check," Charlotte said. "I'll call the county seat. We can't just give up."

I looked across the table at two people in obvious pain. I hadn't known the Owens for long but they had become important to me. I took in a deep breath and let it out slowly. "Ya' know, I've got some money. Maybe I can help, by hiring a lawyer, I mean."

Bob looked up at me with an expression that projected more resentment than gratitude. "Thanks, but no thanks. I'm perfectly capable of taking care of my own family." He rose abruptly from the table. "I've got some stuff to check on." He walked briskly away without another word.

I looked at Charlotte. "I'm sorry if I offended him," I said. "I just wanted to help."

"Bob's a proud man," she said. "He is grateful for what you've done for us and for the town but he could never take money from you. He'd draw the line at that."

"Then, is there anything else I could do?"

She reached her hand across the table. "You've done so much already and we'll never be able to thank you enough."

I took her hand in mine for a moment then stood. "Maybe it would be best if I went."

"Okay," she said. "But Bob will come around. He's not angry with you. He's just fed up with the situation."

"I know, "I said, giving her hand one last squeeze before releasing it. "Just don't be afraid to ask for anything. I don't have a lot of friends. I don't want to lose the two of you."

She smiled but a tear rolled down her cheek. I turned and walked back to the car. I climbed in and took out the grocery list I had convinced Ellie to give me. I started the car and pulled back out onto the highway, driving south to the four lane then west. It took nearly an hour to get to the town where Ellie shopped. The trip was not a comfortable one. I couldn't stop thinking about Bob and Charlotte and about their future. I'd wanted to help them but only ended up insulting Bob. But I did have the ability to help, if only he would let me. I had to find another way to do it. But I couldn't seem to think of a way. I turned the radio on and listened to country music that made me cringe but at least diverted my attention until I reached my destination.

Mount Carter was a mid-sized town on what Midwesterners consider a mountain. Anywhere else it would have been a hillock at best. I drove into the town, past homes that reflected every style, from hundred-year-old farmhouses to midcentury bungalows. Neat lawns came all the way to the curb without sidewalks. Tall, ancient trees lined the street and arched over it like the ceiling of a cathedral. I approached the center of town and found a neat square like Amber Creek's must have been. I turned left and then right again passing a hardware store, a bank, a coffee shop and a gift shop, all tidy brick buildings with ornate cornices and welcoming entrances framed by potted plants and broad benches. The courthouse and library across the square and two churches in front of me completed a scene that seemed like it came out of a classic movie. I was struck with how much the people of Amber Creek had lost.

I turned left again at the corner of the square and then right to take the street that ran between the churches. More homes lined the sides of the street, first rather grand and Victorian then more modest but still well cared for and appealing. A few blocks further on was a more modern business district with a gas station, a pharmacy and the grocery store. I pulled into the parking lot. Entering the store, I surveyed my list and was surprised that Ellie had added condoms to the bottom of the list. Along with Ellie's groceries, I selected several items that I knew Irene needed. I lingered a moment at the head of the liquor aisle, telling myself that I should get a bottle of wine...for Ellie. I turned down the aisle just to look around. Mid way, there was a small sign reading 'Scotch' and I headed there. I'd always preferred scotch, good scotch. Mine was Talisker. Eighty bucks a pop. I scanned the sparse scotch section. No Talisker, of course. It was not a grocery store-level scotch. I have to admit to having been a bit of a booze snob. The most expensive bottle was selling for thirty dollars. I picked it up and hefted it. I lifted it to the light and admired its amber glow. I could almost taste it. I was flooded with sensations I hadn't felt for a long time. The unfortunate interaction with Bob was out of my mind and replaced by the anticipation of oblivion that the scotch promised.

The sound of a loud throat clearing pulled me from my reverie and I looked up at a pleasant-looking young woman pushing a half filled grocery cart . A small girl sat in the child seat. The woman smiled closed-mouthed and glanced down at my cart that crossed the aisle obstructing her progress. It took me a minute to register, then I apologized and pulled my cart to the side. She thanked me rather tersely and went on her way but I had seen the judgment in her eyes. I looked at the bottle in my hand and was instantly ashamed. I hadn't had a drink in two years. What the hell was I thinking? I slid the bottle back on the shelf and headed out of the liquor aisle as inconspicuously as possible, forgetting about Ellie's wine. I should have been relieved that I hadn't purchased the scotch but I wasn't. I was disgusted with myself.

I finished my shopping quickly and, at the checkout, picked up a selection of candy bars to give to Bob's kids. I would like to have gotten something for Bob and Charlotte but I wasn't sure how they would be received. I loaded everything back into the car and headed home.

Funny that I thought of Amber Creek that way, as home. I'd been there less than two months. I really didn't have a place to live there other than my RV. I wasn't related to anyone there. I didn't have a job or really a purpose there, but yet, it felt like home to me. The connections I'd made there felt more real to me than almost any I'd made in my life. Maybe that was because, in Amber Creek, I had allowed myself to be me. No facade, no mask, no pretense. And, much to my surprise, people were okay with that. They accepted me into their fold. They made me feel like I belonged. And I wanted to help them and to become one of them. And I could have blown it all so easily with one bottle of scotch. I thought about this as I drove out of Mount Carter, wiping my moist eyes.

My first stop was at Irene's place. I took a few items into my RV and stowed them. Then I knocked on Irene's screen door. She opened it almost immediately, wiping her hands on her aprons. I lifted two bags of groceries and said, "Something to repay you for all those delicious meals."

"Come on in," she said, stepping aside. "You know that wasn't necessary."

"No, I guess not, but I wanted to do it," I set the bags on the table. "Say, are Bob and Charlotte home yet."

"They were," she said," but they went right out again. Said they were going to talk with some of the other folks around town. I think they were wanting to discuss their insurance payout. They didn't say much but they sure didn't look happy."

"I'm not surprised," I said. "I was at the farm when they were talking with the insurance guy, what's his name?"

"Andy Folger."

"Yeah, that's it. Anyway, he's not offering them a very good settlement."

"No surprise there," Irene said. "If he weren't the only insurance guy for miles around, he'd have very little business. Most people don't like his .... shall we say business practices."

"Bob said that Andy wouldn't cheat him."

"Bob is a little naive. Andy is out for Andy. He may not cheat anyone but he walks the line."

"Well, that sucks," I said. "I offered to help Bob but he got pissed at me."

"That's Bob. Naive and proud. Not the best combination in these times."

"Well, let me know if you can think of anything I can do to help them out. I really feel bad for them."

Irene smiled sadly. "Thanks, Hank. I'll let ya' know." She reached into the first bag and pulled out a bunch of asparagus. "Ooh, my favorite," she said.

I leaned in and gave her a peck on the cheek and headed outside to the car.

By the time I got to the hospital, Ellie was ready to be picked up. We drove to her place and unloaded the groceries and heated a jar of spaghetti sauce and some frozen ravioli. With new ingredients, I made a caprese salad. We sat to eat and I apologized that I hadn't gotten a nice bottle of Chianti...for Ellie. She said that she didn't mind but I felt like she should. My drinking problem shouldn't limit her. To me, a meal without wine was a concession to my frailty. I kept that to myself though and enjoyed listening to Ellie talk about the day's patients and whatever other local news she had. I shared my experience at the graveyard and with the Owens. Ellie encouraged me to give Bob a little time but assured me that he wasn't angry at me but the situation. Of course, that had been said before, but it was nice to hear again.

Meal over and cleanup done, I asked Ellie if she wanted to take me home. She shook the box of condoms at me and said "I want to take you, but not home." She led me to the bedroom for a slightly more slowly-paced replay of the night before.

CHAPTER TWELVE

It was another three days before Dan called me and asked to meet for coffee at the Pump 'n Shop, a gas station-convenience store- cafe combo that had just reopened on the east end of town where tornado damage had been minimal. He explained that the police station and most other city facilities had been destroyed in the storm. A temporary office was being arranged for but not available yet. And, besides, the mayor ran the Pump n' Shop. He told me that he had invited Ellie and she'd suggested I come along. His officers, Father Sam and the Mayor would also be there for a brief presentation from the BCI representative. I told him that I wasn't sure what I'd have to offer but agreed to come anyway.

Ellie and I got there to see two police cars, a few private vehicles and a black, very official-looking SUV with dark windows already parked there. We walked to the door but there was a sign on it that said that the cafe was closed. "Don't worry," Ellie said. "Angie Parker runs the place and she is also the mayor of our fine city." She pushed the door open and I followed her in, trying to ignore the display of cheap whisky near the front of the store.

At the counter, a young woman in a blue apron looked up. "Oh, Ellie," she said. "Grab a cup of coffee and a donut. They're waiting for you in the cafe." She pointed through a doorway just past the counter.

"Thanks," Ellie said, heading to the coffee urn. Under her breath, she told me that the girl was Angie's granddaughter who had worked at the Pump n' Shop since graduating high school. "She's a smart girl, but doesn't want to leave Amber Creek and there aren't a lot of job opportunities around here." We filled our coffee cups, grabbed a donut each and headed into the cafe which was little more than a back room with a few assorted tables and a buffet-style service counter, currently devoid of buffet-style food. At one table were Dan and his officers. Sam sat at another with a late middle-aged, stocky woman who stood and extended her hand.

I reached down to take her hand as she couldn't have been much over four feet tall. "You must be Doctor Pressman," she said. "I've heard so much about you. I'm Angie Parker."

"Nice to meet you, Mayor," I said.

"So you've heard. The fine folks of Amber Creek have elected me four times and for one reason and one only. No one else ran."

I laughed, grasping her hand. Her wit was infectious. She directed Ellie and me to sit with her. We greeted Sam and the police officers.

"So, where are these all-important state guys?", Angie said. "Don't they know I've got a business to run?"

"They were making some last-minute calls out in their car," Dan said. They should be in soon.

"Any news in the meantime," Angie said, to which Dan responded with a shrug. Then he and his officers stood to attention. Two men in black suits, white button-down shirts and conservative ties walked in. One was tall, trim and graying around the temples. The other was a little shorter and solidly built. The tall one stepped over to Dan.

"Hello again," he said. "I'm glad we could get together. Would you mind making introductions?"

"This is Captain Andrews and Lieutenant Pierce of the BCI," Dan said. He then followed through, identifying each of us in turn and our connection to the case. Last was Sam. The BCI men looked stunned.

"Excuse me, Father Cannon," Andrews said, "I don't recall asking you to this meeting."

"No," Dan interjected. "I'm sorry but I asked him to come. After all, the bodies were on his church property, so I thought it was logical."

"I'm sorry too," the captain continued very formally. "But I should have been more explicit. Father, the information I wanted to discuss today is not for public consumption. I'm going to have to ask you to leave."

"Now wait a minute," Dan said. "I don't see any harm in his staying. He has a right to know what you found on his property."

"I believe the church yard is the property of the diocese or, at the very least, the congregation. Father Cannon is an employee."

"That's not how it works," Dan said, more loudly than he probably intended.

"You didn't seem to mind that I was here," I interjected. "You didn't invite me."

"No, I didn't," Andrews said. "But, being that you're here, I may be able to use some of your insight."

"But Father Sam is devoid of insight?" Ellie asked sharply.

"Wait, I understand," Sam said, coming to his feet. "I'll leave but if at any time you do need to talk with me, please feel free to call." He headed to the door.

Dan, obviously irritated, called after him. "I'll fill you in later, Sam."

"Thank you, Father," the captain said before giving Dan a searing look. "Now, if you don't mind, I'd like to get down to why we're here." He and the lieutenant stepped to the front of the room and scanned the little group. "I'm sorry for the confusion, but, once we've talked, I hope that you will understand why I asked your priest to leave and where the investigation needs to go from this point. But first a few questions."

"You've got our attention," Angie said, sarcastically.

Captain Andrews proceeded to interview Ellie and myself about our involvement in the case so far and our impressions. We shared what little we knew then answered a series of more pointed questions that didn't seem to amount to much. He then asked Dan if he or his men had anything else to add.

"You know everything we know," Dan said, "and hopefully a lot more."

"Alright, so let me summarize our case," the captain said, ignoring the tension in the room. "We are aware of the identity of the first victim found in the storm rubble, Sally Franklin."

"The first victim?" Dan said. "So you're saying the others are related to Ms. Franklin's death."

"Yes, we believe that they are. Ms. Franklin was a prostitute who we believe was abducted in Omaha and brought to Amber Creek, where she was held captive, tortured, raped and ultimately murdered by suffocation. We believe that her body was dumped among the tornado debris in hopes that she would be seen as a victim of the storm."

"We know all of that," Angie said. "What about the others?"

'I'm coming to that," Andrews said. "The first body found in the churchyard has yet to be identified. It is the body of a woman who we believe was in her early twenties. She showed the same signs of bone wasting and healing fractures as found in Ms. Franklin but, as there was essentially no soft tissue remaining, there is little else we can say."

"How long was she buried," Dan asked.

"We think she was there for between three and five years. And, interestingly, the headstone indicated that the person buried below her body had died three and a half years ago."

"Oh my God," Ellie said, covering her mouth.

"So you have no idea who she is," I said.

"Not as of yet," Lieutenant Pierce said. "We are continuing to examine the evidence. It's still early."

"And the other two?" Ellie asked.

"They were in a better state of preservation," Andrews said. "We were able to make identifications. Mary Capeheart, a twenty-two-year-old Chicago prostitute, missing for nearly three years. She showed the same signs of physical abuse and deprivation. We could confirm that she had been raped but no DNA evidence of her assailant could be collected. The same for the third woman, one Candy Streckaman, a twenty-year-old prostitute, missing from Minneapolis for approximately eighteen months."

"So you're saying that they were all prostitutes from pretty far away, who were killed in Amber Creek."

"Not exactly," the lieutenant responded. "They were buried here. We speculate that they were also killed here though we cannot assume that."

"And the graves," I asked. "When had they originally been used? I mean..."

"I understand what you're asking, "Andrews said. "One was dated two and a half years ago and the other just a year."

"So the dates of the original burials coincided fairly well with these," I asked.

"Yes," Andrews said. "We are working on the theory that the murder victims were buried very shortly after the original internments."

"The soil would have already been disturbed," Dan noted. "Easy to dig and no one would have thought anything of the loose mounds of dirt."

"Exactly," Andrews said.

"So, do you have any indication of who might have done this?" Angie asked, the sarcasm lost from her voice.

"That's where we will need the help of everyone in this room," Andrews said.

"But why me," I said. "I'm not from here. I've only been around since the tornado."

"We are aware of that," Andrews continued, "but you may be able to provide us with some insight into the personalities you've encountered in the town and, with the help of our forensic team, you may be able to help us understand our killer."

"Well, I'm glad to help any way I can," I said, "but I'm no forensic psychiatrist, as I have said many times."

"We appreciate that Doctor," Andrews said. He turned to Dan. "We would like to coordinate through your office to schedule interviews with persons of interest."

"Alright," Dan said. "Where do we start?"

"We would like to start with Father Cannon," Lieutenant Pierce said.

"So why did you ask him to leave," Angie said.

The BCI men responded with silent steely-eyed stares.

"You don't think that..." Ellie said. "You've got to be out of your mind. Sam is our friend. He has done so much for this community. He wouldn't be capable of what you are suggesting."

"We are suggesting nothing at this point," Pierce said. "We are just collecting information. But Father Cannon did conduct all three funerals. Also, he was the most likely person to have seen an intruder digging in the cemetery yet he never reported anything."

"The hell with you," Angie shouted. "Dan, tell them they're full of shit."

Dan got to his feet and approached Angie. "Please calm down, Angie," he said. "These guys are only doing their jobs. After all, I called 'em in and it's my duty to help them in their investigation."

"I won't hear this," Angie said. "This is insane!"

"Now wait," Dan said. "You and I know that Sam didn't do this. I just want to help these guys clear him, that's all."

"You can all just get out of my store," she shouted, stepping to the door and crossing her arms.

"Chief Gilmore," Andrews said, "if we could accompany you back to your office we need to solidify our plans."

"I don't actually have an office at this point, but we'll make do." He led them out. At the door, Andrews turned back to the assembled group. "And remember that this is confidential information. If any of you share it outside of this group, you may endanger this investigation." He turned and left.

"That son of a bitch," Angie said. "Who the hell does he think he is?"

Ellie put her arm around Angie's shoulder. "Don't worry," she said. "We know that Sam didn't do this. But we do want to find out who did. So please, let the cops do their work. And do what they asked. The sooner this is done the sooner we can get back to rebuilding this town, OK?"

Angie didn't look happy but she nodded and led us out of the building.

Ellie and I climbed into her car. "That was certainly uncomfortable," I said.

``You don't know the half of it," Ellie said, curtly.

We drove a couple of blocks in silence then Ellie looked at me, uncertainty painted on her face. "What do you think?"

"About?"

"Come on," she said, attending to her driving again. "They are all but accusing Sam of murder."

"Oh...that," I said. "I don't know Sam as well as you do. He seems like an okay guy."

"But?" she said.

"But." I continued, treading carefully, "he is a reasonable suspect if you look at the initial evidence."

Ellie pulled over to the side of the road and turned to look at me face on. "You really don't know him. He couldn't have done this."

"I already said that I didn't, so I don't have much to refute the evidence."

"What evidence," she said, her voice taking on an edge. "Is it just because he's a priest, you're assuming he has a dark side."

"Now wait a minute, I didn't say that."

"You didn't have to. I know what you think about the church". She turned and pulled the car back on the road. At the next intersection, she turned toward the town square and not the road out of town.

"Where are we going," I asked. We had spent almost every night at her house since we'd first made love.

"I'll drop you off at your place," she said, eyes fixed on the road ahead.

"Are you angry with me?"

"I don't know," she said brusquely, her eyes filling with tears. "I think I just need time to process everything."

"Listen, you asked me what I thought. I didn't mean to hurt your feelings."

"I'm sorry," she said. "I just don't know what to think."

"You had to have considered the possibility, just looking at the facts."

"I didn't have to consider anything," she said and slammed on the brakes in front of Irene's house. She sat gripping the steering wheel like a life preserver and looking out of the windshield.

I opened the door to get out and leaned to give her a kiss but she turned away, my lips landing on her cheek. "I'll call you," I said and climbed out of the car.

"Ok" she said. Before I could get the car door closed all the way, she gunned the engine and drove away. Watching her fade in the cloud of dust she left behind, I couldn't help but wonder about Ellie's reaction. Was Sam more to Ellie than she'd admitted? Sam may be a priest but he was also a man.

CHAPTER THIRTEEN

I was confused and a little hurt so I didn't want company. I headed back into my RV. For the first time in a long time, I felt like I wanted or maybe even needed a drink. Fortunately, I had not stocked my RV with any liquor. I walked to the back of the vehicle and dropped on the bed, covering my face with a forearm. I hadn't meant to upset Ellie. Hell, I was starting to have pretty nurturing feelings for her. But I also didn't want to start telling her only what she wanted to hear. The old me was a pro at that and it hadn't worked out very well in the end. There had to be another way. Maybe if I could prove Sam innocent. I decided to review the details of the murder case as I knew them. I really didn't have a lot to do in Amber Creek but maybe, if I could use my free time to help find this killer, I could make amends with Ellie. I didn't want to be the town hero really. I just wanted to show Ellie that I supported her and to show the town that I appreciated the welcome they had shown me. Before I got too far in formulating my plan of attack I must have drifted off to a restless sleep.

I woke to a firm knocking on the door. I climbed out of bed and opened it. Bob was there, smiling sheepishly. "I was hoping we could talk," he said.

"Sure, "I stepped aside to let him in. "Can I get you anything,"

"A good stiff drink wouldn't hurt," he said.

"Sorry," I chuckled. "How 'bout a diet Pepsi?"

"Beggars can't be choosers," He said and took a seat in one of the two recliners in what I liked to call 'my den'. Situated between the driver's cabin and a tiny kitchenette, it consisted of the two chairs, a small table separating them and a good view of the wide screen TV suspended over the dinette across the RV.

I handed Bob his drink. "So, what's up?"

"It's about the other day, when you came out to the farm," he said. "Charlotte and I got to talking after you left. She thinks I was kinda hard on you. And I guess she's right."

"Don't give it a thought, Bob," I said, taking the seat beside him.

"No, I owe you an apology. You were only trying to help. Though I can't accept your generosity, I should have at least thanked you." he said. "So... well thanks and I'm sorry."

I smiled, feeling genuine warmth. "Apology accepted. You've got a lot on your shoulders. I just want to help any way I can." We clinked our soda cans and took a swig. Like most men, we were momentarily at a loss for words. Then I seized the opportunity. "Bob, how much have you heard about the bodies they found?"

"It's all over town," he said. "'Course, I don't know how much is fact and how much is gossip."

"Well, I've been asked to be a part of the investigation, sort of. A pretty insignificant part from what I can tell, but be that as it may, I do want to help. Unfortunately, I can't give you any details of the case. Sworn to secrecy and all that shit but I could use your help."

"How's that," he said sitting forward, the soda can gripped with both hands.

"Well, you know the people in this town pretty well, right."

"Yeah, I suppose," he said. "Charlotte was raised here but I've been here since we got married."

"I'm wondering if you know of any men in town who live alone and travel frequently?"

He sat back again and cast his gaze to the ceiling. "Let me think." I waited patiently for a few minutes, nursing my Pepsi. "Well," he said. "There's Andy Folger, the guy you met up at the farm. He's on the road a lot for business. And Pete Miller, he's the new pharmacist. He's single but I think he's got ...well, someone out of town he goes to see a lot."

"How new?' I interrupted.

"Well, you gotta remember, I'm talkin' Amber Creek 'new'. He's been here maybe four years. Bought the drug store from old Mr. Waterson. It's been one of the few places in town where you can get everyday supplies. 'Course, it's gone now. Used to be on the west side of the square. Can't help but wonder where he is now. He lived over the store."

"A real loss to the community," I said, shaking my head. "Anyone else you can think of?"

He took another long draw on his soda and squinted his eyes. "Well not exactly in town but the Paulson boys, Ed and Tom live on a farm just north of town. When you're heading to my place, you turn right at the county road instead of left. They're out about two miles. Both in their forties. Neither one ever married. Lived with their folks till they died then they both of 'em just stayed on. Nice enough guys. Quiet."

"Ok," I mentally filed their names as unlikely suspects. Our killer had been in town during the storm or there would have been no way to plant Sally Franklin's body so quickly.

"Listen, let's ask Charlotte and Irene, they're much better at this than me."

I agreed and we walked out of the RV and into Irene's house. They were both in the kitchen, Irene kneading bread dough and Charlotte at the table doing paperwork. I suspected that, as the family bookkeeper, she was sorting out what assets were left and how much would be needed to get the farm back up and running. I didn't envy her that job.

"Hey, girls," Bob said. "Hank and I were talking." Charlotte looked up with a knowing smile. She obviously suspected Bob had apologized and she approved.

I took the floor and reviewed my conversation with Bob. Charlotte set her pen down, pursed her lips and cocked her head. Irene kept kneading but her creased forehead suggested a mind at work.

"There's Jerry Albright," Charlotte said. "He works with Dan Gilmore. A deputy or something. Anyway, he was married. His wife left him, maybe seven, eight years ago. No kids or anything. He just kept the house here in town. I don't think he's been seeing anyone, but he's on the road a lot, with his work, I suppose."

This sounded like an interesting suspect but a dicey one too. Dan was not likely to want one of his own accused.

Then Irene chimed in. "I don't know if he counts but there's Sam. He's a priest so I guess he's technically single. And he's got those other churches out of town."

There was the prime suspect again. Single, traveled and certainly had access to the church yard. "Who else works at the church?" I asked.

"When I was a kid," Irene said, "there were half a dozen nuns, a groundskeeper and a couple of lay teachers. They've been gone for quite a while. Now Sam does most of the work himself or volunteers help out. I doubt that there's all that much to do anymore."

"Anyone else comes to mind," I said.

"Not really," said Charlotte. "It's not that big a town. We'll let you know if we think of anyone else."

"Well, thanks," I said.

"If you want to talk with Sam, I think he's in town this afternoon. I'm on the church council and we're supposed to get together after lunch. Sam talked to the insurance company and wants to fill us in."

"Yeah," I said. "I saw Andy Folger at the church the other day."

"Oh," Irene said. "He doesn't do our insurance. The Diocese handles all of that."

"Oh, okay," I said. "Guess he was just nosey like everyone else. Do you know where Father Sam is now?"

"No but I can get you his cell number after I'm done here," Irene said. Bob and I sat and made small talk while Irene pounded and rolled the dough until she decided it was done. She shaped it into a ball, dropped it into an oiled bowl and rolled it around a few times. She covered the bowl with a damp dish towel and slid to the back of her counter. She washed her hands, pulled her purse off a hook near the door and removed her cell phone. "Here ya' go," she said and read Sam's phone number. I keyed it into my phone's contact list.

"Thanks," I said, rising to my feet.

"Coming back for supper?" Irene asked.

"I'd like to but don't count on me," I said,

"Eating up at Doc Ellie's again," Bob said, a lascivious tone in his voice.

My face felt suddenly warm. "Ah, probably not tonight," I forced a smile and made a hasty retreat.

Once outside, I vetoed going back to my RV alone so I started walking toward town with no specific goal in mind. Entering the storm-ravaged area, I noted several houses undergoing repair. Most of the homes that were beyond saving had been cleared but no new construction had begun yet. I suspected that that would be several months away. The town square now looked bleak. The west side was a vacant lot. On the north side, the church complex was still as the storm had left it but was now ringed with police tape. No clearing or reconstruction could be contemplated there until the murders had been solved. The east and south sides of the square were undergoing various degrees of restoration. No business had reopened there yet.

The gazebo was once again open but some of the trucks were still parked near it. Dan, his operations center and the entire town administration had found temporary quarters in an old abandoned farm equipment store about five blocks to the east. They'd be moving in soon, once the plywood walls and temporary phone lines were in place. It would be completed soon, but Amber Creek itself was obviously going to need a lot more time, a lot of money and a lot of love if it were ever to be what I suspected it had once been.

I walked into the gazebo and sat on one of the metal benches that circled its interior. From there, I watched as people came and went, some just passing through, others lugging building material. There were no shoppers or people looking for a place to eat. No business being done. There probably wouldn't be for quite a while. I pictured how it must have looked in the past when downtown was the center of business, government and faith that it had been. I imagined people shopping, meeting and praying there. It must have been a vibrant place.

Across the square, a car pulled up in front of the church and Father Sam climbed out. I got up and walked his way, joining him on the sidewalk where he stood staring across the yellow tape at what was left of his church. He looked tired, crestfallen and like another good wind could blow him away. Could this man be a murderer, I wondered. I stood beside him without looking at him. "I'm so sorry for your loss," I said lamely.

He looked over at me and smiled. "Thanks. But we'll rebuild. Maybe not as grand or solid, but we will rebuild. The people of this town need it to happen and I'm going to do my damnedest to see it's done."

I turned to look at him. His red eyes and drawn face made me feel real empathy. He was hurting, not just for himself but for his community. I had walked away from my hurt but it was clear he wouldn't. He was a man with a mission, a passion. Without meaning to, he had told me who he really was. And, I hoped, who he was not.

"I suppose you can't do much here until the police are done?"

"No," he said. "Not till they're done with the place or with me."

"Excuse me," I said, playing dumb.

"Dan and the guys at BCI want to talk with me after the parish council meeting," he said. "I couldn't blame them if they suspected me. There's plenty of circumstantial evidence."

"What do you mean?"

"Well, first, I live here. The rectory is right behind the church, so I had easy access and I didn't report any strange goings on in the church yard."

"Did you see any?" I asked.

"No, of course not. See, the rectory was built for two priests. I've been the only one there for years and I picked the bedroom and study on the street side. The traffic noise was nothing compared to the kids in the playground. The kitchen and dining room were on the side facing the school and I was rarely there in the evening."

"So, you weren't likely to see anything."

He shook his head. "Then second, I did the funerals so I would have known where to put the victims' bodies"

"So would just about everyone else in town," I said.

"Granted. But, third, I live alone and had a lot of space where I could have hidden a captive. And I'm only a few blocks from where the first body was found."

"Still, that doesn't add up to much."

"Maybe not," he said, his face imploring. "How about you come into the rectory and I'll make you a cup of coffee."

I suspected that he had more to say but didn't want to say it outside on the sidewalk. "Okay," I said and followed him around the side of the church to the rectory. It had been sheltered somewhat from the storm by the church and the school buildings so it had suffered only superficial damage. The yellow tape wrapped around the church but didn't limit access to the rectory. We walked up a short flight of limestone steps to a long, pillared porch and an intricately carved set of double doors. Sam opened the door without unlocking it and I followed him in. We walked to a kitchen at the back of the building and he directed me to a metal kitchen table with four worn chairs. As he made the coffee, I looked out the glassless window, now covered with thick plastic sheets. The remains of the gym wall ran parallel to the window. Had the gym still been intact, I suspect that I couldn't have seen any more than a sliver of the churchyard. Maybe Sam could have seen more looking out of the window over the sink but I doubted it.

As the coffee maker gurgled, Sam came back to the table and set two mugs and a plate of cookies on it. "They're not the freshest," he said. "Girl scouts haven't been around yet this season."

I chuckled and he pulled out a chair for himself. "There was something I didn't want to say outside. Something you're likely to hear eventually and something I could use your help with, as a doctor."

"Sure," I said. "Go ahead."

"Well, there is something else the police are likely to hold against me." I just nodded. He went on. "Ya' see, I've been here quite a while but this wasn't my first assignment. I was in a church in the south of the diocese for six years before I was assigned here. Back then they were still sending problem priests," he made air quotes," to treatment and then reassigning them."

"Problem priests," I said. "Like pedophiles, you mean."

"Well, that, yes but not just that. You see, I was young and there was a girl. She was from a bad home and I thought I was helping her. She ended up pregnant."

"Really," I said. Sitting back in my chair.

"But it wasn't mine," he insisted. "She said it was but I knew that she'd been seeing another man in town. She told me so in confession. But I couldn't say anything."

"Even to protect yourself?"

"You're not Catholic, I assume. The seal of the confessional is inviolate. I tried to convince her to tell the truth but she was frightened of the guy and of her family. She claimed that I had raped her when she was in the rectory for counseling. All I could do was deny it."

"Was there an investigation?"

"Of sorts. The diocese paid the family off so there would be no legal charges. The bishop talked with the girl and decided that, implausible as her story was, I should be removed from the parish. He sent me to treatment in Minneapolis for six months and then assigned me here."

"And the girl?" I inquired.

"I heard that she had the baby and ended up marrying the real father. Several years later he went to prison for domestic assault and she took her child and moved away."

"So you were never cleared?" I asked.

"No, and if the police get my file from the diocese, it won't look good."

"So, what is it you'd like me to do?"

'I'm not sure," he said, getting up to pour the coffee. He sat back down and wrapped his hands around his mug, looking into it instead of at me. "I know this is not appropriate to ask. You're not in practice anymore and I barely know you, but I was hoping that you could speak for me." I started to shake my head but he held his hand up. "I'm not asking you to make anything up. I'd be glad to talk with you about anything you want. Make a full evaluation if that's what you need to do. And whatever you find, you have my permission to share it with the cops."

"Are you sure of this," I asked. "Don't you think you should get some legal advice first?"

"Look," he said, finally staring directly into my eyes. "I didn't kill anyone. And I don't want another scandal that will send me off to another parish somewhere. This town needs me here. And I need this thing resolved. Please help me."

His sincerity was undeniable. Of course, to commit these murders would have taken a sociopath and sociopaths are unbelievably good actors. They can make you believe the sky is blue at midnight. But somehow, something about this man got hold of me. For no reason that made any sense, I knew he was telling me the truth.

"I'm not a forensic expert," I said. "But I'll give it a try. I'll need a day or two to process this but I will do an assessment and go from there. Okay?"

"I could ask for no more than that," he said, reaching his hand across the table and shaking mine. As I picked my mug up for another sip, the doorbell rang.

"Oh, God," Sam said. "I forgot, I've worked an appointment in before the council meeting. Would you mind?"

"No, of course not." I rose and walked to the door. Sam opened it and I saw a man waiting at the porch rail, looking toward the north. His back was to me but I was pretty sure it was Andy Folger. I walked away without another word.

CHAPTER FOURTEEN

Walking back through town, I reviewed my conversation with Sam and the impression I was left with. He certainly didn't act like a murderer. He seemed sincere and legitimately concerned. I like to think I'm a good judge of character but I had to admit that history had proved me otherwise. Once before I had encountered a murderer who had been able to pull the wool snuggly over my eyes. As a matter of fact, she was the reason I lost my license and ended up on the road to Amber Creek.

To make a long story short, a young woman back in the town where I'd practiced psychiatry for over thirty years had manipulated me in the hope that I could help her get away with murdering her husband. She'd been clever, devious and an incredible actress. She'd used my own guilt over the death of my wife to trap me in a lie. Fortunately, I'd figured her out in time and exposed her but it still cost me my career, my friends and my home.

To the best of my knowledge, that had been the only time a patient had pulled one over on me. Then again, if I had been duped once how could I be sure it hadn't happened many times before. Obviously, I hadn't been a very good judge of my own competence. Was that same character flaw at play now? Was I letting myself be fooled again? Was I trying too hard to fight my own prejudices against religion in general and Catholic priests in particular? Though I had never been victimized by the clergy, I certainly knew people who had. Holy Orders did not lift a man out of the realm of human emotions and drives. Holy men were capable of doing some very unholy things and then hiding behind their vestments.

I had promised to do a mental health assessment of Father Sam and I would follow through. But I needed to go into it with my eyes wide open and my prejudices in check. I headed back to my RV to start doing some research. After checking that my satellite dish was working, I sat at the table and opened my laptop and began a search that took me to the dinner hour. I would have kept going but one of Bob's kids tapped on my door and invited me to supper with the family. I was glad to take a break.

I sat down to a thick slice of beef roast. One of the perks, I was informed, of farming is having a side of beef in the freezer. The accompaniments were well prepared but mostly out of cans and boxes. Fresh produce was still hard to come by because of the storm so the asparagus I'd bought for Irene was a real treat. Fortunately, the meal was also accompanied by gossip, funny stories and the kind of jokes that kids tell, not very funny, but you have to laugh anyway. No mention was made of Ellie, a fact for which I was grateful. So, I decided to pump the family for more information about the townspeople, in particular the single men we had talked about earlier in the day.

"Irene, let's pick up where we left off at lunch. Tell me a little more about Pete Miller."

"The pharmacist," Bob chimed in. "What about him?"

"He's single and he lives alone," I said.

"Single," Bob chuckled. "If that's what you want to call it."

"Bob," Charlotte said. "Now that's enough."

I directed myself back to Irene. "You said he's been in town about four years."

"Yes."

"And he has a girlfriend who lives out of town," I continued, trying to ignore Bob's sudden burst of laughter.

"Bob," Charlotte shouted. "Knock it off."

"You're not funny?" Irene chided.

"Just ignore him," Charlotte said.

"No, really," I said. "I'd like to know too."

Charlotte shook her head but with a wave of her hand signaled Bob to go on.

"You see," he said, "Pete is a nice guy and all but he's not much of a lady's man, if you know what I mean."

"I'm not sure I do," I said.

"Let me put it this way," Bob said, grinning widely. "His girlfriend's name is Albert."

"Bob," Irene said. "If Pete wants to keep his lifestyle private then that's his business. He's still been a great asset to this community. "

"What story would you use if you lived in a small, very Catholic town with a bunch of closed-minded hicks like you," Charlotte said to Bob. "Besides, how would you know anyway?'

"Bumped into him at the bar one night. He'd already had a few and I had a few more with him. He slipped up about his girlfriend. Ended up telling me the whole story. Albert lives in Omaha. They met in college. Pete said they'd be living together but he wanted his own pharmacy and the only one he could afford was here in town. I suspect that, once he'd made enough money, he'd have sold this store and moved back to Omaha to buy a bigger one, I guess the tornado changed all of that."

Six-year-old Sara broke into the conversation. "Daddy, how can a boy be a girlfriend?"

Charlotte gave Bob the evil eye. "You kids head up to your room. I bet there's some homework you haven't finished. You can have dessert later," They reluctantly left the room and once Charlotte heard their footsteps on the stairs she turned back to me. "It's true. Pete is gay. Most of us figured it out a long time ago but if he wants to keep it a secret, it's not our place to out him."

"I wasn't outing anybody," Bob said, his hands up in surrender. Both Charlotte and Irene rolled their eyes.

"Okay," I said, "Then, how about the deputy, Jerry…"

"Albright," Irene said. "He's a nice enough fellow, considering."

"Considering?"

"Jerry is sorta crusty, especially if he's had a few," Bob said. "He grew up here in town. Married his high school sweetheart but she couldn't take his drinking so, after a few years she left. Moved out of town because she was afraid of him."

"You don't know that," Charlotte said.

"Seems there's a lot I don't know tonight," Bob retorted.

"Has Jerry had any other relationships since his wife left?" I asked.

"On and off," Charlotte said.

"He's just one of the guys at this point, Bob said. "At the bar or watching the game with pals whenever he can. I think he's washed his hands of women."

"Well," Irene said. "Drink is going to be the end of him, just like my Eddie."

Remembering some of my research, I asked "What was he like as a kid?"

"He's quite a bit older than we are," Charlotte said. "He was a big deal on the high school football team when I was in grade school. Got married then went into the Army for a few years. Coming back from the war sorta changed, they say. Harder. Maybe a little paranoid. He joined the police then, though I'm not sure he was cut out for it. Marriage didn't last very long after that."

"Did he abuse his wife," I asked.

"We can't say that," Bob said.

"But she was afraid of him," Charlotte said. "Edna Westerhouse was a friend of hers and she said that Ann, that's Jerry's ex, would come over to her place late at night to hide out when Jerry'd been drinking."

"I remember him," Irene said. "A nice kid, very respectful. His folks were good people too. They're gone now."

"Has Jerry ever been in any legal trouble?" I asked.

"Well, ya see," Bob said. "His dad was good friends with Dan Gilmore. That's how he got on the police force, such as it is. Dan sorta keeps an eye on him especially since his dad passed on. Jerry coulda been hauled in on DUI or public intox on several occasions. Been in a few fights. I don't think Dan looks the other way, exactly. I think he wants to help him get his shit together. And, it actually seems to have been helping in the last little while. Even before the tornado, Jerry was doing better somehow."

"Better how?" I asked.

"Not drinking as much for one thing."

This peaked my attention, considering my own relationship with the bottle. "AA maybe?"

Bob shrugged. "Who knows?"

"How 'bout Andy Folger?" I inquired. "What can you tell me about him?"

"Is this all about those murders?" Irene asked.

"Well, yes," I said. "The police wanted me to help out a little."

Charlotte took in a quick breath. "You don't think it was any of these guys, do you?"

I looked at her frightened eyes. "I can't really say but... well I'm trying very hard to find a couple of suspects to suggest to the BCI people."

"Why?" Bob asked. "What do you know?"

"I'm not supposed to say but..." I went on, speaking more softly, as if someone else might be listening. "They intended to question Father Sam."

"What?" Irene blurted. "Because of what I told you?"

"No, of course not," I said. "They were already planning on talking with him. The three bodies at the church, his church. He lives alone."

"And he's a priest," Irene said. "Is that it?"

"Well..." I said, "Anyway, that's why I'm trying to look into other possibilities."

"I guess we should thank you for that," Irene sighed. "But I just know it couldn't be Sam."

"To be honest, I don't think so either," I said. "Now tell me about Andy.

"He grew up in town too," Bob said. "Between Charlotte and Jerry in school. I'm told he was always kind of odd. Quiet. Not many friends."

His family?" I asked.

"Mom and dad are all I know," Charlotte said.

"Well, there was a brother," Irene said. "Died of SIDS, they said. His mother took it really badly."

"I guess I do remember that, now that you say it" Charlotte interjected, slowly shaking her head. "I can't imagine how she felt, but not that losing a kid isn't horrible and all. It's just that she got to be so controlling with Andy. He musta been like four when his brother died. She barely let him out of the house after that, except to go to school and church. She had him dress like he was going to a funeral all the time. Ya' know, white shirt and tie. I don't even think he owned a pair of jeans."

"She was a very troubled soul," Irene said. "After Andy left for college, she didn't know what to do with herself. And when he got married and moved to Omaha, she was devastated. She and her husband were never on very good terms, even before the baby died. People wondered how she got pregnant in the first place."

"So, how did he end up back in town?" I inquired.

"Well, his father ran the insurance firm," Irene said. "Actually, he was the firm. He died of a heart attack at his office desk. Just like that," she snapped her fingers. "That's when Carol, Andy's mother, called him and begged him to come home to run the office. She promised to bury the hatchet with Andy and his wife. I don't think he wanted to do it but Carol was pretty good at making people feel guilty. I suspect she badgered and threatened him until he finally gave in. He and his wife moved back to town. They didn't have any kids. They bought the house from Andy's mom but she stayed there with them. It's just a couple blocks from the town square."

"Was his house hit by the tornado?" I asked.

"No," Bob interjected. "He was one of the lucky ones. Just superficial damage. And, surprise, his was the first house to get repaired. Wouldn't ya' know it."

"Anyway," Irene continued, "Carol and Andy's wife didn't get along. Too much alike, I guess. It wasn't six months and she left town. I guess they're divorced. Andy still lives in the same house. His mother died about five years ago."

"How's he done since then? "I asked.

"Okay, I suppose," Bob said. "What do you mean?"

"Does he date, have friends? That kind of stuff."

Charlotte stepped in. "He's tried with a few women around town but It never worked out. I know a couple of them. They say he's sort of different."

"How so?"

"I don't know, you'd have to ask them."

"But any indication that he was violent or threatening?" I asked.

"No, not that, but just different ya' know. Sort of creepy."

"Okay, well thanks," I said, coming to my feet. "Can I help clean up?"

"No, "Charlotte said. "I'm going to put Bob on that chore again. He deserves it after what he's said." Bob shrugged, got up and started clearing the table.

"Well, goodnight," I said. I rose to leave but when I opened the door, I could hear a dog barking in the distance and was reminded of my research. I stepped back in the room, "Say, do you know if any of those guys had pets as kids?"

"Let me think," Charlotte said. "Jerry's family always had dogs around. Mostly for hunting. Pete's got a cat now but I couldn't really say if he had any as a kid. And Andy had a couple but they never lasted long. I don't think his mother approved. Why do you ask?"

"Just to get an idea of what kind of person they are," I demurred. "Pets tell a lot about people."

"Just be careful, Hank", Irene said. "It's nice that you want to help Sam, but let the police do the detective work."

I nodded, said good night. I certainly appreciated Irene's concern but I was sure there had to be something I could do to help so I headed back to my RV. Sitting back at my little table, I opened the laptop again and did a few more hours of research before heading to bed. Lying there, I decided that I needed to talk with someone about what I'd learned. I should talk with Dan but who I really wanted to talk with was Ellie. If I called her and told her that I didn't suspect Sam, maybe she would be willing to hear me out. I vowed to call her in the morning.

CHAPTER FIFTEEN

As soon as I was out of bed, I called Ellie and she agreed to meet at the hospital for lunch. The cafeteria was operating again. She sounded unrepentant but at least interested in talking. Hoping I could find Dan and fill him in on what I had learned, I had a quick breakfast of coffee and pop tarts and headed to the town square. From the square I walked east to the temporary municipal building. It was long and low with glass making up most of its front wall. Plywood panels covered some of the places where the glass had been shattered and duct tape traced cracks in most of the other panes. Fortunately, the tornado had given it a wide berth though windblown debris was scattered on the large parking lot where I suspect that new farm equipment had once been displayed. I walked into the lot and between a police car and a couple civilian vehicles. Inside, the space had been jury-rigged with makeshift walls of plywood that didn't quite reach the ceiling. At a folding table, sat the esteemed mayor surrounded by phone equipment, an opened laptop and piles of paper folders.

"Angie," I said, "what are you doing here?"

"I work here," she said sarcastically. "At least some of the time."

"You don't have a receptionist?"

"Yeah, but she took time off to take care of her mother. I fill in when I can," she said. "So. what can I do for ya'."

"I was hoping to talk with Dan," I said.

"Sorry, out on a call. Jerry's here," she said, "For what good it'll do ya'."

"Why do you say that?"

"Let me just say, if he didn't work for Dan, he'd probably not work at all."

"Oh," I said, noncommittally.

Angie leaned over her phone and pushed a button. A male voice came on the speaker and Angie announced me. She broke the connection and directed me to the third door to the left. I felt uncomfortable meeting Jerry, considering what I'd learned about him just the night before and not liking what I'd learned. But I guessed that I was committed now. I walked toward the rear of the building.

There were actually no doors, just spaces between the plywood panels, but who was I to judge. I tapped on the wall and was invited in. Jerry was sitting at another folding table, trying to look busy. He was skinny and, though currently slouching in his chair, looked like he would have stood nearly six feet. His hair was dark and close-cropped. His face was deeply tanned and looked as if it had partially melted in the sun, sagging around the eyes and the corners of his mouth. He didn't bother to get up. "What's up?" he said

"I was hoping to talk with Dan," I said.

"Ain't here," he said. "Back in fifteen or twenty minutes, I guess. Anything you need me to do for ya'?"

I deflected. "Just wanting an update on the murders."

"To the best of my knowledge, there's nothing new," he said. "Course, I'm not exactly in the loop. Since the meeting at Angie's store, Dan has been talking mostly with the BCI guys. Bunch of stuffed shirts, as far as I'm concerned."

"Maybe I'll just wait out front for him," I said.

"Naw, just take a seat," he pointed to a white plastic lawn chair beside the door. "I kinda wanted to talk with you myself."

"All right, "I said, taking a seat.

"You're sorta new around here," he said. "And being a shrink and all, I can't help but wonder what you think."

"About what?"

"About the murders, of course."

"Well, they're pretty disturbing."

"Yeah, yeah, but what do ya' think about the guy who did it?"

"I don't know who did it," I said. "Do you?"

"Course not, but you must have some ideas. Some kinda nut case, right?"

"That's not exactly a clinical term."

"You know what I mean," he said. "Nobody in his right mind would do shit like that."

"I suppose not," I replied. "In all likelihood the killer is what we call a psychopath, a violent person with an antisocial personality disorder."

"Like I said, a nutcase."

"I'm not sure what you mean by that but I can tell you that the killer was not insane, in the legal sense. He knew what he was doing and he knew it was wrong. He just didn't care or maybe he couldn't control his own urges."

Just then, Dan walked into the room and shouted, "Jerry, get out of my chair,"

Jerry got up, showing Dan a guilty smirk and left the room, saying nothing else.

Dan took a seat and noticed me sitting there. "Oh, Doc," he said. "Didn't see you there."

"I was just having a conversation, of sorts, with your deputy."

"That guy is gonna drive me nuts," he said. "I've tried everything I can think of to make a cop out of him. I guess it's true, you can't make a silk purse out of a sow's ear. Though I must admit, he's had a little more on the ball lately. Will wonders never cease?"

I chuckled and then turned to more serious matters. "Listen, Dan, I wanted to talk to you about the murders. I know I'm not an investigator but I've talked with some folks and I wonder if you've considered a few suspects."

"The BCI is in charge of most of that, but they have talked with Father Cannon."

I said only, "Oh."

"They talked with him last evening, for quite a while. Of course, he didn't say anything incriminating but they said that he seemed awfully nervous, almost defensive."

"Well, they were accusing him of murder," I said.

"That's just it. They were just asking general questions. They didn't accuse him of anything. But they're more suspicious now than they had been. They thought he was hiding something."

"What do you think?"

He paused, planting his elbow on the table and scratching his forehead. "I don't know. I can't believe that Sam is involved. Fuck, he's my friend. But a lot of things point his way. To be honest though, I haven't had much time to think about it. With the storm and now the panic about a murderer being in town, I've been swamped."

"I can imagine."

"I just got back from visiting three different single ladies. They all wanted me to inspect their homes for security and to reassure them that they were not going to be the next victims. The calls are coming in pretty steady. Everyone's worried."

"I guess I can't really blame them."

"So, ya' see, I haven't much time to actually investigate the murders."

"That's why I wanted to talk with you, Dan. I've been able to give it some thought. Besides Sam, there are likely to be other people to consider. Like Pete Miller or Andy Folger or..." I cleared my throat. "Or even Jerry Albright."

Dan sat erect and cut into me with steely eyes. "That boy may be a loser and a lazy son of a bitch but he's no killer."

"Okay, but all three of those guys fit a pattern," I said. "They're single, they live alone, they go out of town a lot. And they all have relationship issues."

"That doesn't make them killers," he said, dialing it back a little.

"No, it doesn't but doesn't it at least earn them a closer look."

"Well, Mr. Detective," Dan said, "I'll have you know that the BCI and I have pulled together a list of persons of interest and all four men are on it, plus a few more. We are investigating, so thanks for the help but please let us be the cops. If we need your particular skills we'll ask.'

"Okay," I said, holding my palms up. "I didn't mean to step on any toes. But the BCI guys did say they could use my help."

"I know that,' he said. "But not on the investigation. They were hoping you could sit in when they have a clearer idea of who the killer is. Maybe give them some insight into personality and stuff like that."

"As I told them, I would be happy to help in any way I can," I said. "By the way, I talked with Sam."

"About what?" Dan said, skeptically.

"Don't worry," I said. "I didn't talk about the investigation. But he did. He knows that he will be a suspect. He wanted me to do a mental health assessment on him so he could help defend himself."

"He did, huh? And what did you say?"

"I said I would do it."

"Well, I think it's a lousy idea. You could actually do him more harm than good."

"Why do you say that?"

"Come on, Doc. Don't play stupid. He may incriminate himself. He may not have told you a few important details, not yet, at least."

"Such as?"

"Such as his history of rape. We already talked with the diocese."

"He told me about that already. As a matter of fact, that's why he wants my help. He claims that the girl lied."

"Well, we'll see when the records come from the church. Meanwhile, for your own good, don't get involved until you're asked to. Okay."

"I've already been asked," I said, getting to my feet. "But thanks for the warning." I turned to leave but Dan stood and stepped toward me.

"I'm sorry, Doc," he said. "I didn't mean to come down on you like that but this is real hard on all of us."

I smiled. "I know that, and all I want to do is help." I shook his hand and walked away.

I left the building, waving at Angie as I did. I walked north across the blighted path of the tornado and on to the hospital. It was a little early for lunch so I strolled east for two blocks and encountered more of the storm debris. It surprised me how close the tornado had come to destroying the hospital. If it had, what would Amber Creek have done? What would have happened to Ellie and the staff and patients in the building? I shuddered to consider it. On the more self-centered side, I would never have met Ellie and the last few weeks with her would never have been. I was once again glad that I would have a chance to talk with her and maybe to get back to where we had been before our meeting with the BCI.

I returned to the hospital and walked to Ellie's office. Her door was closed and a young couple was sitting on chairs across from her door. "Waiting for Dr. Sparks? " I inquired. The young woman smiled and touched her rounded abdomen. Her companion looked at her with an impish grin.

"Congratulations," I said. "I'll just wait for her in the cafeteria."

I walked back down the hall and turned into the cafeteria. It looked much busier than when I'd first been there. Several tables were occupied and the food lines were staffed. I took a Diet Pepsi out of the cooler, paid for it and found a seat. I checked my phone for messages. There were several from back home. I guess I had forgotten to check them once the service came back up. There were texts from my old nurse, Phyllis. She'd been more than my nurse though. She was a friend who I used to call my office mother. The first messages were chatty, then concerned and finally panicky. Not wanting to talk on the phone in public, I responded with a text that reassured her and filled her in on a few of the details. There were also several messages from Jeannette, a woman I'd dated but who was now a close friend. I answered hers too. It made me think about the life I'd left behind, the people I'd hurt and the chances I'd missed. I really didn't want that again. I recommitted myself to doing better.

I was so lost in thought that I didn't notice Ellie until she cleared her throat. I looked up and she was standing beside the table, dressed in tan slacks and her white coat. Sun coming through the window sparkled in her hair and her eyes looked welcoming. "Where were you, just now?" she asked.

"Memory lane, I suppose." I got up from my chair, leaned in and gave her an innocent peck on the check.

"Let's eat," she said, turning away. "I'm starved."

Unsure if that was a mild brushoff or a sincere expression of her hunger, I shrugged and followed her through the cafeteria line. Trays in hand we returned to the table and Ellie started into her plate of mystery casserole as if it were ambrosia. I guess she'd not been kidding. I admit that I didn't have much appetite, my stomach being too busy processing anxiety.

When Ellie started to slow down, I decided it was time to speak up. "Ellie, I was glad you wanted to meet. I didn't like the way we left things last time."

She put her fork down gently. "I'm sorry I was so...I don't know, irritable."

"No, It's okay, really," I said, leaning forward. "I just want you to know that I see why you were so sure about Sam. I talked with him yesterday. He's no murderer and I agreed to help him prove that."

"How are you going to do that?" she asked.

"He wants me to do a psychiatric assessment of him and make a formal report."

"But you're not licensed."

"Maybe not, but I haven't forgotten everything I ever learned. Besides, I've done a little research about serial killers. I can use that as a guideline."

"What have you learned?" She said and then picked up her fork to continue eating while still listening intently.

"Well, first of all the information I found was sort of sparse. There were a lot of professional articles but all I could get were brief abstracts unless I wanted to pay for the full journal."

"Seems kind of mercenary," she said.

"Yeah, well, I guess that's the way the world works now. But I did find information that was meant more for the general public but written by informed folks who did their research."

"Okay, what did you find?"

"It appears that most serial killers, if not all, are psychopaths, people with little or no moral structure and a complete lack of empathy."

"No surprise."

"They tend to be from very chaotic families with domineering and often sadistic mothers and passive or absent fathers. Their own violent instincts start showing up as animal cruelty, often mutilation. They may have a history of sexual assault before going on to murder but a lot of them are sexually inexperienced and insecure, feeling rejected or taunted by the opposite sex. Some of them have tried to fit in by forming families of their own but they are rarely successful. It seems to be these failures that fuel the rage that expresses itself in violence."

"So, they aren't just insane?'

"Of course, some are. Some are delusional or experiencing command hallucinations ."

Excuse me, Ellie interjected, "It's been a while since my psychiatry section in med school. What are command hallucinations?"

"Oh, sorry," I said. "That means auditory hallucinations that tell the person what to do. You know, like a command. But, to be honest, they seem to be uncommon among serial killers. Most are just very angry people who have perverted sexual drives and no scruples. They are often clever though. They can be very charming and disarming. They can be excellent actors, playing whatever role they need to get what they want. I guess, if you're willing to kill, lying is not such a big sin."

"But, how does it start, the actual killing, I mean," she asked, no longer interested in her meal.

"It's usually triggered by a specific event, a trauma, an insult, something that fuels the rage to a new level. The first murder may be impulsive. But then, the killer finds out that he derives pleasure, sexual or otherwise, from the killing. I can become like a drug addiction. The later murders are more likely to be planned and more organized. The serial killer learns to milk every ounce of pleasure out of the murder. He then will have a cool-down period of days, weeks or even months when his memories of the assault can be revisited again and again. At some point though, that isn't enough so he starts planning the next murder. For a while the planning is all he needs, but eventually, the compulsion builds to the point that he acts. And the cycle repeats."

"So how does all of this help you to evaluate," she broke eye contact for a second before finishing her thought. "A suspect."

"I look for signs of sociopathy like lack of empathy. I ask about history of traumatic childhood events, possibly a history of sexual abuse. And of course, the best predictor of future behavior is past behavior so I ask about previous assaults, animal mutilation and so forth."

"And you think a serial killer will be honest about those things," she said, incredulity clear in her tone.

"I don't know. I'm new to this stuff. A garden variety psychiatrist doesn't deal with these issues on a regular basis, thank God. But I do know that psychopaths like to brag, like to impress or to intimidate, so who knows what they might say, given the right opportunity."

"Are you sure you want to get involved in all this," she said. "It sounds like it could get dangerous."

"Well, fortunately, I'm starting with Sam."

She nodded and reached her hand across the table to mine. "Thank you for helping him. He's very special to me."

"I got that impression already. Would it be okay if I asked you why?"

She let go of my hand and cupped her face in her palms, massaging her forehead. "Sam and I, we came to Amber Creek at nearly the same time. Of course, I came with my husband. He wasn't interested in making friends but Sam and I bonded. We were outsiders together, sort of. It was never anything romantic, more like family, I guess. Anyway, then when

Brad, that's my ex, ran off, I guess I leaned on Sam. Maybe more than I should have, but he was there for me. He always has been and he never asks for anything in return. He was probably the one who convinced me to stay here. He reminded me how much I was needed and how much good I could do. I guess he helped me find a reason to go on. I think he and I know each other better than anyone else. And I know he would never, could never, harm another human being, no less kill one."

"That explains a lot," I said. "Thank you for telling me. And you know, that only reinforces my impression of Sam. It would take a good person to have that kind of relationship with someone like you."

She smiled and reached her hand out to mine again. "Let's forget what happened and get back to where we were. Come to my place tonight."

"I have to admit that I was hoping you would say that."

We got up and we wrapped our arms around each other before heading our separate ways, her back to work and me back to my RV for more research.

CHAPTER SIXTEEN

The next two days with Ellie were like we'd never argued and maybe even better than that. We ate together, slept together and made love several times. She went to work during the day and I went back to my RV to continue my research and prepare for my evaluation of Sam. Irene fed me breakfast and stopped in from time to time. Once she brought a tray of cookies to my RV and sat to share a few. I know I shouldn't have but I explained what I was doing and why because I knew how important Sam was to her.

"I just hope it will do some good," she said. "Sam is a good person. And your help means a lot to him, and to me."

"He's very special to you, isn't he?" I asked.

"He's been there for me and for my family. My husband Eddie's illness was hard on all of us. Long and drawn out. Funny thing was that he'd stopped drinking just before we found out how ill he was. Cirrhosis. It was too late. We considered a liver transplant but he'd been a smoker too and his lungs wouldn't have been able to take it. It took two long years for him to die. It was like he shriveled up and rotted away right in front of us." Her eyes sparkled with restrained tears. "And Sam was there with us the whole time. He prayed with us but he also sat with us, ate with us and sometimes stayed with us at Eddie's beside throughout the roughest nights. No heartless serial killer would have done that. There was nothing in it for him."

"I agree, '' I said. Uncharacteristically, I took her hand in mine and held it gently. "He couldn't have done these terrible things and I will do all I can to help him prove that."

She smiled tightly. "I thank you for that. But be sure to be careful. I wouldn't want you to put yourself in danger."

"How so?"

"We know that Sam didn't do this but someone else did. And he's out there."

"I'm sure the police will find him eventually," I said.

She squeezed my hand. "So let them. You're not a detective. Once you're finished helping Sam, you need to step back. Those other men you asked about? They're the law's problem. Not yours."

"Yes mother," I said.

She shook her head, picked up her tray and left me alone in the RV.

A few more hours of research, and I felt I was finally ready. I gave Sam a call. He was at one of his other churches for the morning but agreed to meet with me at the rectory after lunch.

I loaded my shoulder bag with my laptop, a notepad and various potential testing materials. As I walked across town to the church, I noticed a number of the previously vacated lots had simple mobile home-like structures on them. FEMA signs were posted to reassure us that the government was doing its duty, I guess. No actual rebuilding was going on yet but the cleanup had nearly finished. Repair crews were at work on many of the homes that had not actually been demolished. It looked like Amber Creek was going to recover, but it was going to take time.

I crossed the town square and around the church to see that Sam's car was parked in front of the rectory. I walked up the steps to find him sitting in a plastic lawn chair on the porch. He rose and we shook hands.

"Been here long?" I asked.

"A bit," he said. "I guess I was nervous to get this started."

I smiled to reassure him. "It won't hurt much." I followed him into the house and back to the kitchen.

"Is this okay?" he said, pointing at the worn metal table.

"Sure," I said. "Take a seat and we'll get started."

"Coffee or ... anything?" he said, unintentionally broadcasting his anxiety. I shook my head and he took a seat.

With most psychiatric evaluations, there is an obvious starting point. "What brings you here to see me?" We call that the chief complaint. In a situation like this, we both know the reason we're meeting. No need to pretend we don't. So, I started with what we refer to uncreatively as the history of present illness. As there was no obvious illness, I started into general questions. How's your appetite, your sleep, your energy. He admitted that he hadn't slept well since his visit with the BCI. Appetite was poor and he had to push himself to get through the day but he was getting things done. He denied feeling sad but, instead, he was very anxious. He said that he felt like there was always someone looking over his shoulder, though he knew this was ridiculous. He wasn't hearing or seeing things that other people couldn't. Most importantly, he hadn't thought about harming himself. I asked about that several different ways, mostly to reassure myself. Suicidal thoughts often accompany severe anxiety, depression and emotional trauma and were an indicator that immediate intervention was called for. More intervention than I was really in much of a position to provide.

Satisfied that I'd covered all of those bases, I went on the family and social history. There was no history of mental illness or substance abuse in Sam's family that he knew of. He had been raised about as far from Amber Creek as possible without being out of state. Oddly enough, he'd not been raised a Catholic. His parents were atheists but his grandmother, with whom he had a very strong bond, was Catholic. He would go to church with her sometimes, especially on church holidays. His parents tended to look the other way but his brother and sister teased him mercilessly so he didn't share a lot of his evolving religious ideas with them. At one point, he'd decided to ask his grandmother if he could be baptized. She'd smiled and told him that he already was. Like a lot of grandmothers she knew, she had secretly baptized each of the children when their parents weren't looking. She'd never shared this with Sam's folks or siblings but she felt she had preserved them from spending eternity in Limbo. Sam had later learned that the powers that be in the Catholic church had eliminated limbo and purgatory some time before that. He never told his grandmother.

Sam had attended public grade school and high schools but went to a Catholic college in Omaha, qualifying for enough scholarships that his parents didn't complain too much. While there he made friends and dated girls. He'd even gone to bed with a few. But he'd felt a pull that he couldn't understand. He attended Catholic services and was taken with the pomp and ceremony but that wasn't all. He could also feel the depth of the sincere faith he saw around him. He didn't understand it. It wasn't logical. But it felt right. After his second year in college, he was formally baptized. His grandmother was the only family member he invited but her pride and delight were all he needed.

He received the other sacraments in succession, finally deciding to take Holy Orders, which required another four years of schooling. His parents and siblings were not supportive, though, with time, they were at least accepting. After ordination he received his first assignment in a rural parish. Initially, he did very well there, bonding with parishioners and developing a real talent for youth work. That's when the roof fell in and he was falsely accused of rape. His anger over this gradually evolved into pity for the girl and resentment of the church. He considered leaving all together but his grandmother was ailing and he didn't want to disappoint her more than he already had. As a result, he agreed to a six-month treatment program in Minnesota. He assured me that he would grant access to his records there if I needed them, but that he had been given a clean bill of health by the treatment team. That had been about fifteen years ago. And that's when he came to Amber Creek, actually being assigned to three affiliated parishes because of a shortage of priests in the diocese and declining attendance in the churches. He felt he adapted well and rediscovered what he referred to as his vocation. He now felt that he'd found a home, especially in the Amber Creek rectory where he'd chosen to live. He regretted that since the storm, he'd had spent little time there, focusing his attention on duties in the other two parishes.

At this point, I directed myself to questions more specific to serial killers. Had he had pets as a child? Yes. Had any of them been abused or killed? No. Had he any criminal record? No. Had he had friends and was he liked? Yes, and as far as he knew no one disliked him. Had there been any sexual relations since becoming a priest? He'd paused on that one before breaking eye contact and almost whispered "No." I filed that reaction aware for later study and continued. Had he considered any such relations? That's when he reminded me that he was only human. He admitted that his eyes had wandered and, in his dreams, he'd sometimes followed them. But in reality, he'd resisted temptation. I was tempted to ask him if his eyes had ever wandered in Ellie's direction but that would have been pretty self-serving and unprofessional so I buried that thought. Had he ever fantasized about rape? He was obviously offended by the question but cooperated saying he hadn't nor had he ever fantasized about other violence towards women or anyone else.

Then I focused in on the murders themselves. Had Sam known any of the women identified so far? No. Had he been aware of any unauthorized activity in the churchyard? Not

anything more than family visits and childish pranks. Did he have any information about the murders that he had not shared? Here he paused, focusing on his hands that were clenched on the table. He finally looked me in the eyes and said, "There is nothing more that I can share about the murders."

I sat back and studied him. He held eye contact, unwavering. "That is sort of a vague answer, wouldn't you say?"

'It's all I can say." His eyes seemed to shift from conviction to imploring.

"Alright," I said, fumbling with my notes. "How about if we change direction for a bit? I have a personality inventory on my laptop. It has several true or false questions. Would you mind completing it?"

He looked relieved. "No, of course not."

I slid the computer across the table and showed him how to complete the questionnaire. "While you're working on that, I'd like to take a walk around the block. Okay?"

"Sure. I'll call you when I'm done." I nodded and walked out to the porch and down to the street. As I walked away, I couldn't help but consider Sam's reaction to several of my questions. Throughout the rest of the interview, he had been open and cooperative, actually seeming to relax as we proceeded. But two questions, "have you ever had a relationship with a woman since becoming a priest?" and "do you have anything else to say about the murders?" had created reactions in him that surprised me. Was that the same reaction the BCI investigators had seen? Was that why they were so suspicious? Was Sam hiding something? I had to think about that before I could consider my evaluation complete. I'd walked for nearly an hour before I got Sam's call. Fortunately, I'd been walking in circles around the town square so I was able to get back to the rectory quickly.

I found Sam sitting at the table with a cup of coffee and a paperback. He'd pushed the computer across the table but left it on and open. "Any concerns?" I asked.

"No," he said. "But I have to admit some of the questions were tough to answer. For example, it asked if you ever thought you'd like to be a florist. Ok, so who hasn't but would I really like to be one? No."

I chuckled and admitted that some of the questions were sort of odd but that the test was verified and statistically supported. I closed the program and the laptop. "That's probably enough for today," I said and stood up.

Sam walked me to the door and extended his hand. "Doc, I want to thank you for doing this."

"My pleasure," I said, shaking his hand. "But don't think we're done. I suspect I'll be back for more."

He flinched a little but said, "Sure, anytime."

I walked down the steps and headed back toward my RV. I wanted to review the test results and just try to pull the whole evaluation into some sense of order before Ellie came to pick me up at five.

I opened a diet Pepsi and sat at my little table with the laptop open in front of me. I accessed the personality inventory that Sam had completed and ran the diagnostic program. Manually scoring this kind of test would have taken over an hour but the modern program made it almost instantaneous. Interpretation was a little more complex and required the organic circuitry inside my skull rather than the metal and silicon of the computer. I reviewed the data several times to reassure myself that the personality profile it provided was essentially normal. Yes, it showed Sam to be an anxious person and one with a tendency to spirituality. No surprise there. It showed him to be sensitive and empathetic. He appeared to have heterosexual orientation but rather little sexual experience. It did not suggest a tendency to anger easily or to being judgmental or egocentric. There were no indications of violent fantasy. This was not the profile of man prone to sexual violence. Of course, he could have lied in his answers. Fortunately, the test had verification protocols that, though not foolproof, could reliably indicate deception. I believed the test to be valid and, thankfully, reaffirming my own clinical impression. I closed the computer, feeling a sense of relief though Sam's answer to those two questions I had asked him still lingered in the back of my mind.

I got up, took a quick shower and dressed, in anticipation of Ellie's arrival. I was just slipping into my shoes when she knocked on my door. I welcomed her in and offered her a soda. She sipped at it while I collected a couple of changes of clothes into a gym bag. I figured I might as well have them at her house considering how much time I was spending there. Then I grabbed a soda for myself and sat across from Ellie at the little table. She smiled at me with uncharacteristic coyness.

"What?' I asked.

"I'm not sure if I'm allowed to ask," she said, "but did you see Sam?"

"I did, but I can't really share anything with you," I said. "As a physician, you already know that."

"Yes, of course, but...well you know."

I rested my hand on hers. "Yes, I know." I took a minute to collect my thoughts. "The one thing I can say is that I am more sure than ever that Sam didn't commit these murders."

"Thank God. I knew he was innocent."

"I didn't say that...exactly," I said. "He didn't commit the murders but he knows something, something he isn't sharing. Not with me and not with the police."

"What do you mean?"

"I think he knows something about the murders, but won't or can't say."

"Do you think he knows who did it?"

"Possibly. I suspect someone talked to him, probably in his capacity as a priest."

"In confession maybe?"

A sudden image flashed into my head. The first day I went to the rectory. The man on the porch who had come for confession. I was pretty sure it was Andy Folger. "Of course, and Sam would be bound by, what is it called..."

"The seal of the confessional.".

"Yes, and he won't reveal what was said."

"Can't reveal," Ellie said emphatically, "He didn't even reveal what was said in confession to protect himself from a charge of rape."

"He told you that?" I asked.

"No, but it didn't take an Einstein to figure it out," she said. "So, what now?"

I shook my head. "I don't really know." I got to my feet and grabbed the gym bag. "For the time being, I just want to get out of here and think about something else. We walked out of the RV, got in Ellie's car and headed out of town to find a decent restaurant meal.

The restaurant was on the old highway about six miles east of town. It was actually a bar that served food but the menu was more varied and appetizing than I expected. We ordered steak and baked potatoes. I encouraged Ellie to have a drink if she was so inclined but she demurred and had an iced tea. I had a diet cola. We chatted while waiting for our food, talking loud enough to hear over the din. At the bar was a group of three men shouting, laughing and punching each other in the shoulders. One was Jerry Albright. While I watched, the bartender brought another beer to each of Jerry's companions and set what looked like a club soda in front of Jerry. I pointed him out to Ellie. She gave me a closed lip grin and said nothing but it was obvious that she was acquainted with him.

"An old beau," I teased.

"Hardly," looking into her tea.

Jerry was one of my suspects. I wondered if he had done something to Ellie. If he was the killer, perhaps Ellie was in danger. "Is there something I should know?"

She shook her head subtly. "You have professional confidences and so do I. Let's leave it at that."

If our food hadn't come just then, I might have pushed harder but instead I just nodded and returned her tight grin.

The food was good and the conversation lightened up again. As we were just finishing up, I noticed Jerry dangling a set of keys in front of his companions. They staggered behind him as he led them out the door. He appeared to be the designated driver. Good for him.

CHAPTER SEVENTEEN

Two days later, Ellie was in the bathroom, getting ready for work. I was still lounging in bed when the doorbell rang. She popped her head around the corner of the door. "Would you mind getting that?"

"But, what will people think," I said, feigning shock.

"Just do it, you knucklehead," she said and shut the door.

I climbed out of bed and slipped a robe over my boxer shorts. I padded barefoot to the front door and, in standard small-town style, swung it open. There stood Captain Andrews and Lieutenant Pierce of the BCI.

"Hello, Gentlemen," I said. "Doctor Sparks is getting dressed. Would you like to come in and wait?"

"We aren't here to talk to Doctor Sparks," Andrews said.

"You want to talk to me?" I asked, surprised. "How did you know where to find me?"

Pierce snorted. "It's a small town, Doc. It's not easy to keep a secret around here."

"Unless you're a murderer," I said, chuckling. Neither man broke a smile. Perhaps I'd taken it a step too far. I cleared my throat. "Come on in and take a seat. I'll just let Ellie know you're here. I walked back to the bedroom and when I returned I was wearing a t-shirt, khakis and a pair of loafers. I sat on the sofa, facing the two men who were seated stiffly on a pair of occasional chairs. "So, what can I do for you?"

Andrews started. "We have some concerns. We understand that you have met with Father Cannon to do a psychiatric evaluation."

"Yes, I did," I said, a little apprehensively.

"And who authorized that evaluation?" Andrews said.

"Well, Sam, of course. Who else would have?"

"Doctor, do you recall that you were asked to be available to assist us in our investigation?"

"Yes,"

"Do you also recall that you were asked to talk with no one about the case without our authorization?"

"Well, yes, but..."

Pierce injected himself into the conversation. "But nothing, Doctor. You violated our agreement."

"That was not an agreement so much as an order," I said, as Elie walked into the room. "And I don't really like being given orders."

"Excuse me, gentlemen," Ellie said, probably in hopes of cutting the tension that was building in the room.

The BCI men stood. "Ma'am, we are very sorry to intrude so early in the morning."

"That's okay," she said, breezily. "I was going to make some coffee. Would you care for some?"

Both men shook their heads, embarrassed. Andrews said "Ma'am, if you wouldn't mind, we were hoping to have a private conversation with Doctor Pressman."

"No,' I said. "Why don't you sit right here beside me, Ellie." I patted the sofa cushion and she followed my lead, sporting a disarming smile.

The two men didn't look happy. "Perhaps we should go," Andrews said. "The long and the short of what we wanted to say was that we will no longer be needing your assistance on the case, Doctor Pressman,"

"And absolutely no more investigation on your part," Pierce said.

Ellie looked at them and then at me. "What's this about?"

Pierce and Andrews ignored her question and walked away, closing the front door loudly behind themselves.

Ellie followed them with her eyes then returned her concerned gaze to me. "What the Hell?"

"They found out that I met with Sam and, apparently, they don't like it."

"They haven't arrested him or charged him have they?"

"Not that I know of."

"So what business is it of theirs?"

"That's what I thought." Suppressing my own building frustration, I said "Forget about them. I'll talk with Dan this morning and clear it all up. Meanwhile, how 'bout I take you out of breakfast at Angie's."

"Breakfast at a gas station, wow," she feigned a girlish giggle. "What more could a girl want?" We grabbed our jackets and jumped in the car with me behind the wheel. Ellie didn't seem to mind my obsessive need to drive. As I turned the key, my phone buzzed in my front pocket. I chose to ignore it, assuming the caller would leave a message if it was anything important.

The Pump 'n Shop was actually a popular breakfast stop, being the only place open nearby and at that hour. Several cars were parked out front already. We walked in and passed a display of beers, wines and liquors, none of them high end. I tried to avoid looking at them but I must admit that my mouth had almost immediately begun to water. Pavlov's dogs were not a legend. But those dogs didn't have my resolve to stay sober.

In the back room, there were only a few empty tables. We took one and soon Angie's granddaughter, Cindy, came to the table and took our beverage orders; coffee and OJ. We helped ourselves to the buffet of scrambled eggs, bacon and simple pastries. Neither of us chose the biscuits and sausage gravy, though it appeared to be going fast. We'd just sat back at our table when Dan Gilmore came from across the room and stood by us. "Morning, Hank, Ellie," he said. 'Mind if I join ya' for just a minute."

"Of course not," I said.

Dan pulled up a chair and planted himself on it. "I just wanted to give you a heads up," he said.

"About what?" Ellie asked.

"The BCI guys are pissed about you talking to Sam."

"We know," I said. "They came to visit bright and early this morning. It looks like I'm off the case."

"Well, don't say I didn't warn you," Dan said. "I just want you to know that I appreciate you trying to help Sam and all but they have a point. You are not a criminal investigator and you shouldn't be involved in the case unless you are asked to be."

"Well, that's not likely to happen now," I said.

"I'm sorry about that, Hank," Dan said. "But would it be okay if I pick your brain from time to time, off the record of course."

"No problem," I said. "I realized that you're all just doing your jobs."

"Thanks," he said and rose. "Enjoy your breakfast." He walked back to his table where Jerry Albright and another cop were eating.

"Nice of him to try to warn me," I said.

"He could have stood up for you," Ellie replied. "Are you okay with this?"

"I suppose so. I mean I've said a half dozen times that I'm not a forensic psychiatrist. Still, they said they could use my help. I guess it irks me that they wanted me to help them and no one else. I'm not sure that I'd help them now if they came back on their knees."

"Not even Dan?" she said.

I just shrugged and dug into my breakfast.

After eating, I told Ellie to go ahead to work. I would pay the bill then walk back to check on my RV. Before heading to her car, she kissed me as if it didn't matter who was watching. I liked that.

I watched her drive away and walked to the counter to pay for our meal. Beside the cash register was a pile of big city newspapers. The headline read 'Socialite Killer Dies in Prison'. I picked up the top paper and scanned it. A large picture of Carla Parker appeared under the headline. She was the woman who cost me my medical license, but she didn't look like she had the last time I saw her. New lines crossed her face and her hair was very short and graying. I was stunned. I couldn't move.

Cindy, standing at the register, cleared her throat. "Doc, can I help you?"

I flashed her a look of wide-eyed, open-mouthed disbelief. I must have worried her. She said, "Are you okay, Doc?"

I mumbled something, handed her a twenty and returned to my table in the back room, the paper in hand.

I laid the open paper on the table and read the lead article. Carla had gone to prison for murdering her husband. This I was well aware of, being that she had used me to try to avoid the conviction. She had tricked me into believing that her husband had repeatedly assaulted her. She had hoped that I would testify to her victimization in court, getting her off with a plea of self-defense. When I'd started to question her story, she sealed the deal by drugging me and tricking me into bed with her. Of course, I admit that I was as responsible as she was for that. I nearly allowed her to get away with it too, until having a last-minute change of heart while still on the witness stand. She'd been in prison for less than two years now. The article was unclear about the cause of death, speculating that she may have killed herself. But I knew Carla. She was not the type to take her own life. Taking someone else's was no problem but her own, never. I suspected she'd gotten the wrong inmate or guard angry enough to take it out on her. She was good at that. After I'd figured her out, I had had fantasies of doing it myself.

But now she was dead. And I was part of it. If I had gone along with her, would she be alive today? Then again, even if I had, she might still have been convicted. And if she hadn't been convicted, would she have been a danger to anyone who crossed her in the future? I didn't know. She had come to me as a helpless, frightened victim, not the scheming murderer she had become. I was still torn between the helpless waif I had first met and the witch she had turned out to be. I could imagine her lying on the floor of her cell, bruised and beaten or bleeding from a knife wound. The woman I saw was as much the waif as the witch. My heart raced with the mix of relief and regret. I felt beads of sweat forming on my forehead and the edge of the paper shook in my fingers. I felt like I couldn't breathe. I remembered these feelings. They were what I had felt when I'd had my heart attack. I pushed the paper aside and tried to catch my breath.

Dan was still across the room, finishing his coffee. He stood and called to me. "Doc, are you okay?"

I turned to him and I must have looked like death warmed over. He rushed to my table. I struggled to my feet and held my palms out to him. "I'm fine," I said. "I just need some air."

"Are you sure," he said, taking my arm.

I pulled away from him and headed for the door. I blurted out, "I'll be fine." and rushed away, intending to leave the building all together but was once again confronted with the sight of the liquor display. Suddenly my mouth filled with saliva again and I felt a rush of hope. I grabbed a bottle of cheap whiskey, took it to the counter and paid for it. I barely gave Cindy time to slip it into a paper bag but I knew I couldn't waste time thinking. I rushed through the door and to the side of the building where I reached into the bag, unscrewed the lid and took a long, fiery drink. I gagged and spat out a mouthful of my first taste of booze in nearly two years. I was disgusted with myself and I didn't want to take another drink, but I did anyway and then another. Temporarily satisfied, I considered throwing the bag and all into the garbage. Instead, I screwed the lid back on, sealed the bag and walked toward town, feeling warmth flow through my veins, the familiar cloudiness starting to fill my head and the pain of Carla's death already beginning to numb.

I got to the town square and crossed to the gazebo where I stood behind a column and downed another few ounces of whiskey. I was now feeling more nothing, which I had to admit was my goal. I resealed the bottle and resumed my walk home. Before I got there, my vision had started to get fuzzy and I couldn't seem to keep myself walking in a straight line. Reaching my RV, I swung the door open and stumbled up the three steps, barking my knee on the last one. I left the bag and its contents sitting at the top of the steps, pulled myself to my feet and staggered to my bed where I dropped into a dreamless sleep.

I woke up with a start and checked the clock. I'd been asleep for maybe two hours, though it felt like I'd barely closed my eyes. I slid to the end of the bed and stood unsteadily. With a sudden rush in my head and spasm in my gut, I stumbled into the bathroom and dropped to my knees just in time to empty the contents of my stomach into the toilet. Even though my stomach was surely empty, I continued to retch again and again, making the back of my throat feel like I was bringing up a razor blade. Finally done, I leaned back against the wall and struggled to breathe. I had to admit to myself that I deserved this. Sober for nearly two years, what had I been thinking?

Then I remembered. Carla. She was dead and I had played no small role in her death. The guilt cut into me but I also burned with anger because she had used me and I had let her. But she had killed her husband. I hadn't. She had put herself in prison. I hadn't. And at the same time, she had ruined my life. But I had to admit that I had done that to myself as much as she had. I was torn. My mind went in circles between guilt and rage and I couldn't stop it. I realized that that had been the reason to get drunk. And it still was.

I got to my feet, ran cold water over my face and left the bathroom in search of the whiskey. I saw it on the top step by the door. I was still pretty unsteady on my feet, so when I leaned over to pick it up, I fell forward, catching myself on the door frame. I stepped down to steady myself, then turned, picked up the bag and stumbled to the banquette. Before I'd even seated myself, I had the lid off of the bottle and to my lips. I took in a big mouthful but my stomach lurched and I puked it out on the table top. I sat back, closed my eyes and took a few deep breaths. Then the merry-go-round started up again. Carla dead. Me to blame. Her to blame for my fucked-up life. It went round and round in my head. So, stomach or not, I picked up the bottle and took another swig, forcing myself to keep it down this time. Then I took another and that was the last thing I can remember from that day.

CHAPTER EIGHTEEN

When I woke up, I had no idea where I was. I sat up quickly and my head spun inside. I dropped back on the bed. Then I realized that I wasn't in my RV. I was in a real bed. But where? I looked around me. My vision was cloudy but gradually clearing. I could see that I was in a bedroom, not a hospital room. Well, that was a plus. I saw my pants draped across the end of the bed. I was wearing the T-shirt I had put on the morning the BCI people showed up. I sat up again, more slowly this time. A stab of pain ran through my hand and I looked at it mystified. It was neatly wrapped with gauze and paper tape. I still felt light headed but I was able to wait it out. The other side of the bed had not been slept in. Another plus. I swung my legs over the side of the bed and gradually worked my way to a standing position, bracing myself against the furniture. There was only one door other than the closet sliders and I needed to find a bathroom. I opened the door slowly and took a peek outside. Relief flooded me. I recognized the place. I was in Ellie's house. I must have been sleeping in her guest room. I padded to the bathroom, did my business and returned to the hall, nearly running into Ellie.

"Well, look what the cat drug in," she said.

"Ah, hi," was the best I could come up with.

"I was afraid you'd maybe died in there," she said. "How are you feeling?"

"Like my insides want out," I said. "How did I get here?"

"Let me fix you some breakfast and I'll fill you in."

I wasn't sure about breakfast but I followed her to the kitchen and took a seat at the table. She set a tall glass of water and two ibuprofen tablets on the table in front of me. "First things first," she said. "You need some hydration and the meds speak for themselves."

I popped the pills in my mouth and took a sip of the water. It went down okay so I drank the rest in one long gulp. I pushed the glass forward and, in a pitiful voice, asked "May I have some more, please?"

She took the glass, refilled it from the tap and slid it back to me. "Take it easy," she said. "I'll get you some toast." She popped two slices of bread in the toaster and poured herself a cup of coffee. When the toast popped up, she buttered them lightly, put them on a plate, and set the toast in front of me. She sat opposite me and looked sternly across the table. "So, how's the hand?"

I studied it. "Hurts some but not bad. What's wrong with it?"

"You tell me. You had a pretty big cut but thankfully not deep. It wasn't hard to dress it, after you passed out."

"Thanks," I said vaguely, "I guess."

"Okay, so what happened?"

I shook my head, which brought the queasiness back temporarily. "I'm not really sure. Last I remember, I was in my RV."

"So, you don't remember anything about Angie's store?"

"Well yeah. I took you to breakfast."

"After that."

I took a minute to collect my thoughts. "Oh yeah. I guess I got drunk."

"Ya think," she said. "But why? I haven't seen you take a drink since I met you."

I planted my elbows on the table and rested my head in my hands. After a long pause I said "You remember I told you about that woman back home who killed her husband?"

"I thought that might be it," she said. 'I saw it on the news last night."

"Did they say how she ah… died?"

"No. They're not releasing any of that information yet." she said. "Listen. I know it's hard to lose a patient but I don't understand why her death drove you to drink."

I looked into her eyes. "Because it feels like it was my fault."

"Your fault, how?"

"If it weren't for me, for what I said in court, she wouldn't have gone to prison."

"Okay, so it would have been better if she had gotten away with murder?"

"No, of course not but maybe if I hadn't been involved, she wouldn't have killed her husband."

"Now wait a minute," she said. "She didn't kill her husband because of you. She killed him to get his money. She just wanted you to get her off the hook. Which, thankfully, you didn't."

"You don't understand," I said. "I could have stopped her...somehow. I could have done something."

"Hank, listen," she said, taking my hand in hers, "you were foolish, you were off base but you didn't kill anyone. If you hadn't been there, she would have found some other way to cover her tracks. You've got to realize that."

I sighed and looked away. "It's not that easy. I should have known."

"Maybe so, but there's no going back. And going on a bender will never fix anything." She got up from the table. "You finish your breakfast. I've got to call Jerry."

"Albright? Why?"

"Because he brought you home yesterday. He could have arrested you but he didn't. You should be grateful. He asked me to call him when you came around."

"Why would he do that? And why would he arrest me?"

"You eat," she said. "I'll let Jerry explain everything." She walked out of the room and left me staring at the toast in front of me.

After eating my breakfast, I was feeling a little more clear headed and a little less like shit. I put my dishes in the dishwasher and headed to the bedroom for a shower. Afterwards I went to Elie's room for a fresh set of clothes. My keys, wallet and phone were sitting on the bureau. Ellie must have taken them out of my pocket to launder or possibly destroy the clothes I'd been wearing the day before. I picked up the phone, seeing that there was an alert on it. Whoever had tried to call me the prior morning had left a voicemail. I opened it and listened, feeling sick all over again.

The message was from Phyllis, the woman who had been my office nurse and receptionist back home. I often referred to her as my office Mom. She had called to warn me about the news of Carla's death and to ask me to call her. I froze for a few seconds, unable to decide what to do. Phyllis was one of the people I cared most about in the world. She was also one of the people who had been hurt by my involvement with Carla. To top it all off, she was the one who, after getting to know Carla, had seen right through her. She had encouraged me to break ties with Carla and to have nothing to do with her legal case. If I had listened, I would probably still have my practice, my home and the woman I had fallen in love with. But I hadn't listened and here I was, struggling to start a new life and doing a piss poor job of it.

As was so often my solution, I decided not to decide. I opened my text app and sent Phyllis a message claiming that I was okay and I would call her when I got the chance. I knew that that chance was not likely to come soon. I was ashamed of my cowardice but I pushed the send button anyway and slipped the phone into my jeans pocket and hurried out of the room.

By the time Jerry had gotten there, I still felt queasy and lightheaded but breakfast and the shower had helped a lot. Ellie showed Jerry into the living room and then put a jacket on and walked outside. I looked at Jerry unsure of what to say.

He broke the ice. "Hey champ, feeling better?"

I took a seat, "Yeah, I guess so. I'm sorry if I caused any trouble."

He sat across from me. "Nothing that can't be fixed," he said. "But you do owe Angie an apology."

"Why's that?" I asked, not sure if I wanted an answer.

"You don't remember, do you?"

I shook my head, initiating a brief burst of nausea.

"I've had black outs, too. It's scary not knowin' what ya' did."

I nodded.

"Okay, well yesterday afternoon you walked into the Pump 'n Shop, drunk as a skunk. You tried to buy a bottle of booze and Angie wouldn't sell it to ya'. You raised quite a stink. Broke a few things too. Angie called 911 and, lucky for you, I was on duty."

"So you brought me here," I said. "Why didn't you take me to jail?"

"Cause Angie was nice enough to not file a complaint. Besides, I've been where you were," he said. "I'm a drunk too. Fortunately, I haven't touched a drop in over two months."

"I didn't know,' I said. "But thanks."

"I was hoping that, if I brought you here, Doc Sparks would take care of you. Then, when you were sober, I could talk you into coming to AA with me. She told me you had a drinking problem before."

"She did?" I said, "Well yeah but I hadn't had a drink for over two years."

"Well, now you're back to ground zero. Have ya' been to AA?"

"Yeah, back home."

"And?"

"And it helped...a lot."

"So, there aren't any meetings in town since the church was hit but I know there's one in Halston tomorrow night. I'll pick you up at seven." He stood to leave.

"Wait. Why?" I asked. "I didn't think you ..."

"Listen, Doc. I know that I'm a fuck up. I know what people think of me. But I'm trying to change. And part of AA is helping your fellow drunk. This is as much for me as for you. So, seven?"

I stood and reached my hand to him. "Sure," I said. "And thanks."

We shook hands. He left and drove away in his police car. Ellie must have been just outside because she stepped back in before I could close the door. "How'd that go?" She asked.

"I guess okay but I don't understand why he's bothering," I said.

"He gave me permission to tell you that I've been treating him for a couple months. He's had a drinking problem for years. Since he got out of the service. I put him on disulfiram so he could get a handle on the drinking."

"Really, I stopped prescribing that years ago. Too punitive. You drink so you deserve to get sick. There are better options."

"Well excuse me," She said, brushing past me. "I'm just a country GP so I'm not up on all the newfangled treatments."

I followed her to the kitchen. "I'm sorry. That's not what I meant. It's a good thing that you were able to help him. He says he's been sober for two months."

"Well, it's a start," she said. "I really want him to go to the VA and start counseling. I think he's got PTSD big time."

"Maybe I can talk to him about it tomorrow night," I said.

'Oh yeah?"

"He's going to take me to an AA meeting."

"Oh," she paused. "I guess that's a good idea. But it was just one relapse, right?"

"Yes, but it wasn't the first time I thought about drinking so I think it will do me some good."

"Well, I'm glad then," she said, wrapping her arm around my waist. "I really don't want to see you like that again."

"How bad was I?"

"Frankly, I was surprised you were standing up. And I didn't know you had a mouth on you like that. I took a bit of a struggle to get you in bed, but once you vomited you seemed more than willing."

"Ellie, I'm so sorry."

"It's okay but please, next time try to make it to the toilet before you puke. The last thing I want to do after work is clean the carpet."

"I promise you there won't be a next time," I said. "Wait, why aren't you at work now?"

"It's Saturday and there's no one in the hospital, so I'm all yours."

"Saturday? I lost a whole day."

"Jerry brought you home just after five yesterday. Once you got to bed you slept straight through. I even checked on you a few times to make sure you were breathing."

"The last I remember was being in my RV. It couldn't have been later than ten or eleven. That's a lot of time to lose."

"What do you last remember doing?"

My face felt suddenly warm. I suspect I was blushing with embarrassment. "I was drinking. I passed out on my bed and when I woke up, I found the bottle and, well you can guess the rest."

"Maybe we should take a look at your RV," Elie suggested.

I agreed and she drove me there. The door was ajar and when we stepped in the smell of whiskey was overwhelming. On the floor by the banquette lay the remains of what must have been a half-full bottle of cheap rotgut. In my mind's eye flashed an image of me setting the bottle down too close to the edge of the table and watching it tip and fall to the floor, almost in slow motion. I'd grabbed for it too late and a glass shard had sliced across my hand. A smear of blood on the tabletop confirmed my recollection. That explained my going back to Angie's store, too. I'd needed more booze. And she knew better than to sell it to me. I must have been a sight.

"Well, that explains a lot," Ellie said surveying the mess. "Let's get this cleaned up."

A knock on the door interrupted our efforts. I opened it to find Irene. "Oh, hi," I said, meekly.

"I saw you pull up," she said. "Is everything okay?"

"Yeah, I just needed to pick a few things up."

Irene looked past me. "What the hell? Did you two have a fight in here?"

"No, nothing like that," I said. "Ellie's just helping me clean up."

Ellie stepped forward. "Hank is your typical bachelor. Housekeeping is non-existent."

Irene looked further into the RV, concern on her face. "That looks like blood to me."

I raised my hand showing her my bandages. "I'm a klutz, too."

"If you say so," Irene said. "But you both know that I'm right next door. If you need help, all you need to do is call."

"Thanks," I said. "But we've got everything under control here."

"That's not what I meant," she said, looking deeply into my bloodshot eyes. "If you need help of any kind, I want to be there. You've both been there for me and mine. I may not be an MD but I've learned a lot in my life. I know where the potholes are and if I can help you avoid them..."

"Thank you, Irene," Ellie said. "Hank and I appreciate it, more than you can know. But right now, we're okay."

"Alright," Irene said, "You're welcome to come over for supper tonight, if you're not busy." She gave us a half smile and closed the door. Through the glass of the door, we watched her walk away, her head slowly shaking.

Ellie turned to me. "That lady is pretty smart. I don't think she misses a thing. Let's not give her anything else to worry about. Okay?"

I nodded. "Okay."

We finished the cleanup and an hour later, we were back at Ellie's house. Soon after that, I was back in bed, swearing to myself to never drink again. Alcohol had not affected me like this since I was a kid. I guess two years of sobriety had eliminated my tolerance. I closed my eyes but images of Carla swam in my head, mixing with ones of Ellie and of my deceased wife. My guilt was strong but not as overwhelming as it had been the day before. Though forgiving myself was far beyond my ability at that point, at least I was able to see that I, over the past two years, had made some positive changes in my life that could provide a foundation for the future. I fell asleep considering the possibilities.

CHAPTER NINETEEN

When I woke, it was still light out. Was it morning and had I lost another whole day? Or had been asleep for only a short time? I pulled my phone from my pocket. It was a little after one so I'd only napped, not hibernated. I noticed a text message waiting and opened the app. It was from Ellie. She'd been called to the hospital to see a patient in the ER. I closed the message and saw the one from Phyllis right beneath it. I'd promised to call her but was still not sure that I wanted to. The two things I was sure of were my full bladder and my empty stomach. I eased myself out of bed and proceeded to deal with both issues.

After making a quick lunch and downing it, I cleaned the kitchen and started back to the bathroom to get civilized. My phone buzzed again and I pulled it out. It was another message from Ellie. She'd be tied up for most of the afternoon so I was on my own. I closed the message and there it was again, the text from Phyllis. I took a deep breath and headed into the bathroom, committing myself to calling her as soon as I'd cleaned up.

Showered, shaved and dressed, I sat on the edge of the bed and pulled my phone out. I stared at it for a time, trying to frame what I'd say to Phyllis. She'd been my nurse and my receptionist, but so much more than that. She was my friend, my confidant, sometimes even my confessor. She'd been there when my wife died and through the whole Carla mess, even when I hadn't deserved her support. It had been a couple of months now since I'd last talked with her. There was a lot I could tell her. And some that I didn't really want to tell her. I took a deep breath, pulled her number up and hit the call button.

The phone rang, once, twice then a third time. A part of me thought that maybe I was off the hook. I could leave a brief message and put the conversation off again. Then Phyllis picked up. "Doc, hello. I was hoping you'd call, eventually."

"Yeah, well," I said. "You know me. Don't do today what you can put off till tomorrow."

"Same old Doc," she chuckled. Then after a pause. "How are you doing, really?"

"I can't say that great. I was getting along pretty well until..."

"Til' Carla died. I know what you mean. I had sorta convinced myself that it was all behind us."

"Yeah, well. Now I guess it really is. Carla is gone for good."

"You can't fool me, Doc. I can guess what you're going through. You're looking for a way to let yourself off the hook but you're having trouble finding it."

"You know me pretty well, Phyllis."

"Doc, she was to blame for the whole thing. Like I've said so many times before, she planned it and she acted it out. You were a pawn. Admittedly you should have known better but you didn't, so what's done is done."

"Yes, but it's not like you didn't warn me."

"Warnings are pretty ineffective with a guy like you who has all the answers. I hope you've learned your lessons."

"I think so but then again, I can't always be wrong."

"No. You actually have a lot on the ball when you can keep your ego in check."

"Well thanks, I guess."

"But, you sound like you're handling things okay now. Are you?"

"I'm working on it. I'll admit I flipped out a little after reading about Carla in the newspaper."

"Flipped out?"

"Went on a bender. The first in two years."

"Oh, I'm so sorry. Is there any way I can help?"

"No, but thanks. I met someone here who goes to AA. He's taking me to a meeting tomorrow night."

"Well, that's good. AA always seemed to help you," she said. "By the way, you haven't told me where you are."

"Oh, I'm in Amber Creek."

"Why does that name ring a bell?"

"Lots of reasons. Take your pick. There was a devastating tornado a couple months ago and then they discovered there was probably a serial killer in town."

"Oh, Lord, yes. I read about that. How the hell did you end up there?"

"Luck of the draw. I was passing through when the storm hit."

"Oh god. Were you injured?"

"No. Camper's okay too. But there was a lot of damage in the area and, considering I didn't really have anywhere else to go, I stuck around to help out."

"Of course, you did. You've always tried to hide that side of yourself but it has a way of leaking through."

"I've met some good people here too. I like the place and I think they like me."

"I don't see you living in a small town."

"Neither do I, but for now it's good," I said. "The real reason I called was to apologize for not keeping in touch. I meant to. The phones were out for a while but that's no excuse."

"Well, I'm just glad you're calling now."

"How are things back home?'

"I've settled into my retirement. Doing some volunteer stuff. I'm really quite content."

I cleared my throat. "And Jeannette?" Jeannette and I had dated. More than that actually. I'd considered asking her to marry me. But then the whole Carla thing ruined it. We broke up but somehow, she'd found a way back to being my friend.

"Jeannette? Well, she's fine. She's...seeing someone."

"Oh?" I said, hoping that my disappointment wasn't showing. "Good for her, then." I was pretty sure I didn't want any details. It had been over for some time between Jeannette and me but I still missed what we had had together.

"You know you really screwed up a good thing with that one. She was a catch."

"I guess I hope I learned a lesson at least." I was ready to change the topic. "Especially since I met someone, too."

"Oh, do tell."

"She's the town doctor. I think she's pretty special."

"Well good luck this time and watch your Ps and Qs."

"Come on, Phyllis."

"Come on yourself. You know I love you like a son but you have a way of stumbling over your ego and ruining a good thing. And I don't just mean Jeanette." Phyllis had been well aware of the way I'd flouted my marriage vows. She was also one of the few people who saw the insecurity I tried so hard to hide and that fueled my self-important facade.

"That's the real reason I called. I missed your motherly criticism."

"At least with me, you always know what you're getting," she said. "Tell me about this lady doctor."

"She's divorced and has been pretty lonely, romance wise. I hope that's not the only reason she's interested in me. But we have a lot in common. And... she knows about my past and is okay with it."

"Well, I'm glad you were up front with her."

"I have to admit that she sort of figured it out on her own but I didn't try to hide anything and, when she asked, I told her the whole ugly story."

"Good. It's always best to start with a clean slate. And to keep it clean." I could imagine her shaking her head as she always did when giving me advice that she suspected I would not follow.

"I'm doing my best," I said. "And I've been trying to help with this murder thing."

"Playing detective, are you?"

"No but I've been helping on an assessment of a suspect who I'm pretty sure is innocent. He's the local priest."

"Maybe he can return the favor and bring you back to the church."

"Not likely, but he does seem a pretty good guy. There are a few other suspects, especially one guy. I've been sort of looking into things."

"You better be careful."

"Yeah, that's what everyone is telling me. Leave it to the professionals, they say."

"Sound advice, I'd say."

"Sure, but what if they're not seeing what I'm seeing? What if they miss something?"

"Something that only you, the brilliant Doctor Pressman can discover."

"No, not that but..."

"But nothing," Phyllis said. "You always think you're the smartest guy in the room. Admittedly, you occasionally are. But you're not a detective. The real detectives have procedures, and rules. They don't need an amateur messing things up."

"But I just want to help."

"Sure, but you wouldn't mind being the hero, would you? Sometimes you can be just like a little kid, playing at life. Rules and consequences be damned."

"Now that's not fair."

"No. You've forgotten pretty quickly. If you'd followed the rules with Carla and considered the consequences, you'd still be here and I'd still have a job in your office."

"You said you liked being retired."

"Oh bullshit, Doc. I like it because it's what I've got. If things could be like they were, I'd be working in that office till I dropped over dead. I loved it. You know that. But it was because of you that I'm not there. And sometimes that still pisses me off."

"I've told you how sorry I was."

"And just like a little kid, you think that makes it all okay. But it doesn't."

"I don't know what else to say or do."

"Say you'll do better.... then do better. I know you can."

"Thanks for the vote of confidence," I said with a good dose of sarcasm.

"Come on, Doc," she said. "I know that you can do the right thing when you decide to. You did with Carla."

"And look where that ended."

"Where would it have ended if you hadn't exposed her? Neither of us can know for sure, but I bet it would have turned out bad for somebody. You did the right thing. The consequences were hers. Now see to it that you keep doing the right thing."

"Yes mother," I said.

"Wait a minute. I'm being serious. I know you, maybe better than you do. I've seen the tough exterior crack more than once. And underneath is a kid who felt rejected by the world. A kid who learned to play the game in order to get by. You put on whatever mask it took to convince people that you were who you wanted them to think you were."

"Okay, so where are you going with this?"

"I'm going to the truth. You couldn't have pretended to be the empathetic doctor, the caring husband, or even the considerate lover unless there was already some of that in you. I was there a lot of the times when your mask fell away and behind it I saw the scared kid but also the empathetic doctor and the caring husband. I saw when your heart burst with joy and when it broke. And that was real. And that was why I cared so much about you. Don't put the mask on again. Don't be the genius or the hero. Just be you."

I wiped moisture from the corner of my eye. "Phyllis, I don't know what to say."

"Don't say anything. Just promise yourself that you'll be the best you can.

"Thanks. Really. You've given me a lot to think about."

"You're very welcome. Now I better get back to my busy life."

"It's been good talking with you. You'd make a good moral compass if only I'd pay more attention."

"Doc, you don't need me to show you what's right and wrong. You just need to decide to play by the rules because when you do, things work out better."

"I'm working on it," I said. "And I promise I'll try harder to keep in touch."

"You do that," Phyllis said. "And thanks for calling. It sets my mind at ease."

I disconnected and dropped the phone on the bed beside me. I couldn't help but admit to myself that Phyllis was right, on all points. She knows me as well as just about anyone. She knows my many weaknesses as well as my few strengths. And she was right about how I loved to play the detective. In some ways it had been my strength as a psychiatrist. I liked to dig for puzzle pieces and figure how they fit together. I liked to solve problems. But some problems weren't mine to solve. Yet, here I was, doing it again. Being the hero, the smartest guy around. If I was willing to back off and let the professionals do their job, we'd all be better off. But what the hell. I did have some insights they might not have. I did have something unique to offer. And so I did have a few more things I needed to check out. But once I did, I'd back off. I made a promise to myself. And I hoped I could keep it.

That night, I lay in bed beside Ellie. I struggled to sleep but my conversation with Phyllis spun around inside my head. Here I lay beside a beautiful, kind woman who, for some reason, had invited me into her life. Other women who had opened their hearts to me had only found pain or death. I certainly didn't want that for Ellie but, of course I hadn't wanted it for Jeannette or Marie. But that didn't alter the outcome.

Ellie stirred beside me, mumbling in her sleep. She hadn't said much after coming home from the hospital. Usually, she and I would discuss her work over supper. She would talk about patients, their ailments and treatment, knowing that I understood the parameters of confidentiality. That night she'd been quiet, answering questions with as few words as possible. Of course, I assumed she was angry with me about the drinking and I couldn't blame her. Besides, it seemed that I was always thinking that whatever was going on was about me. We had gone to bed without making love or doing our usual pillow talk. So what else could I think. When I apologized again, she tried to reassure me that I wasn't the cause of her funk but she just left it there, with no further explanation.

I was just rolling to my side when Ellies called out unintelligibly and came up on her elbows, wide awake and trembling. I sat up and took her in my arms. "It's okay," I said. "I'm here." She looked around confused for a few seconds then buried her face in my chest. I felt her tears soaking into my T-shirt. I held her until the sobbing abated. She pulled slowly away and looked up at me. In the semi dark I had trouble reading her expression.

"Okay now?" I asked.

She nodded. "Just a bad dream."

"Want to talk about it?"

"No, doctor," she replied with mild irritation.

"I didn't mean to be your shrink. I wanted to listen as your...I guess your lover."

She paused and I waited. "It was a dream about what happened today."

"I said I was sorry." I always came back to my ego.

"No, not that. It was at the hospital."

"Yes," I nudged.

"A patient of mine. She had a miscarriage."

"That's a shame."

"It's not that. Not just that. She was thirteen."

"Oh," I said, lamely.

"Her parents hadn't even known she was pregnant and she won't discuss the paternity."

"Is she okay, medically I mean?"

"Yes, but she's understandably upset. And her parents...well I spent most of the afternoon talking them down, especially when I explained that I needed to make a report to social services."

"That couldn't have been easy."

"No, I wasn't," she said flatly. Then the tears started to flow again. "I just feel like I should have been able to do more, ya' know. Say the right thing to make it all better."

"Oh, Ellie," I said. "You're a good doctor and a caring person but you can't fix everything."

She pulled away. "But they're my patients, my responsibility. You can't understand."

I realized two things then. First, that I didn't understand. Some of my patients had tragic outcomes too. But because of their own actions and choices. Not because of me. It wasn't my fault, except for one possible exception. And, second, that Ellie had a bond with her patients and this community stronger than any I had ever had with mine. She cared deeply and hurt just as deeply. "I'm starting to understand," I said. "And, I want to be here for you."

She looked up into my eyes and forced a weak smile. "Thank you. It's good to have someone to talk to about these things."

"It's my pleasure," I said. "Now, let's try to get some sleep. We can talk again in the morning."

I eased her back on the bed and, lying beside her, wrapped my arm across her, my face buried in her hair. Her sobbing slowed and she drifted off. I lay there, awake thinking of how much I loved that woman, though I hadn't admitted it before, even to myself. I knew that I had to be careful to not ruin a good thing, like I had before. I finally fell asleep too, holding her. Protecting her.

CHAPTER TWENTY

Seven o'clock the next evening, Jerry pulled up in front of Ellie's house and beeped the horn. Ellie and I had been clearing the table of supper dishes and she waved me toward the door. I kissed her goodbye and headed out to his car. He wasn't driving the police car. He was in an aging Camaro, a little worse for the years but still sporty. I climbed into the passenger's side and thanked him for picking me up. He just grunted, threw the car into gear, made a quick narrow turn and sped out, throwing up gravel in his wake. He drove down the hill and onto the old highway, heading west. At least he slowed down while going through town but once he was across the creek that bordered the west end of town, he hit the gas hard.

I double-checked my seat belt and asked," Are we in a hurry?"

"Nope," he replied. "I just hate to waste a big engine.

I shrugged and focused my eyes on the road ahead. "Say, can you tell me what I did at Angie's Friday?"

"It's like I told ya' before, you walked in drunk and picked up a bottle of booze but Angie could tell you'd already had plenty to drink so she refused to sell it to ya'. You started yelling and she asked you to leave. You grabbed the bottle and headed for the door. That's when she picked up the phone to call 911. You must've heard her. You spun around but lost your footing and fell over the liquor display. Broke a good twenty or so bottles."

"Oh jeez, I'm so embarrassed. Angie's a nice lady. I guess I do owe her an apology."

"And about a couple hundred bucks. Good thing it wasn't the good stuff ya' broke."

"After the meeting, maybe we could stop and talk with her."

"Nah, she won't be there that late. Try tomorrow."

I nodded and about thirty miles of embarrassed silence followed until we pulled into another small town. Halston was built on the same basic plan as Amber Creek. The tornado hadn't been through there but that didn't mean it was in that great a shape. On the way into town, with the dimming early evening light, I could make out several run-down homes. A long low motel that looked like it had been built in the fifties and untouched since. There was a town square but most of its buildings were empty with for sale signs and a few boarded-up windows. There was a bar and gas station. The church was on the square too. With its gray weathered stone facade and short steeple, it looked smaller and older than St. Michaels in Amber Creek. It didn't have all of the accompanying campus buildings and was hemmed in by overgrown shrubbery. A small gravel parking lot had six or seven cars parked in it. Jerry drove the Camaro in and parked a little away from the other vehicles. We got out and he led me to the side door that took us to a short flight of dark stairs to the church basement.

In a back room, we found three guys and two women seated in a circle. They all looked up when we entered and welcomed Jerry. This obviously wasn't his first time here. He introduced me just as Hank, no last name as is the tradition. We pulled two more chairs from a rack near the wall and squeezed into the group. A guy who looked young enough to be my son welcomed me. "Is this your first meeting," he said.

"Hardly," I replied. "Just my first one here."

"Well, we were just getting started," he said. "Mind leading us in the serenity prayer, Jerry." From that point the meeting followed a familiar pattern. Review of one of the steps, I don't remember which, followed by testimonies. I perked up when Jerry's turn came.

"Hi, I'm Jerry and I'm an alcoholic." The group greeted him in unison. "I haven't had a drink in over two months. I can't say it's been easy but I've had a lot of help. You folks, my doctor and even my ex. I called her to make amends and she was nicer to me than I deserved. 'Course, she's married and has a couple of kids now. And I've got nothing thanks to the bottle. But I'm workin' on it, little by little. I just know it's gotta get better."

"It does" and "it will" passed through the group in support of Jerry. I just looked at him and pursed my lips. This was not the loser I'd seen before. This was a man in pain. A man I suddenly wanted to help. But I had to remind myself that he could also be a man who had brutally killed four women, that I knew of.

I passed on giving testimony and, this being my first meeting, they let it go. After the meeting I got to know several of the members over weak coffee. They weren't the same people I'd met at my AA meetings back home but their stories weren't all that different. They all faced the same devil I had, and apparently still did. These were good people, probably better than I was. I made myself a promise to return.

In the car on the way home, I decided to break the silence. "Thanks for taking me to the meeting. I think I needed it more than I realized."

"I go every week," He said. "You're welcome to come along."

"Thanks," I said and several minutes of uncomfortable silence followed. "Listen, I'm a psychiatrist ya' know and if ever you want to talk about ...well, whatever. I'd be happy to listen."

"Thanks," he said, looking straight ahead at the road. "I'll pass for now."

"Sure," I said lamely. "Just let me know."

Another uncomfortable silence followed, then Jerry broke it. "It's not that I don't appreciate the offer, it's just...well there's been a lot of shit that I don't like talking about."

My training kicked in and I just said, "But maybe it would help to talk about it?"

He looked at me, "I ain't your patient, Doc."

"I know that. Besides, I don't have a license to practice anymore, so ..." I shrugged.

He smiled a second then turned back to the road, face blank again. To my surprise, he wasn't done talking. "I drank to forget. I suppose a lot of people do. Now that I ain't drinkin'...well it's hard."

"When I stopped, I found myself remembering all the things I drank to forget."

"No shit," he said. "I think that's why most of us drink, to forget or to hide out."

"That was my excuse. I had a lot to forget. I was a shitty husband. My wife died before I could make it up to her. I screwed up my practice and hurt some people who were very special to me. When I stopped drinking, all of that was waiting for me. A lot of it still is."

"I know what you mean," Jerry said. "When I left the army, I was pretty screwed up but I had the idea that I could just go home and pick up where I left off. You can imagine how that worked out."

"I suspect things didn't go as planned."

"Ya' think," he grunted. "I figured everyone had changed; my wife, my folks, my friends. No one was the same. Not even where I worked. To cope I found the bottle again. And people just kept getting stranger around me."

"When did you figure it out?" I asked.

"Figure out what?"

"That it was actually you who had changed."

"Oh, that. Not til it was too late. My wife left me because she said I was too cranky and never talked with her. She was right, I guess. But her leaving just gave me more reasons to drink. I lost my job. My family wouldn't talk to me. I didn't have a friend in sight, except for other drunks. God knows where I'd be if Dan hadn't stepped in when he did. And he's stood by me even though I've disappointed him at every turn. I didn't go for help til' he said something that made me think he was ready to give up too. So here I am, two months sober."

"And having trouble with that, too."

"Yup. All the things I drank to forget didn't just disappear." He shook his head. "They were waiting just where I left 'em."

"You were too impaired to process any of it. I was in the same boat. I guess I still am."

"Yeah, but it wasn't just that I had to cope with what happened since I got home. Believe me, that was bad enough."

"But the things that happened in the Army, they flared up too, I imagine," I said trying to sound sympathetic but suspecting that what Jerry had to say could explain the murders, if he was indeed responsible.

"Yeah," he said and hit the gas pedal harder. We were well over the speed limit at that point and I could see the remains of the Amber Creek grain elevators in the distance.

"Jerry, please let up a little. You don't want to get us killed."

"S'pose not," he said. He slammed on the brakes and the car spun around. He regained control and pulled onto the side of the road. He kept his eyes directed straight ahead. "Doc, maybe you coming with me isn't such a good idea. Next time you should find your own way there, or maybe find a different group altogether."

"I'm sorry, Jerry. I didn't mean to upset you."

"It's not that," he said. "I... I buried some pretty awful shit from the war. I saw people killed - friends, kids. Hell, I killed people. And me, I didn't get a scratch. I came home and a lot of other people didn't."

"That's called survivor guilt," I said.

He turned to look directly into my eyes. "I don't care what it's called, I just don't want it anymore. I don't want to be afraid every time I meet someone that they're gonna hurt me, or worse, somehow I'm gonna hurt them. I hurt people and I killed people and I don't like it. Before that happens again, I'd rather kill myself. I almost did a bunch of times."

"But you didn't. There's got to be a reason for that."

"I can't honestly tell you what it is."

"Don't give up looking," I said.

He turned back to the road and gave the car gas, driving past the elevators, across the creek and back into town without another word. When he dropped me off in front of Ellie's house, I got out of the car and turned back to him. "Next week, same time, if you're willing?"

He didn't look at me but he nodded. I closed the door and he spun the car around and drove down the drive. I watched until his tail lights vanished at the turn. Then I just stood there, processing what I had learned. Jerry was a damaged soul. But somehow, I couldn't believe that he was a killer. Sure, he'd killed in wartime. Unfortunately, that had been his job. But that had obviously affected him so much that he'd pulled away from people he had cared about. He drank to suppress terrible memories, worse than I had ever experienced. He was afraid for himself and, more importantly, of himself. I couldn't imagine that he was a man who could plan to kidnap, confine and murder four women. It would have torn him apart. I'm pretty sure he would have killed himself first.

Just then, Ellie opened her door and shouted, "Are you coming in or what?"

I turned and walked into the house with her. We went into the kitchen and sat across from each other at the table.

"How'd it go?" she asked.

"The meeting...it was good," I replied. "People were nice and the routine was just like at home."

She studied my face for a moment. "What is it?"

I shook my head. "Jerry. He's not the killer. He's hurting. Racked with guilt. Psychopaths don't feel guilt. And serial killers are psychopaths."

"That's a good thing then," she said.

"Yes, of course it is. But then who is the killer?"

"That's not your job to determine," she said. "Let the police figure it out."

"I know, I know. But they still seem to want to focus on Sam and I know they're wrong about him."

"Dan said that the BCI is looking at several suspects. Not just Sam."

"They need to look at Andy Folger. He's the only one that's left. And I can see him as the killer. I watched him talk with Bob and Charlotte about what little the insurance company could do for them. He was as cold as a dead fish. And I saw him at the rectory. I bet he confessed to Sam, knowing that Sam wouldn't be able to tell anyone. He also knew that the secret would eat at Sam and make him look guilty to the BCI."

"Wait a minute, Hank. I think you're jumping the gun."

"I don't think so. And I'm going to talk to him."

"Who? Andy? Don't you dare."

"Someone has to."

"The cops. Let them do their job. If you have to, just talk with Dan about your suspicions but then let it drop."

"I'm not sure I can," I said.

"Well you better, because it's really none of your business and you're just going to get yourself in trouble," she insisted. "Now forget it and let's just get to bed."

I nodded, got to my feet and followed her to the bedroom. I had made a decision then and there. I was going to keep digging but I just wouldn't tell Ellie. This was my burden alone.

CHAPTER TWENTY-ONE

The next day, I dropped Ellie off at the hospital so that I could borrow her car for the day. In exchange, I promised to take her out for a nice dinner, though I didn't have a clue where. My first stop was at the temporary municipal building. No one was at the front desk but luckily, Dan was in his office. I tapped on his plywood door frame and he asked me in.

"To what do I owe the honor?"

"Well," I said, clearing my throat. 'It's about the case...the murders."

"I seem to recall asking you to stay out of police work."

"I know but."

"But nothing. Do you hear me?"

"No, really, this is important. Jerry took me to an AA meeting last night."

"I thought one of the A's was for anonymous."

"Of course, you're right but hear me out. Jerry and I had a long talk and I don't think he killed anyone."

"I could have told you that."

"But, listen. That only leaves one suspect."

"I'm not going to tell you again, Hank. The BCI is handling this. They know who to look at and how to do it. You sticking your nose in can only mess things up. Like with Sam. Remember?"

"Okay, but just tell me, are they looking at Andy Folger?"

"You are no longer involved in this investigation in any way. So, to you, that information is confidential."

"Come on, Dan. Give me a break. Are they, yes or no? That's all I need."

"If I tell you, you'll just start snooping around him and screwing up the investigation."

"That sounds like a yes'" I said.

"You didn't hear it from me," Dan said. "Now, is there anything else you needed. I'm sorta busy."

I stood and thanked him, turning back before exiting. "Hey, Dan. Where would you take your wife for a really nice meal?"

"Paris, if I could afford it," he chuckled.

"No really."

"I don't know," he paused thoughtfully. "There's a place in Mt. Carter, about an hour west. Don't remember the name but I bet Angie knows. You could give her a call on your way out." He emphasized the last part and I got the message.

That reminded me of my need to talk with Angie about the other night. The Pump 'n Shop was a half block away so I walked over. Angie was at the counter and I approached feeling exposed. She looked up. "Hi, Doc." She cocked her head to the side and raised her eyebrows. "How ya' feeling?"

"Fine," I said. 'And I understand that I have you to thank at least in part for that."

"Oh," she said, not helping me in any way this morning.

"Jerry told me what happened. I can't remember any of it myself, but I think I owe you an apology and some cash."

"You were pretty tanked when you walked in here."

"Apparently. And if you had done the easy thing and sold me another bottle, who knows what would have happened."

"I have a policy," she said. "Based on past experience."

"Well thanks, anyway," I said. "What do I owe you for the breakage?"

She smiled. "The best way to pay me is to promise you'll never buy another bottle of booze from me again."

"That's a promise," I said, taking two hundred dollar bills from my wallet and extending them to her. "This should cover it." She waved me off so I slipped the bills into a charity box on her counter. "By the way, Dan says there's a nice restaurant in Mt. Carter. He didn't know the name but he thought you would.

Angie did indeed know the name. The Grey Goose. Pricey for the area but being the only nice place for miles, it could be busy. She offered to call and make a reservation for me. "I've got contacts," she said. I thanked her and headed out. I got in the car and checked the grocery list Ellie and I had pulled together. I backed out of the parking space and started the long drive to Mt. Carter to get the groceries and maybe check out The Grey

Goose. It would give me plenty of time to think. I needed a way to talk with Andy Folger without pissing off everybody in town.

Purchases stowed in the trunk, I left the grocery store and drove by the Grey Goose. It looked like it would just fit the bill, not Michelin-rated but on a landscaped lot with ample parking and a stylish entryway flanked by faux gas carriage lights. I hoped Angie had been able to get those reservations.

I headed out of town, considering the plan I'd hatched in my head. Andy Folger ran an insurance agency, right? I was new to town and my RV was new. Suppose I'd been dumb enough to forget to insure it. Of course, I was probably over insured, a practice recommended by most medical organizations because doctors were seen as having deep pockets. Anyway, I would contact Andy to see about a policy. Meanwhile, I could scope him out.

It was noon by the time I got to Ellie's house. I unloaded the groceries, made myself a ham sandwich and sat at the table. After lunch I wasted ten minutes searching the house for a phone book before realizing that such things were antiques. So, I checked the internet on my phone, looking for reference to the Folger Insurance Agency. There was a very basic website with minimal information but at least I got the phone number and the address. I dialed the number and after several rings a man answered.

"Folger Agency," he said rather brusquely. I hadn't had much contact with Andy but it sounded like him.

"Yes, is this Mr. Folger?" I inquired.

"Yes, how can I help you?" He didn't sound very helpful to me.

"This is Hank Pressman. We met at the Owen's farm."

"Yes." His enthusiasm was underwhelming. He was lucky that he had no business competitors around.

"Well, I have an RV. As a matter of fact, it's pretty much all I have right now. And, like an idiot, I didn't get around to insuring it. The tornado reminded me how important insurance was, so I wonder if we could meet some time to discuss purchasing a policy?"

"Yeah," he replied. "I'm on the road right now but I'll be home around three. My office is at my house so you could meet me there."

I agreed and told him I had the address from his website. He hung up and I left the house to drive to my RV to get the registration and whatever paperwork I might need. I had no intention of buying anything from him but I had to go through the motions.

When I got to Irene's house, I noticed that she was hanging laundry on a line in the yard. She waved and called, "Hey stranger, where ya' been?"

I walked over to her and she gave me a quick hug. "Mostly at Ellie's," I said.

"You're good for her," Irene said. "I had my annual a few days ago and she seemed happier than I've seen her in a long time."

"Well, she's been pretty good for me too."

Irene took the last towel from her basket and pinned it to the line. "Could ya' use a cup of coffee," she said.

"Sure could," I answered and picked her basket up to follow her into the house. I sat at the kitchen table and Irene poured us each a cup of coffee that I suspected had been sitting on a hot plate most of the morning. It had probably been great when freshly brewed but the aroma was no longer enticing. I added a generous spoonful of sugar to mine and stirred. It tasted terrible but Irene didn't seem to notice.

"You been keeping yourself busy?" she asked, raising her eyebrows again.

"Yes and no," I replied. "Since the storm cleanup has progressed there isn't much for a guy like me to do. I still help out where I can."

"What I really meant was anymore drinking?"

"Oh, that," I said. "Can't hide much from you."

"You forget about my Edie. I learned what to look for. Besides, news gets around fast in small towns."

"Yeah. well, I admit I didn't do myself proud the other day. But it's not going to happen again."

"I hope you're right. You and Ellie seem to have a good thing going. It would be a shame if booze got in the way."

"I promise, I'll do my best. I've screwed up a lot of things in my life. I need to do better and I will."

"So, any long-term plans?"

'Not sure," I said. "I like it here but I don't know if I could make it my home. I'm used to a lot more going on."

"I know what ya' mean," she said. "Small towns are not for everyone. I think it took a while for Ellie to adjust too."

CHAPTER TWENTY-ONE

I nodded. "But I'm getting to know people around here. Nice folks."

"For the most part," she said.

"That reminds me," I said. "I've got an appointment with Andy Folger this afternoon, to talk about insurance on my RV. What sort of guy is he?"

"Kind of an odd duck, always has been."

"What do you mean?"

"It's hard to explain. Even as a kid, he was different. Didn't have a lot of friends. Didn't do sports or clubs. Just about everyone in town was either in the 4H or scouts, but not him. 'Spose it was his mother. She didn't let him out much. His dad wasn't a lot of help."

"How so?"

"Let's say he didn't exactly wear the pants in the family. He was a nice enough guy. Ran a good business and was active in town affairs but once he got home, he was under her thumb, just like Andy."

"She's gone now, isn't she?"

"Yes, five, six years ago. We thought Andy might move on once she'd died. But he didn't. Just stayed in the same house and kept the insurance agency going. Sometimes I feel sorry for him."

"Sometimes?" I asked.

"Well, he's kinda hard to sympathize with. Sorta, I don't know, cold. Doesn't seem to have much of a sense of humor either. I doubt anyone would have a lot to do with him if not for the agency."

"Sounds like a shame," I said, taking my last sip of Irene's uncharacteristically awful coffee.

"I suppose, but he only has himself to blame at this point," she said. "Can I pour you another cup?"

I waved my hands. "No thanks. I should get going." I rose to leave.

Irene stood too, but she grabbed my arm before I could leave. "Hank, you're not still looking into the murders, are you?"

"Why do you ask?"

"Because, if you are, I want to know that you're being careful about it."

"What do you mean?" I asked

"Hank, I'm not stupid. I know why you're asking about Andy. If you think he's involved in the murders, then tell the cops. Don't go looking into anything on your own."

"Why? Do you think Andy could be involved, somehow?"

"I don't know, but Charlotte and I talked about him, after you asked about single guys in town. We agreed that he gives us both the creeps."

I sat back down. "Why do you say that?"

"It's nothing you can get a handle on. It's just a feeling." She sat again beside me.

"That's sorta vague," I said.

"Okay, for example, there was a time when I was at church. Charlotte and the kids too. Well, a bird flew in. It's happened before. Well Andy, he's a church usher. You know how they are. Like to push their weight around. Anyway, Andy grabbed his collection basket. One of those with a long handle and, after a few tries, he caught the bird in it. He covered the basket with a hymnal and went out the side door of the church. He was gone a few minutes then came back. And sat down at the back of the church like always."

"So, what's creepy about that?" I inquired.

"It wasn't that. It was afterwards. After mass. We walked out and I heard a little girl scream. She was with her folks at the curb. Of course, everyone looked at her but her mom looked down at the pavement and then rushed the girl away. And, wouldn't you know it, Charlotte's boy, Bobbie, had to run over to check things out. There was a bird in the gutter, or at least what was left of one. It looked like it had been crushed, blood and guts mixed with the feathers."

"And what makes you think that was the bird Andy had caught?"

"I can't prove anything. But it was beside the sidewalk we take to church. Bobbie being a boy, wouldn't have missed something like that. I don't believe it was there when we came in."

"You think Andy killed it."

"Let me say, it wouldn't have surprised me," she said. "So, my point is be careful around him. If you're just buying insurance then I wouldn't worry. If you're playing detective, watch out. Or better yet, just don't."

I got up again. "Thanks for the warning, mother. I'll be a good boy."

She rose and gave me another hug. "See to it that you are," she said.

I left to get the paperwork from my RV but I didn't forget what Irene had said. I had been reminded of my research on serial killers who often started out by torturing animals. Was this another indicator of Andy's personality? I needed to keep that in mind and to be careful, like Irene had said. I got into the RV, changed clothes for dinner and picked up the information I needed for my meeting with Andy.

I arrived at Andy's house about five minutes early and parked out front. Andy lived a couple blocks east of the church and a couple south of where the first body had been found. I stored those locations in the back of my mind as I approached his front door. The house was dated and plain but neat and well-maintained. I stepped up on the small porch and rang the doorbell. I waited a minute then heard a voice to my right. It was Andy.

"This way" he said, from the driveway. "My office is behind the garage."

I followed him around the side of the house and to a door at the back of the garage. He opened it and directed me inside. He had walled off the rear eight feet of his deep garage and turned it into a sparse office space with a desk, a few side chairs and a line of filing cabinets that stood against the wall behind his chair. On his desk were a phone, a laptop computer and a desk light. No framed pictures or knick knacks. There was a large map on the wall but no art. The space was about as sterile as possible. Andy directed me to a side chair then took his behind the desk. "What can I do for you?" he said, monotone.

Just then, my phone buzzed. I held up my index finger and the screen. A text message from Angie confirmed that she had made dinner reservations for me. I forwarded the message to Ellie, hoping that Andy couldn't tell who I was texting.

"Sorry,' I said. "Well, like I said on the phone, I need to insure my RV."

"I checked the database," he said. "It appears you already have a policy with one of the companies I deal with."

"Oh, well, yes, "I stuttered. But I'm on a fixed income now and I hoped that you could help me get a better rate."

"That's not what you said on the phone," he said, glaring at me.

"No, I guess I didn't want to sound...I don't know. Cheap maybe."

"Alright," he said, unconvinced. "Because you already had a policy with asset details, I was able to work up a few offers. But frankly, your current rate is pretty good, unless there are assets you hadn't listed."

"No," I said. "Well, yes actually. My computer, my TV, my clothes. Did I list those?"

"They are all covered." Then he stood and walked around the corner of the desk to sit on its edge where he towered above me. "What is this visit really about?" he said.

"I don't know what you mean," I said, looking up at him uncomfortably.

"I'm not a fool, Doctor Pressman. I know that you were asked to help the police look into these horrible murders. I know that you talked with their prime suspect, Father Cannon. I also know that, before you came to Amber Creek, you were involved in one of the biggest murder cases in the state. Your reputation is, shall I say, shady at best."

I stood and was now looking down on him. "Listen, I had nothing to do with that murder, directly. And my reputation is none of your business. I just came here for an insurance quote."

He slid a piece of paper across the desk. "Here ya' go," he said. "I printed 'em up for you to peruse at your leisure." He gave me a very toothy smile. "Anything else I can do for you.:

I took the paper, folded it and slid it into my pocket. "No, but thanks," I said and walked out the way I'd come in. Andy followed and stood in the doorway watching me. In the space between the house and the garage, I noticed two basement windows, flanking the stoop at the house's side door. They were heavily frosted. I doubted that they admitted much light. I walked past, climbed into my car, and drove away, but those windows haunted me, as did my meeting with Andy.

CHAPTER TWENTY-TWO

I had a good half hour before I was to pick Ellie up so I swung by the church to see if Sam happened to be there. I wanted to reassure him of the results of his tests and maybe ask what he knew about Andy Folger. His car wasn't parked on the street but I pulled over and walked up to the front door. After ringing the bell three times with no answer, I guessed he wasn't there. I got back to the car but, as I opened the door, a gray sedan sped past me, missing me by mere inches. After cursing the unseen driver, I climbed into my car and headed to the hospital. Maybe Ellie would be done early. The same gray, late model sedan cut me off at the turn to the hospital. I hit the brakes, cursed and went on my way. I tried to see into the car but it sped away before I could make anything out through its tinted windows.

Ellie was still with a patient when I got to her office, so I went to the hospital cafeteria for a diet Pepsi and a bag of chips. There was no one else there at that time of day so I ate my snack and played games on my phone til' five then walked back to Ellie's office. She was just locking up. I wrapped my arms around her and kissed her. She pushed me away gently. "Not here," she teased.

"Okay, but wait til' I get you home."

She laughed and took me by the arm. We walked out to the car and I drove us to Ellie's house. She'd gotten my text message about our restaurant reservation but assured me that we had plenty of time before we had to leave. Then she pulled me into the bedroom.

At six o'clock, showered and dressed, we got back into the car and headed through town. The sky was overcast and unusually dark. "I sure hope that doesn't mean another tornado," Ellie said.

We crossed the creek heading west to Mt. Carter on the old highway. I turned on my headlights and my wipers as heavy raindrops started splattering the windshield. Before long the rain grew steady and visibility became limited. I slowed and headlights appeared in my rearview mirror. They approached rapidly so I tapped the brakes to signal to the driver behind me. He didn't seem to care as he came up on my rear and tailed me way too close for comfort. I tapped my brakes again and he dropped back a bit, only to accelerate again and pass me, then hit his brakes once he was in front of me. I slammed mine on to avoid rear ending him and blasted the horn. With the dark and the rain, I couldn't make out who was behind the wheel. He sped up again. I waited a bit to give him time to get well ahead of me and then drove on. I turned to Ellie. "What the hell was that guy's problem," I said. Then Ellie screamed. I turned back to see headlights coming right at me. I spun the wheel and went off the road as the other car passed, mere inches from us. Unfortunately, there was a ditch parallel to the roadway and with the turn, the car slipped into it and flipped on its side. My head slammed against the car window and I suspect I passed out for a few seconds.

When I came to, I could feel blood dripping from my forehead. I looked over at Ellie. She was laying on top of me unconscious, her legs crumpled against the center console. I tried to rouse her with no response. Then I dug into my pocket to find my cell phone and pulled it out. The signal was weak but I dialed 911 and hoped for the best. A dispatcher came on the line but I could barely hear her over the rain. I shouted to explain what had happened and, as best I could figure, where we were. I begged her to hurry. She instructed me to stay on the line while she messaged the local emergency services.

I'd been able to rouse Ellie to a state of semi consciousness. She was alert enough to tell me she was having a lot of pain in her left leg but then drifted back to sleep. It seemed like I'd waited for hours, but it had probably been only fifteen or twenty minutes. The dispatcher had kept me talking the whole time but signed off when I told her that emergency services had arrived. A police car got to us first, its siren screaming. I couldn't see it well but recognized Dan when he got to the car and looked in through the windshield. The rain hadn't let up much and still pummeled the car so I couldn't hear what he was trying to shout to me. I pointed to myself and made an okay sign with my thumb and forefinger. Then I pointed at Ellie and shook my head too vigorously, causing me a wave of nausea and pain in my forehead. Just then, Dan turned and signaled toward the road.

The ambulance had arrived and he waved them over. The emergency workers were able to open the passenger door of our car and carefully extract Ellie, who screamed in pain when they moved her. I climbed out after her, the rain beating down on both of us. An EMT took my arm and helped me to a gurney beside Ellie's in the ambulance. He climbed in between us and the ambulance sped back the way we had come, to the Amber Creek Hospital. The EMT informed me that a helicopter was coming to take us to the University hospital, as Ellie was the only doctor around.

The ambulance approached the bridge over Amber Creek while the EMT placed an IV line, EKG leads and oxygen sensors on Ellie and then me. I looked over at Ellie and she seemed to have lost consciousness again. Her EKG monitor showed a steady but rapid rhythm and her oxygen level was good. Her blood pressure, on the other hand, was low. I feared that she was going into shock. I looked down at her leg and, though it was covered in blood-stained gauze, I could see an odd bulge on her shin. Her injuries were obviously worse than mine. My monitor readings looked relatively normal. My pressure was up but considering what was happening that was no surprise. When the EMT tried to check me for injuries I redirected his attention back to Ellie. She obviously needed it more than I.

We crossed the creek and slowed slightly going through town. The ambulance pulled into the covered emergency entrance at the hospital. The rear doors swung open and, with the help of two nurses who had run out of the hospital, Ellie's gurney was taken out and rolled into the ER. The EMT attempted to help me get out as well but I shouted at him to follow Ellie. He looked uncertain until I sat up and swung my legs over the side of the gurney. "I'm fine," I said. "Go help her." He was obviously reluctant but left anyway. I quickly pulled the EKG patches from my chest and dropped the pulse oximeter on the gurney, I pulled the IV bag from its hook and, hoisting it above my heart, clumsily made my way out of the ambulance. I was in a lot of pain, so I knew I was probably more banged up than I wanted to admit. The police car had parked beside the ambulance and Jerry jumped out of the driver's side door as Dan got out on the other. They rushed over to support me and guided me into the ER. Jerry leaned close to my face and seemed to sniff. He looked up at Dan and shook his head. I suspected he'd been checking for the smell of alcohol. "Not a drop," I said.

I was led to a small, curtained bay in the ER and placed on another gurney. Dan took the IV bag from me and hung it on a nearby pole. Then he leaned close to me. "What the hell happened?" he asked, with concern in his voice rather than anger.

"We were driving to Mt. Carter for dinner. Then this car came at us head on. I had to pull off the road to avoid him."

"Can you describe the car?"

"Not really," I said. "It was raining so hard." Then an image flashed in the back of my mind. A gray sedan. An older model. And I'd seen it before but where? I told Dan what little I could recall. Of course, he asked if I'd seen the driver. I had to admit I hadn't. Then a nurse came in and sent Dan out. She helped me out of my clothes and into a gown, inspecting me as she went. No bruises yet but there was a gash on the left side of my forehead where I'd hit the window. She did a quick manual exam. I had several areas that felt sore but nothing suggestive of a fracture. There was no tenderness in my abdomen or chest that would have suggested internal injury. She drew blood and I gave her a urine sample which didn't look grossly bloody. I was sure that I would hurt for a while but there was no significant injury.

"I'm not a doctor but I think you're just banged up," the nurse said.

"That's great," I said. "But how about Ellie, I mean Doctor Sparks?"

"There appears to be a compound fracture of her left tibia. Her vitals are stabilizing. She hit her head pretty hard, too. She's been coming in and out of consciousness."

"The cops said a helicopter was coming."

"Yes, the weather has slowed it down but it should be here soon."

"Where will they be taking her?"

"University Hospital. We talked with them and they'll be ready for her."

"Can I go with her?'

"I doubt it," she said. "They don't have a lot of space."

"Then, can I see her before she goes?"

"I'll check but you stay here for now." She left, closing a curtain behind her. She was gone for several minutes when I heard the sound of frenzied movement outside my room. I called out "What's going on?" without a response.

I swung my legs over the side of the gurney, and walked unsteadily to the curtain. I felt a sudden yank on my arm and remembered the IV. I took hold of the pole and, using it as support, walked past the curtain. I saw the nurses, cops and EMT guiding another gurney, I suspected Ellie's, toward the door. "Where are you going?" I called, stumbling trying to catch up with them. Dan turned back and hurried over to support me.

"The helicopter is landing. We're taking her to it now."

"I've got to go with her," I shouted.

"No," Dan said. "There's no room. You need to get back to your bed."

The ER doors opened just then and I could hear the roar of the landing helicopter. The nurses rushed their charge through the doors which closed behind them, muffling the sound. I started to sob like a child but allowed Dan to lead me back to my gurney. Within minutes, the nurse came into my alcove. "They're off," she said. "Ellie was awake and responding. Her bleeding has been stopped. I'm sure she'll be fine."

"This is all my fault," I said.

"It was an accident," Dan said.

"No, that's just it," I said. "That car. I saw it before. It was coming for me."

"Now, Doctor Pressman," the nurse interrupted. "Try to relax. I can get you something for pain. It will help you rest, too."

"No, wait," Dan said. He looked at me. "Where, where did you see this car?"

I thought for a minute and rubbed tears from my eyes. "It was...let me think. At the rectory. Earlier today I wanted to see Sam but he wasn't there. I went to get back in the car and this old gray car buzzed past me. I think it was the same car."

"Did you get a license number?"

"No, but I know who it might have been." I looked up at the ceiling and closed my eyes.

"Okay," Dan said. "Who?"

I took a deep breath, knowing what Dan was likely to say. "Andy Folger."

"Why Andy?"

"Because...because I went to see him this afternoon."

"You what!," he shouted.

"I was checking out insurance... for my RV."

"The hell you were," Dan said. "I told you to keep your nose out of this case, didn't I."

"Yes but..."

"But nothing. You may have gotten Ellie killed, don't you realize that?"

"I'm sorry," I said. "I didn't mean to."

"Oh, well then that makes it all better," he snarked. "Ya' know I could arrest you for that and if you pull anything like it again, I will." He turned and stormed out of the room. The nurse stepped out of his way and then looked back at me, confused.

"I could use those pain meds now," I told her. "Enough to knock me out."

I spent the night in the ER, sleeping on and off. Images of the accident haunted my dreams when I could sleep and, when I couldn't, guilt flooded over me. I knew Dan had been right. If Ellie died, it would surely be my fault. If I hadn't been so arrogant to think that I could solve the murders better than the cops could, Ellie and I would have just gone out for a nice dinner and come home to her bed and all that implied. But now, look at where we were. My self-flagellation was interrupted by a new nurse entering my cubicle.

"How are you feeling this morning?" she asked.

"Any word about Ellie?" I blurted.

"Yes," she replied. "All good too. They gave her some blood and she had surgery on her leg. It was a compound fracture. She came through it well. Word is she's alert and her vitals are stable."

"Thank God," I said. Just an expression, not a prayer. "When can I get out of here?"

"Back to my question," she said, "how are you feeling?"

Throwing the sheet aside, I sat up with some effort and pain that ran from my left leg, up my side and into my neck. "Like I was hit by a car."

"Fortunately, the x rays don't show any fractures. But you're pretty bruised up," she said pointing to my left arm and leg.

I hadn't noticed the black and blue patches on my arm and leg. "Oh shit. I see what you mean."

"But your vitals are good. There's no broken skin, except on your forehead. That's been cleaned and dressed. Of course, we don't have a doctor to clear you but we talked with our telemedicine doc. He reviewed the data and said that if you think you're ready to go, we should call someone to pick you up."

"Great, Bob Owens, let's call him."

"Fine," she said. "I'll call him for you and then we can disconnect the IV and the monitors. I'm afraid your clothes aren't going to be much use to you. I'll ask Bob to bring a change."

Bob was there a half an hour later. He waited outside my cubicle while I struggled into the clothes he'd brought. Then I pulled the curtain aside and limped out.

"Let's get you home," Bob said.

"No," I said. "I need you to take me to University Hospital. I've got to see Ellie."

A nurse stepped over from her desk. "No, Bob. You need to take him home and get him to rest. We have meds for him, ordered by the telemedicine doctor. Directions are on the bottle. He's to rest today and come back tomorrow to have his bandage changed. Got it?"

"Yes sir," Bob said, saluting.

"And before you go, I'll need you both to sign a few forms." She pushed several pages forward on the desk, and grinned with mock menace. "That way, if you fall and break something on the way out, I'm in the clear." That's when I remembered her and her sense of humor. We had worked together just after the tornado.

"Oh come on, I'm fine," I said. We filled in our names and pushed the papers back to her.

"We'll see about that tomorrow," she said. "Meanwhile, go home. Doctor's orders."

So that was that. Bob helped me into his truck, drove me back to my RV and helped me out of the car, wrapping my arm around his strong shoulders. We began a slow walk to my RV. The pain pills I'd been given were obviously wearing off and every step sent a bolt of lightning through my left side. We hadn't made it to the RV before Irene burst through her kitchen door. "Where the hell do you think you're taking him?" she shouted.

"I'm supposed to put him to bed," Bob responded.

"Of course," Irene said. "But not in there. I have a bed ready for him in here."

I looked her way, pain stabbing my neck. "It's okay, Irene. I just need a little rest."

"You need someone to keep an eye on you," she said. "Bob, bring him in here then you go back to his place and get a pair of PJs."

"No, really," I mumbled.

"Don't argue," Irene said.

Bob shrugged and turned me toward the house. "Once she's got her mind made up, there's no changing it,"

I had to admit there was no fight left in me so I let him walk me inside. Irene guided us through the kitchen and into a small room off the parlor. A bed was waiting there, the bed clothes pulled back and ample pillows against the headboard. "You didn't have to go to all this trouble," I said.

"It was no trouble," she replied. "This was my Eddie's room when he got too sick to climb the stairs."

I felt a little ashamed to have resisted her invitation. This was obviously hard for her but she was determined to help me. "Thank you, Irene," was all I could think to say.

Bob sat me on the edge of the bed. "I'll run and get those PJs for you," he said.

"Don't bother," I said. "I don't have any. But if you could help me out of my clothes, I can just sleep in my underwear. He complied, tossing my clothes on the other side of the bed. He helped me swing my legs onto the bed and lay down. Then Irene took over, tucking me in. She handed me two of the prescription pills and a glass of water and wouldn't leave until I'd downed them. After she left, I dug my phone out of my pants pocket and called the University Hospital. I asked for Ellie's doctor but of course, he wasn't available and the nurse said she couldn't release information to me. I asked to talk directly to Ellie but was told that she was resting comfortably and shouldn't be disturbed. I ended the call and dropped the phone beside me on the bed. I carefully rolled on my side and closed my eyes, falling asleep almost immediately. At least I slept better knowing Ellie was okay.

CHAPTER TWENTY-THREE

I have no idea how long I slept before a firm tap sounded on the door. I rolled carefully onto my back. "Come in."

The door swung open, driven by Irene's back side. She turned to me and displayed a covered tray. "I thought you might be hungry."

"What time is it?" I said, pulling myself painfully to a half sitting position against the pillows.

"Nearly five o'clock, "she said.

"I've slept all day."

"Guess you needed it," she said. "Now you probably need something in your stomach."

"Yes, but there is something else I've got to do first. Is Bob still around?"

"Won't be home til' six," she said. "Don't be shy though. I can certainly help you to the bathroom if that's what you're talking about."

"No that's okay, I can get there by myself." I slid my legs to the edge of the bed, grimacing all the way.

"Don't be a hero," Irene said as she placed one arm behind my back and one under my legs, bringing me smoothly to a sitting position.

"You've done this before," I said. "Were you a nurse or something?"

Sadness flashed across her face and was gone. "Like I told you, this was Eddie's room. His last year was hard for him... for all of us. Hospice came in. They showed me what to do to take care of him."

"I'm so sorry," I said.

She shook her head. "Past is past. Now let's get you to the bathroom." With her help I stood unsteadily and limped to the bathroom off the kitchen. "Sorry, there's no shower or tub but I left a washcloth and towel there if you want to clean up."

"Thanks," I said. "You really didn't have to do all this,"

She smiled. "Just tell me when you're done and I'll help you back to bed."

Once I was back in bed, sitting up against the pillows and tucked in, Irene took the dish cloth off of her tray. There was a mug of tomato soup and a grilled cheese sandwich on it, alongside a glass of water and two more pain pills. She set the tray on my lap, tucked the dish cloth under my chin and handed me the pills. I popped them in my mouth and swallowed them down with half a glass of water. I set the glass down and picked up the mug to sample the soup.

"Careful," Irene said. "It might be hot."

"Probably when you brought it in," I said. I took a sample sip. "It's just right now."

"Well, you enjoy," she said, turning to leave.

"No wait," I said. "I could use a little company."

She pulled a chair over from the wall and took a seat. "What's on your mind," she said.

"Nothing special." I continued to work on my meal as we talked.

She turned her head knowingly to the side. "Really?"

"I suppose you'd like to hear about the accident."

"Well," she said, leaning forward.

"You mean it's not already the talk of the town."

"Yes but no real details. Just that there was an accident and that Ellie was helicoptered to University," she replied. "By the way, have you heard how she's doing?"

"Yeah. She had a serious fracture of her lower leg but they did surgery and she's going to be okay."

"Thank the Lord. So, tell me what happened."

"Okay. Ya' see I was driving Ellie's car. We were going to that upscale restaurant in Mt. Carter."

"The Grey Goose?" She pretended to be impressed.

"Yeah, that's the one," I said. "Well anyway we were on the old highway heading west. It was raining pretty hard so I slowed down. Then this car pulled up behind me. I let him pass and the next thing I knew, a car was coming at us head on. I think it was the same car. I did the only thing I could and pulled off the road but there was a ditch and I rolled the car."

"Oh, my lord," she said.

"Fortunately, I had my phone and called the ambulance. They took us to Amber Creek Hospital. Like you said, Ellie was flown out and I spent the night in the ER."

"And they thought you were well enough to go home?"

"Well, I kinda pushed and they didn't have a doctor on site anyway. So here I am. And thanks again for that."

"Well, you finish up your meal. I'll be back in a few minutes." She rose and headed to the door but then froze in place. She turned back to me. "The car that ran you off the road. Did you recognize it?"

"No," I said, "Not really."

The wrinkles around one eye bunched up and she sat back down. "Not really," she said, as if she wasn't believing me.

"Alright. I do think I saw it earlier that day after I..."

"After you went to Andy Folger's place. Am I right?"

"Yes ma'am," I said, like a repentant schoolboy.

She jumped to her feet. "Hank, you idiot. You poked the bear. Even after being warned...more than once."

"I was trying to help Sam."

"Baloney. You were trying to be the big man who caught the killer."

"No that wasn't it."

"Be honest, Hank, at least with yourself."

"Okay, maybe you're right. But I did want to help Sam."

"And look where it's got you. You and Ellie both could have been killed." She leaned over and took the tray from my lap.

"I'm not finished with that," I said.

"You are now," she said, carrying the tray away. Before closing the door she looked back at me. "Just promise me that you'll mind your own business from now on." I nodded and she closed the door, shaking her head.

I leaned back against the pillows and covered my eyes with my good forearm. I was angry but not as much at Irene as at myself. She hadn't been far off the mark. I was playing the hero, the smartest guy around. I was going to solve the murders and show everybody how clever I was. Sure, I wanted to help Sam and I hoped that that had been my primary motivation. But I did want to prove something. I had always wanted to prove something. If I was honest, that was why I went to medical school, why I went into a specialty that my classmates had shunned, why I had taken Carla as a patient three years ago. I was going to show everyone that I was not that worthless kid from a broken home who would never amount to anything. Yes, and I was proving something every time I broke my marriage vows. I was the hottest guy around and every woman wanted to fuck me, even though I couldn't find anyone to love. The few people who did love me, I wouldn't let get close enough to me to see who I really was. So, what did I prove anyway?

I thought that I had somehow gotten past all of that. I left it all behind when I left my career and my home. Here in Amber Creek, I had discovered a purpose. I had made friends. I found Ellie. I was a better man than I had ever been. But still, I was trying to prove something. It hurt me to think what that something was...or wasn't. Did the missteps I'd made outweigh all the good I'd done since coming to Amber Creek? I hadn't thought so but now, once again, my need to be the hero was putting other people at risk. Ellie could have died because of it. If she had, Amber creek would have lost its only doctor. Who else would I have hurt then? And for what?

These were things I spent most of my life trying to not think about. These were the things that haunted me when the lights were out. These were the fuel that fed the fire of alcoholism. And they were the reason that I wanted a drink right then more than I had in a very long time. Fortunately, there was no way to get any. I was in no condition to get a bottle myself. Irene sure wasn't going to mix me a cocktail. But maybe I could talk her into giving me a few more pain pills. No, that was not going to happen either. I just had to lay here and suffer it out. But of course, that was me feeling sorry for myself again. More reason to beat myself up. That's how depression sets in. I rolled painfully to my side and buried my face in the pillows and, as the pills I'd already taken finally kicked in, fell into a restless sleep.

CHAPTER TWENTY-FOUR

The next morning, I was already awake and sitting at the side of the bed when Irene knocked on my door. She waited until I asked her in and then opened the door holding a tray with a glass of water and my pills. "Good morning," I said as nonchalantly as I could.

She gave me a strained smile. "And how are you feeling this morning?"

"A little better, I think," I replied. "And you?"

She stepped forward and presented the tray to me. "I'm okay...I mean ...I've thought about what I said yesterday and, though I'm still frustrated with you, I may have been a little out of line."

By then I'd swallowed the pills and drained the water glass. I set the glass back on her tray and held my hands up in surrender. "No. I gave it some thought too and I have to admit that what you said hit home with me. I do like to play the hero."

"On the other hand," she said, "you were helping Sam and the rest of us. I have to thank you for that. But please, from here on out, leave detective work to the real detectives. Okay?"

I grinned back at her. "Deal. But that means I have to find some other hobby."

"How about I teach you to crochet," she said, chuckling at her own humor.

"I'll get back to you on that."

"So do you think you're ready to come to the table for some breakfast?"

"Sure, but let me get cleaned up first."

"Of course," she said and stepped to the closet and grabbed something from a hook on the inside of the door. She came back with a well-worn plaid robe. "This was Edie's. It probably won't fit but give it a try."

I took it from her and came stiffly to my feet, trying not to let her see that I was still in quite a lot of pain. I slipped into the robe and tied the sash around my waste. It hung just above my knees and bunched up at the waist but it was warm and covered what absolutely needed covering. I saw that the sight of me in Edie's robe had touched Irene's heart. I thanked her and gave her a peck on the cheek before limping past her to the downstairs bathroom.

After breakfast and interrogation by Irene's grand kids, Bob helped me up the stairs to the bathroom where I climbed cautiously into a warm bath that felt like slipping into heaven. When the water started to cool, I called for Bob's help. He helped me out of the tub and into the change of clothes he'd collected from my RV.

Bob helped me back down the steps and into his truck under Irene's watchful eyes. We drove back to the hospital for my dressing change. Afterwards, I asked him to take me to see Dan. I limped into the municipal building and found a young woman sitting at the front desk.

"Hi, I'm Hank Pressman," I said. "You must be new."

She smiled. "Not really. I've been away with my mom. She got pretty banged up in the storm."

"Oh, I'm sorry."

"No, that's okay. She's doing much better now so I was able to come back to work."

"That's good," I said. "Say, is Dan in?"

She called him on the intercom and sent me back. I stepped into his office and he immediately directed me to a chair. "Hank, what the hell are you doing out of bed? You look like shit."

"Thanks," I said. "I just wanted to know what you've learned about the...accident."

"Not much," he said. "I did stop over at Andy's place. He was a little pissed that I was there but did let me see his car."

"A gray sedan?", I inquired.

"Sorry. It's tan."

"Maybe I saw it wrong. Maybe that's the car."

"No way you could mistake it for gray. Yellow maybe, but not gray. It wasn't his car that ran you off the road. And he says that he was home that night, doing paperwork for the agency."

"And you're sure he doesn't have another car?" I asked.

"Checked the garage. It's a double but only one car. There was an oil stain on the floor in the other parking space. Could have been another car or maybe he doesn't always park on the same side. Doesn't prove anything. Sorry."

"Okay, but that doesn't mean it wasn't him."

"Hank, will you just drop it. I told you the BCI is on the case. It's their job. Not yours. All you're doing is making a mess. So, if I find you snooping around again, I'm locking you up."

I looked around, surveying the very temporary space. "And where would that be?"

"Don't be a smart ass." He said. "Maybe our jail is gone but they have a nice one in Mt. Carter and plenty of empty cells. I checked."

I waved my hands in surrender. "Okay, okay. I'll be good."

"See that you are," he said, "and get yourself back to bed before you collapse." He helped me to my feet and showed me back to the lobby where Bob was waiting. He walked me to his truck and helped me climb in.

"Home?" he asked, hopefully.

"How busy are you today?"

"Not very, considering I don't own a farm anymore."

"What do you mean?"

"I'm selling," he said. "Not much choice. Insurance isn't even covering my debts."

"Bob, I'm so sorry." I thought about offering to make him a loan but I remembered what had happened the last time I made an offer like that. "So, what are you going to do?"

"Not sure. Maybe I can get a job with the corporation that's buying me out, though it wouldn't feel right. I've got a family to feed, so I may have to swallow my pride."

"I don't understand why the insurance isn't helping."

"I'm not sure either. Some trick clauses I hadn't noticed."

"And Andy hadn't gone out of his way to point it out until you needed the coverage."

"Let's not go there, okay?" he said, starting the engine and giving it too much gas. "I don't need to get more pissed off than I already am. So, where to?"

"I'll pay you the price of gas and a hundred bucks to take me to the University Hospital."

"I won't take your money, Hank."

"Then I'll find another way," I said, staring him down.

Finally, he shook his head. "Alright, just let me stop home and tell Charlotte."

It was nearly a three-hour drive. We pulled into one of the many parking ramps surrounding the main entrance to a complex of hospital buildings that covered more ground than all of downtown Amber Creek. Bob insisted on finding me a wheelchair to take me the city block to the entrance. Once I was seated, he handed the small suitcase I'd prepared for Ellie and wheeled me inside. At the information desk, he asked for directions to Ellie's room. Then down a long hall to a bank of elevators, up three floors and down another longer hall, we finally arrived at what was hopefully the right nurse's desk. I jostled out of the wheel chair and came to my feet, leaning heavily on the counter.

"Excuse me," I said to a young woman behind the desk. "I'm looking for Ellie Sparks. I believe she's a patient on this floor."

Without looking up, the woman grumbled, "Family?"

"No but she and I are very close," I said.

"I'll call her nurse," the woman said, picking up her phone. She dialed a few numbers, waited for a minute, spoke unintelligibly and hung up. She finally looked up at me. "Wait over there," she said, pointing to a few chairs by the wall. She immediately went back to processing a tall stack of papers on her desk.

I started to walk over to the chairs but Bob reminded me of the wheelchair and I lowered myself carefully back down. He wheeled me to the wall and said "I saw a pop machine by the elevator, need anything." I shook my head and he left me there in the wheelchair.

Before Bob got back, a woman in white skirt and smock walked to the desk and then came over to me. "I'm Ellie's nurse." I tried to stand but she waved her hands. "Don't bother. How can I help you?"

"How is she?'" I asked.

"I would need her permission to talk about her case. I can ask her, if you'd like."

"Please," I said. "And ask if she wants me to visit."

"Sure," she said. I gave her my name and watched as she wrote it on a notepad she'd pulled from her pocket. "I'll be right back." She walked back down the hall she had come from. Bob returned, guzzling a Coke. I was telling him about the nurse when she returned.

CHAPTER TWENTY-FOUR

"She said she would like to see you."

"Me too," Bob said, imploring.

"He seems to be your caretaker so, sure," she said and led us down the hall and to Ellie's room.

Bob stopped the wheelchair outside the door, took the suitcase from me and leaned down. "I should have asked. Do you want to see her alone?"

"I think she'll be glad to see that I have a chaperone," I said. Bob laughed and we followed the nurse into the room.

Ellie was lying in the bed by the window, her left leg suspended from a support structure over the bed. The right side of her face was black and blue. She looked over at us, forcing a smile. "Hi guys," she said. "Thanks for coming all this way."

Bob set the suitcase on the floor and, with his assistance, I got out of the wheelchair and limped stiffly to the bedside. I leaned in and gave her a kiss, which she returned. "How could we not come?" I said.

Dan stepped to my side. "So how are you, Doc?"

She looked up at her leg and back at us. "I've been better,"

"Ya, well," Dan said and then held his tongue.

"What have the doctors said?" I asked, taking her hand.

"They think I'll be able to go home in a couple of days. They plan to put me in a cast once the swelling goes down. They tell me I'll be fine but it will take a while."

"And, are you in a lot of pain?"

She pointed to the IV pump beside her bed. "Morphine on demand," she said. "But really, it's not so bad as long as I stay still. Using the bedpan isn't much fun. How are you doing?"

"Sore and a little black and blue but I really can't complain... considering."

"Well, I'm glad for that at least," She smiled ruefully.

"I just need to tell you how sorry I am about this."

"It wasn't your fault, Hank.".

"But, I think it was," I said. "I think I pissed somebody off and they came after me."

"Who?" she asked, her smile fading.

"Andy Folger."

"What," Bob blurted. "That son of a bitch."

"Wait," I said. "I can't be sure it was him. It's just a hunch. Dan checked his car out and it's not the same one but I still think it was probably Andy."

"But why?" Ellie said.

Here's where things got difficult. "I went to his house, his office really."

"Why on earth would you do that?" Ellie said as she tried to sit up and winced.

I gently eased her back down on the bed. "I told him I needed to look into insurance on my RV."

"I wouldn't recommend you buy insurance on your last shit from him," Bob said.

"He wasn't buying anything," Ellie said, an edge in her voice. "He was investigating, in spite of numerous warnings."

"Investigating what?" Bob asked.

"Dick Tracy here thinks Andy Folger is the serial killer," Ellie said.

Bob shrugged his shoulders. "I guess I could see that. Especially since the tornado."

"But it's not Hank's job to find the killer," she said. "And if Andy did run us off the road, which I'm not saying he did, then Hank is to blame for this." She pointed to her leg.

"I said I'm sorry. If I had known that this would happen..."

"Sorry doesn't fix my leg," she said.

"I know, and I promise you that I'm done investigating. Besides, if I'm not, Dan's going to put me behind bars."

"And I wouldn't blame him," Ellie said.

"So, you're just gonna let that son of a bitch off the hook?" Bob asked.

"No, I'm going to let the cops do their job, like I should have been doing all along."

"Here, here," Ellie said. She looked up at the ceiling and sighed. "Ya' know, I'm awfully tired all of a sudden. Maybe you guys should just head home."

"But Ellie ..." I implored.

She gave me a look that made her message clear. "I have a lot of thinking to do," she said.

"Okay, but call me if you need anything. Okay?"

"I've got your number," she said. "In more ways than one."

I leaned over to kiss her goodbye but she turned her head and my lips landed on her cheek. "I'm so very sorry," I said and I climbed back in the wheelchair. Bob said goodbye to Ellie and wished her a speedy recovery. Then he backed me out of the room. On our way down the hall, he leaned down by my ear. "You really messed that up," he whispered. I just nodded.

On the long drive home, Bob grilled me about my suspicions and any evidence I might have. I was ashamed to admit that I really had no evidence, just suspicion. He said that if Andy was guilty, he'd volunteer to be his executioner. At least his prattle distracted me from my own guilt.

We got back to Irene's house. When she came to the door, I could see the sadness on her face. Bob came around, opened my door and helped me down from the cab. I limped to the side stoop but stopped. I wasn't ready for more questions and anyway I'd already burdened Irene and her family enough.

"You've all been great," I said looking from Irene to Bob and back again. "But I think I could use a little alone time. Would it be okay if I just go back to the RV."

"But Hank, we don't mind having you, " Irene said, stepping down from the stoop. "And you're certainly not well enough to take care of yourself yet."

"Don't worry. I'll be okay," I said, pulling my phone from my pocket and displaying it to her. "And if I need you, I know where you are."

"At least let me bring you something to eat."

"Sure," said. "That would be great." I forced a broad smile and turned to the RV. Bob helped me up the narrow stairs and inside, planting me in my recliner.

"You okay?" he asked.

I nodded. "And thanks for everything."

He patted me on the shoulder and left me alone.

I sat there, reviewing the mess I'd made of things. I had fooled myself into believing that I was a new man, more introspective but less self-absorbed. That what I was doing was an attempt to be helpful. Now I had to admit once again that it had been an ego boost, a way to show myself to be the smartest guy around, which I obviously wasn't. I had gotten myself way in over my head and this wasn't the first time. The last time had cost me my career, my home and my friends. I feared to think what it would cost me this time.

I was watching mindless drivel on the satellite TV when I heard a knock on the door. I shouted "Come in", not wanting to struggle with getting out of my recliner.

Irene came in, popping her head around the half wall beside the stairs. "Are you settled in?"

"Yeah, I may even spend the night here."

She got to the top of the steps and set a covered tray on the table. "That is a very bad idea. And so is spending the day in the chair. You need to move around a little. Work the kinks out or you'll never heal right."

"So you're my nurse now?"

"No, but if I was, I'd be kicking your ass right now. At least get out of that chair and come over here. I brought you something to eat and your meds."

"Okay, okay," I said, lowering the foot rest and struggling from my chair. She could have given me a hand but instead she just stood and watched. Her brand of tough love I suppose. I finally got to the table and settled myself onto the bench. Irene pulled the cloth away and revealed a sandwich, cut on the bias like mothers do, a pile of potato chips and a tall glass of some yellow liquid. I picked up the glass. "And what the heck is this."

"Apple cider, the non-alcoholic kind. It's good for digestion and has lots of vitamins. Take your pills and drink it down."

I complied. It tasted sour and musty. "Tastes great," I said. "Thanks." I started into the sandwich and chips, realizing how hungry I actually was.

"Mind if I sit for a minute," Irene said.

"No, be my guest. Want a few chips?"

"No thanks," she said, sitting on the bench opposite me. "Bob told me about your visit with Ellie."

"Oh." I put the sandwich down, not sure I wanted it any more.

"I'm really sorry it went that way but you can't blame Ellie."

"I suppose you're right."

"But listen, she'll get over it. Give her time and make sure when she is ready you are too."

"I don't know. I wouldn't blame her if never wanted to see me again."

"I don't think that is going to happen. I've seen the way you two are together. There's something special there. Ellie knows it too. She'll forgive you, as long as you listen to her and respect her."

"That's what I plan to do from here on," I said. "And I'm going to do the same with you. You're a smart lady. I should have listened to you all along."

She gave me a strained smile. "Well, you enjoy your meal. And after you're done come to the kitchen for a slice of pie. The walk will do you good." She patted my hand, got to her feet and left me alone.

I looked at the food in front of me and suddenly felt lucky. Irene, and Bob were good and forgiving friends. If I played my cards right, maybe I could get Dan Gilmore back on my side too. That left Ellie. I hoped to hell that Irene was right and that Ellie and I had a chance at happiness. I lifted the sandwich and took another bite.

CHAPTER TWENTY-FIVE

Ellie didn't call me for several days. She was obviously very upset with me and I was in no position to blame her. When she finally did, it was to tell me that she was being discharged from the hospital and would be brought back to Amber Creek by medical transport. She wanted me to be at the house when she arrived, to help get her settled, which seemed positive to me, but also to talk, which didn't. By that time, I myself was up and about and feeling better overall, with only an occasional twinge here and there, almost indistinguishable from the effects of my age.

In the meantime, Sam had stopped by to see me. He was thrilled to hear that Ellie was coming home and that I was able to finally review his test results. He was relieved that I believed in his innocence. "I'm not sure anyone else does," he said.

"What do you mean?" I asked.

"The BCI guys have come around several times. They've checked my travel records. They've contacted my other parishes. They've discovered gaps in my record, times when they think I could have gotten to Omaha, Chicago or Minneapolis to kidnap those poor girls."

"Gaps?" I asked.

"Yeah, well. I have to admit that my records aren't one hundred percent accurate. There have been times that I just had to get away."

"I suppose we all do," I said, "but can't they verify where you went? There have to be records."

"My only credit card is through the diocese. I'm allowed to use it for whatever I want. But I'm always afraid that someone may figure out that I'm not on official business. So, I pay cash. I wear lay clothes and register under an assumed name."

"I suppose you can see why the BCI is suspicious. I'll be honest, it sounds fishy to me," I said.

"I know, but I can't explain it to them. See, there's someone else involved."

"A woman?"

He nodded. "A married woman. I knew her before I went into the priesthood. If she had agreed, I would have married her then. As much as I wanted to be a priest, I would have gladly abandoned my vocation for her. But her family was rigid and very conservative. She wasn't ready to defy them so we parted."

"Parted or went undercover?" I asthemked, dubious.

"No really. I went into the priesthood and tried to forget her. She married someone her family approved of, a Baptist minister. Irony, right."

"So how did you and she..."

"We met at a mutual friend's funeral. I met her husband too. He's actually a really nice guy, for a Protestant," he chuckled uncomfortably. "Anyway, they have three kids and he has a big church in Omaha. Pillar of the community and all. Nothing happened between her and me for a while but we did start corresponding, the old-fashioned way, by snail mail. We didn't want to risk exposure online. She said she loved her husband and her family but that she had never forgotten about me. Of course, I told her I felt the same. A year after the funeral, I was in Omaha for a meeting and she and I got together for lunch."

"Lunch, huh?"

"Well, yes. That was the plan at least. But I was having a sort of crisis of faith at the time and she and her husband were in a rough patch. We hadn't planned anything but ...well neither of us is proud of what happened."

"But I'm guessing it wasn't the only time."

"If only it had been, but we were, what can I say, weak, foolish, greedy. She can't imagine leaving her family. I hate to admit it, but I'd probably leave the church in a minute for her. My crisis of faith is far from resolved."

"So, you could explain all of your side trips but it would destroy her family. Have I got that right?"

He turned his head away but I could see tears glistening in his eyes. "I'm only telling you because I know you'll keep it to yourself."

"Are you willing to risk imprisonment to keep this quiet?"

"I'm hoping it doesn't come to that. The police will surely find out who the real killer is."

"One can only hope. But I've done a little investigating of my own, much to my personal detriment."

"And?"

"I think I know who the killer is but I have no way to prove it." Then I filled him in on everything I had done and all I knew. He listened, patiently, not saying a word. But his face turned pale and he could not maintain eye contact. I knew the signs. I knew he had a secret, a different kind of secret. And I knew that he wouldn't be able to reveal it to me. So I guessed.

"I saw Andy, that day I came to the rectory. He was there for confession, wasn't he?"

He remained silent, but his eyes pleaded to me as they flowed with new tears.

"He confessed to the murders, knowing you couldn't expose him."

"I think I should leave," he said, wiping his sleeve across his cheeks and coming to his feet.

"Wait," I said. "Can't you see. He used you. He knew you couldn't reveal what he said in confession but that, knowing the truth would make you so uncomfortable, the cops would see your response to them as suspicious. He set you up."

"Please, let's just drop this," he said, heading to the door.

I followed him and caught him by the elbow. "But you don't have to keep this a secret. Hell, you told me you were having a crisis of faith. I bet you don't even believe this confession bullshit yourself."

"Hank, back off," he shouted. "Being a priest is all I have left. Don't tell me to give that up too."

"What about the woman you're in love with?"

"We broke it off, months ago. Her husband was starting to get suspicious. And frankly, neither of us could handle the guilt anymore. Now all I have left is my vocation. So, if there is a God and if He is ever going to forgive me for breaking my vows in the past, I have to keep them now."

"And she can just go on with her life," I said.

"As long as I keep our secret, yes. And don't make it sound like she's not hurting too."

"Does she even know you're being investigated for murder?"

"No and I don't plan to tell her."

"When your picture hits the front page, I suspect she'll put two and two together."

He glared at me; his fist clenched as if he was planning to slug me. Instead, he turned and walked out of the RV, without another word. I felt lousy for what I'd said, but then again, I knew it had to be said. And he had to have been thinking it himself. This was obviously a no-win situation for him. The type of situation I'd found myself in only a few years before. My heart went out to him but there wasn't much I could do without betraying his confidence. Besides, I was only assuming that Andy had confessed to him about the murders. Sam had neither confirmed nor denied it. And any supposed evidence I had was flimsy at best. I had no idea what to do now so I did nothing, except think about getting drunk. Instead, I called Jerry and asked him when the next AA meeting was.

When Ellie called again to tell me she'd be on her way home the next day, I borrowed Bob's truck and drove to her house. I cleaned the kitchen of any spoiled or outdated food, made myself a grocery list and drove to Mt. Carter to replenish the supplies. I had to pass the site of the accident going and coming back. Of course, it looked completely different in the light of a cloudless day but I could see where our car had gone off the roadway. Deep tread marks and the collapse of the sides of the drainage ditch showed where the car had plowed down into it. I must have been going faster than I thought, or maybe accelerated to get out of the way of the oncoming car. Details of the accident were still foggy. The consequences, though, were all too clear. That event and all I had done to cause it would haunt me the rest of my life.

Back at Ellie's, I put the groceries away and found vases for the various bouquets I had purchased to scatter throughout the house. I wanted Ellie's homecoming to be bright and welcoming. I hoped that my efforts wouldn't look like over compensation. I debated whether I should just stay at the house, but somehow it seemed wrong to sleep there without her. I considered packing up the belongings I had brought to the house when we were more or less living together. Would that give the right message? Did I want to be able to just walk away if she told me to? Or did I hope that somehow we could find a way around the mess I had made? I couldn't decide what to do, so I did nothing and just got into Bob's truck and drove back to the RV.

The next morning, I got up early, had a quick pop tart and coffee breakfast and walked to Ellie's place instead of depriving Bob of his truck for another day. I suspect that he would have gladly driven me there but I needed more time to process what I would say and do when Ellie finally got home.

The medical transport pulled up just before noon and I hurried outside to meet it. The driver got out and opened the sliding door on the passenger side of the van. Pushing a few buttons unfolded a flat platform. I could see Ellie inside the van, seated in a wheelchair, her casted left leg on the extended foot rest. She looked my way and gave me a Mona Lisa smile that told me nothing. The driver climbed in behind her, maneuvered the wheelchair onto the platform and got back out. He pushed another button and the platform slowly lowered to the ground. Then he slid the wheelchair onto the gravel driveway and operated the controls to return the platform to its starting position. While he did, I stepped up to Ellie. "Welcome home," I said. "I missed you."

"I'm glad to be home," was all she said.

The driver handed me a couple of bags of medical supplies, a pair of crutches and the suitcase I'd brought to the hospital for Ellie. He got behind the wheelchair and headed to the front porch. Bob, with me handing him tools, had built a ramp to her front door. The driver commented on how sturdy it appeared and Ellie gave me a somewhat more endearing smile. We got in the house, the driver reviewed instructions with Ellie and had her sign several pages of paperwork. Then he was gone and it was just Ellie and me. I couldn't help but explore her with my eyes. Her face was a little thinner, but her eyes were still a piercing blue. Her graying blond hair was pulled back in a ponytail. Her skin was smooth and pale yellow with the resolving bruises. I imagined how soft it would still be to my touch. She was so beautiful and I had to admit that I was in love with her, something I'd yet to actually say to her or to myself. I hoped it wasn't too late.

"Looks nice in here," she said. "The flowers are beautiful."

"How about lunch," I said, knowing that this was not the time to profess anything. "Ya' hungry?

"Sure, but how about something to drink first? Maybe a tall glass of ice water."

I pushed her wheelchair into the kitchen, sliding it under the edge of the table where her chair usually sat. I brought her the water and she took a long drink. "The driver gave me a bottle of water in transit but it was warm as bathwater. This really hits the spot."

I set about making a couple of sandwiches and rinsed a bowl of grapes. After I put the food on the table, I pulled a chair up opposite Ellie and sat.

"So, how are you feeling, really," I said.

"I won't say I'm not in pain and this cast is inconvenient at best, but, all things considered, I'm okay."

"Are you able to walk at all?" I asked.

"No, not while I have this cast on. I go back in two weeks for x- rays and maybe they'll give me a walking cast then."

"I'd be happy to stay here and take care of you until you can do it all on your own."

"I was sort of counting on that," she said, "But for now, I'd like you sleeping in the guest room."

"Of course," I said, not able to hide my disappointment.

"It's not because I'm upset with you, though I have to admit I was. It's just the cast. I don't want to hit you with it if I roll over in bed."

"All right," I said. "So... you're not upset with me?"

"At least not as much as I was. I've had time to think. I realize that part of why you were investigating was to help Sam and I understand that. It's the cowboy part of it I don't like."

"Cowboy?"

"You know... going it alone, doing it your own way. That rugged individualist crap."

"Oh," I said. "I've had time to think too and I realize that being a cowboy has gotten me into a lot of trouble over the years." I looked down at her cast. "Case in point."

"Yeah well. We'll get past that in time as long as you're willing to change your ways."

"Done," I said. I knew that, no matter what Ellie said, my behavior had put a barrier between us. One that I couldn't argue with. But I was committed to change because, now that she was home, I knew that I was committed to her too. I loved her and wasn't ready to drive another good woman out of my life. I accepted that it would take time and I was ready to put in the work it would require. I looked across at her beautiful face. "Now let me see you eat something," I said. "You got kinda skinny on hospital food."

She laughed, and we both dug into our meals.

CHAPTER TWENTY-SIX

After a few days, Ellie and I had gotten into a routine. I had left a bell at her bedside that she could ring for help, getting to the bathroom or whatever. In the morning, I provided her with supplies for a quick sponge bath and helped her get dressed. While she was in the bathroom, which was reasonably handicapped accessible, I would go to the kitchen and pull together a breakfast which we frequently enjoyed on the deck while taking in the view of the forest behind the house Before lunch I would set her up in her study with her computer so she could catch up on email and communicate with the hospital staff. A fourth year resident physician had been hired to cover for her during her convalescence and she liked to keep in touch with him. After lunch, I would help her get back into bed for a nap and then I'd sit in the living room with a cup of coffee and a book, close enough to respond if she needed me for anything. She had several callers and I had taken the responsibility to monitor their visits so they wouldn't tire Ellie out too much. I wondered if she might start to feel like I was hovering over her, but decided that it would be her job to tell me if I was.

Sam stopped by every day to talk, to laugh and to pray. His discomfort being around me was apparent, especially after I told him my suspicion about Andy Folger causing the accident. This only seemed to confirm my theory about Andy's confession. I decided to let it all drop because Ellie enjoyed Sam's visits. She gladly prayed with him while I looked for other things to do. I have to admit, I suddenly found myself a little uncomfortable around Sam too, prayer or no prayer. The whole serial killer thing had been weighing on me and I was unsure how the cops would deal with my continued contact with Sam. Besides, we now shared some secrets that I was pretty sure he didn't want me to share with Ellie.

I stood to hold the front door open for Sam to leave after his last visit. We shared a tense smile and he walked out but before I could even close the door, he had turned back and extended his arm to restrain me.

"Listen," he said. "I know this has been hard for you but you need to know how glad I am that you're here for Ellie. She means an awful lot to me."

"Yes, it's been...difficult," I said. "But Ellie thinks a lot of you too. And...I know why. You're all the things a priest should be but damn few are."

"Thanks, but I'm not sure I agree."

"I'm not talking about all the religious crap or the trappings. I'm talking about the way you care and how much you are willing to give."

He demurred. "Well, thanks anyway." He offered me his hand and I shook it appreciatively. Then he turned and walked away. I wish I'd said more, now that I know what was to follow.

In the middle of the second week, while Ellie was working in her office, there was a knock on the front door. I got up to answer, finding the police chief on the front stoop.

"Dan," I said. "What brings you here?"

"Well, I haven't seen Ellie since she got home," he said. "And, ah, there's something I'd like you to do for me."

"Come on in. I'll let Ellie know you're here."

A few minutes later, the three of us were sitting around the kitchen table chatting like old friends. It felt good. After twenty minutes, Ellie announced that she had to get back to work so I wheeled her back to her sturdy. When I came out, Dan was standing by the door waiting.

"Thanks for coming by, Dan," I said.

"My pleasure," he said, "but there's that other thing I wanted to ask you."

"Oh, sure. What was it?"

"We got a lead. There's an old garage out on some acreage that Andy Folger's folks owned, east of town. A neighbor out that way sees Andy coming and going from time to time. He said he saw Andy drive out there a few days ago but he didn't see him drive back again."

I held my breath.

"We got a search warrant and checked it out myself. There's a car in that garage. It's gray. I wonder if you could drive out with me and take a look."

"Oh god," I said. "So, you want me to see if it's the one that ran us off the road?"

"Yeah, if you don't mind."

"Of course not, When do you want to go?"

"How 'bout right now?"

I felt a sudden rush of dread mixed with exhilaration. I felt like I was back on the case in spite of myself. Of course, I wanted to help. But I didn't want to get involved again for fear of Ellie's reaction. After a moment's thought, I said, "Let me talk with Ellie for a minute."

I walked back into the study. Ellie was on the phone and held up a finger to let me know to wait. After she hung up, she looked at me, a strangely knowing concern on her face. "What's up?"

I explained what Dan had said. She listened with her lips pursed. Then she said "Of course, you have to go. We have to find out who's responsible for the accident, and maybe everything else. But please, don't try to play detective. You're a witness. That's all. Got it."

"I promise," I said and kissed her. "You okay without me for a while?"

"I'll be fine, mom," she said.

I rejoined Dan at the door and said, "Let's go."

We drove down to the old highway and turned east. Another mile or so out, Dan turned onto a gravel road, going south through farmland and past a barn and a few outbuildings. "That's the old Folger place. It's rented out to the folks who called us. There's a shed in a wooded area at the back of the property. That's where I found the car."

We approached a copse of trees and stopped outside a rundown building nestled among them. We climbed out and approached it.

"Why would anyone build here?" I asked.

"Beats me," Dan said, "Unless someone wanted to hide something."

"But Andy couldn't have built this," I observed. "This has got to be way older than he is."

"This farm had been in the family for years. Maybe Andy wasn't the only one with a secret."

We walked to the sliding door of the shed and I helped Dan push it back. It was dark inside compared to the bright summer day outside but I could easily make out the shape of a car. I entered and Dan reclosed the doors. As my eyes adjusted to the dim light from a few high windows, I began to feel a prickle in the hairs on the back of my neck. The car was gray, probably thirty years old but in fairly good condition. Dan asked me to stand by the door while he climbed into the car. He turned the headlights on and the sudden glare in front of me was startling. The image of that night on the highway came immediately to mind. "That's it," I shouted. "That's the car."

Dan stuck his head out of the car window. "Are you sure?" he asked.

"Yes. The headlights. They're squarish but one's sort of dim compared to the other. That's like the car that night. I'd forgotten those details."

"No surprise," he said, turning the lights off and climbing out of the car. "You had a pretty good bump on the head."

Dan slid the shed doors open again and the outside light flooded back in. We stepped out and he reclosed the door. "It belonged to Andy's mother. Plates are still good. He must have renewed them under her name. The registration is on file at the county courthouse under her name too. We never thought to look."

"So, what do you do now?" I asked.

"I'll inform the BCI. They'll impound it and take it to their lab. I'll have a talk with Andy but only about the accident. I don't want him thinking that we link the car to the murders, not yet anyway. I will have to tell him you identified the car, though."

"No way you can keep that under wraps?" I asked.

"Sorry. If I want to focus on the accident, I've got to bring your name into it."

"I understand, but I have to admit it makes me pretty uncomfortable. I mean, the accident was only hours after I'd talked with him. And he knew I wasn't there to talk insurance, not really."

"Well, I'll do what I can to protect you and Ellie. Unfortunately, we don't have the staff to put a watch on her house. You need to make sure things are secure there and be ready to call us if anything comes up."

I agreed and Dan drove me back to the temporary police station where I wrote an addendum to my original accident report. Then he dropped me at Ellie's house. As I got out of the car I asked him when he planned to talk with Andy.

"I need to get a hold of the BCI first but I'll let you know."

I thanked him and watched as he drove away. I couldn't help but scan the area with a new perspective. Where could someone hide? How could someone get onto the property or into the house without my knowing? I suddenly felt sympathy for the paranoid patients I'd treated over the years. I went into the house, making sure to lock the door behind me. Before looking in on Ellie, I did a quick check of the other doors and windows. They were all locked. Ellie, as a single woman living alone in an isolated house, had always been careful.

Then I went into Ellie's office. She was looking at records on her computer but turned and smiled up at me. "How'd it go?" she asked.

"It's the car," I said. "It belonged to Andy's mother."

Ellie's smile melted. "And you're sure?"

I nodded and she rubbed her chin. "So, what now?" she asked.

I explained Dan's plan and that I had already done a quick security check of the house.

"Well, let's just hope," she said.

"It's lunch time," I said, intentionally changing the subject. "Are you hungry?"

"I was," she said. "But I need to get away from this computer for a while anyway."

I wheeled her to the kitchen and pulled together a light meal that we ate in silence.

CHAPTER **TWENTY-SEVEN**

I didn't hear from Dan until the next day. He called to let me know that he'd talked with the BCI. They had impounded the gray car and taken it to their lab. He was planning on talking with Andy that afternoon but just about the accident. The BCI would wait until testing was done on the car before approaching Andy about the murders. But they were keeping an eye on his house. I thanked Dan and went about my day, more alert to sounds in the house than before.

I had just helped Ellie into bed for the night and was reading in the living room when my phone buzzed with a text message. I opened a message from Sam that said he needed to meet with me ASAP. I tried to call him back but got only his voice mail. I reread the text message and decided something was so wrong that he couldn't talk. I couldn't imagine what it might be. I texted him, 'What's up". I, of course, wanted to help but I didn't want to leave Ellie alone. Waiting for Sam's response, I went back to Ellie's room to find her already asleep. Then my phone buzzed again, with a one-word message. PLEASE. I looked at Ellie's sleeping form and back at the message. I knew that the house was secure. Doors and windows locked. There had been an alarm system but at some point the service provider had gone out of business and Ellie had never found another. God, I wish she had.

I secured the lock on the inside of Ellie's door and closed it. I went to the kitchen and grabbed a handful of cans to stack at the head of the hall. If someone tried to come to Ellie's room in the dark, they would make a hell of a racket. Ellie had her cell phone at her bedside so the warning and the locked door would give her time to call for help. I hoped.

I made sure all of the outside lights were on and left through the front door, checking that it was locked behind me. I got into Ellie's car and drove toward town. The sound of sirens filled the valley and random lights flickered a few blocks from the church. I tried to ignore them but couldn't help wondering if they were the reason Sam had texted me. I hit the gas and sped to the rectory.

Mounting the steps to the rectory, I was able to look east where smoke billowed, lit by flames from below. It looked like a house was afire a few blocks to the east. I hoped that the fire department had found a way to deal with this disaster, considering their fire house and most of their equipment had been destroyed by the tornado along with the rest of the municipal buildings. Departments from nearby communities were likely to respond, but they would take at least half an hour to get to Amber Creek. I couldn't help but wonder if the home owners had been able to get to safety. Was this what Sam had called about? It seemed odd but only he could explain, so I walked to the door and rang the bell.

I had waited nearly a minute, listening to muffled voices behind the door, before it finally opened a few inches. Sam stepped into the gap. He looked upset, maybe even panicked.

"Sam," I said.

He stared for a few seconds, his overly wide eyes darting to his left. Then he shouted, "Run!"

I stood, too confused to move as suddenly Sam lurched against the door slamming it into the wall And Andy appeared behind him, a gun pressed against the priest's back. "I wouldn't do that, if I were you," he said, a sardonic grin crossing his face. "Unless you want your friend's blood all over this door, I would suggest you come inside. We need to chat." He pulled Sam away from the door and backed into the room. I admit I took a minute to decide before reluctantly following them into the house.

"Would you mind getting the door," Andy said. "Don't want flies in the house, do we?"

I complied and Andy dragged Sam backwards into the kitchen where he pushed him down into a chair. Andy stepped back, the pistol now aimed at me. His expression was stoney with the slightest hint of a grin. Somehow, he looked taller, more solid. Maybe it was the gun and the confidence it gave him.

"Okay," Andy said. "You see that rope over there." He pointed to a coil of a braided laundry line on the table. Sam's phone lay beside it, the last message still filling the screen. Andy continued. "What I'd like you to do is take it and tie his holiness to this chair." He couldn't help chuckling at his own humor.

I shook my head. "What the hell is this all about?"

"Rope first then we chat," he said. "And be aware, I'm gonna check your work, so the rope better be nice and snug."

"If you think I'm going to help you..." I said. But Andy turned the barrel of the gun to the back of Sam's head and my breath caught. I took a moment to assess Andy. His eyes were cold and unfeeling. His hand was as steady as a rock. He was not afraid and he was not bluffing. I walked to the table, picked up the rope and stepped to Sam's chair. Andy backed away, the gun still pointed at Sam's head.

"Arms first," Andy said. "Tie them together. After that, loop the rope around his waist and the back of the chair, then under the chair to his legs. Tie them to the chair legs."

"Sam said quietly, "It's okay, Hank." He looked so deeply into my eyes that I could hardly stand it. His face communicated resignation to the inevitable but also a sort of peace.

Moving slowly, my mind racing to find a way out for both of us, I reluctantly followed the instructions. I knelt beside Sam's chair. He held his hands up, palms pressed together as if in prayer. I wrapped the ropes around in a loose figure eight but Andy kicked me in the ass. "I said tight."

I snugged the rope and ran it around Sam's waist, twice.

"Now, back between his hands and then around his feet," Andy said, clearly enjoying his command position.

I crawled to the front of the chair and ran the rope between Sam's hands and down around Sam's ankles, securing them to a chair leg with a double knot. Finally, I sat back on my haunches and looked up at Andy, hoping my rage was making itself visible. "Will that do...sir."

"Don't get smart with me," Andy barked. "Remember, I'm the guy with the gun. Why don't you take a seat over there." He pointed to a chair on the other side of the table. I pushed myself up from the floor and took a seat. His gun still pointed at Sam, Andy stopped to examine my handiwork and appeared satisfied. He stood and directed the gun at me. "Nice job." He pulled up another kitchen chair and straddled it, facing both Sam and me. "So, I suppose you're wondering what this is all about,'

"I think I have a pretty good idea," I said. I looked at Sam. "See, Andy is the serial killer, but I guess you already knew that."

Andy looked at Sam, actually surprised. "He guesses. So you didn't tell him after all?"

Sam stared straight ahead and made no response.

"No, he didn't," I said. "But it didn't take a lot to figure it out. And the cops will be on your tail very soon."

"Perhaps but I'm gonna make myself pretty hard to find. After I've tied up a few things of my own."

"Meaning," I said.

"Meaning you and the holy father here. I have a hunch that the two of you have been way too helpful to the cops. And even if you haven't, I don't like you much anyway. So, my plan is to kill you. Maybe I can make it look like you killed each other. I could put the suspicion back on Sam. He was the killer, you found out and he tried to shut you up but it all went wrong, for both of you"

"Don't you think there will be more evidence against you, the car or your house." Then a realization hit me. "Your house. It's on fire, isn't it?"

"Yeah, sorry to say. I guess I left the space heater on. I'm a crappy house keeper. Lots of paper and junk all over the place. Probably went up like a bomb. And with no fire department, it's likely to be a total loss. What a shame. Mom loved that house." He wiped away a feigned tear.

"Are you forgetting the car?" I asked.

The corners of his mouth drooped. "I was very careful. They won't find a thing."

"I wish I had your confidence," I said.

Andy stepped forward and swung the gun, slamming it into my left cheek. "You're really asking for it," he said. "You know, after I'm done here, I might just pay a visit to your girlfriend."

Hearing that, Sam's face suddenly blazed with rage. Using all his might, he threw his chair forward and rolled at Andy, knocking him to the floor. I jumped to my feet and grabbed at Andy's gun which went off with a deafening blast. I kicked Andy in the head and was able to pull the gun away from him. Only then did I look over at Sam. He was lying face down, the chair atop him. Blood was pooling on the floor beneath him.

"Sam," I shouted and lurched toward him. I rolled him onto his side. His eyes were wide open and his breathing labored. I called his name again and he seemed to want to respond but only gurgled, inflating a pink bubble that popped on his lips.

While I was distracted, Andy was able to get to his knees and lunged at me, grabbing my gun arm. It swung around and, feeling a flood of rage, I pulled the trigger. My hand flew back and Andy's head came up with a jerk, blood spraying from what was left of his right eye. I crab walked away from him as fast as I could and froze when I hit Sam's chair again. I sat there for a time, stunned and struggling to believe what I had done. Then I remembered Sam and spun around to him. His eyes had closed and he wasn't moving. I untied him as quickly as I could and rolled him on his back. I felt his neck and, finding no pulse, started CPR but each chest compression only produced a fountain of blood from the gaping wound in his side. I stopped pumping, pulled my phone out and dialed 911.

Some time later, I was back sitting in the kitchen chair. Both Andy and Sam were gone, having been rushed to the hospital by ambulance. Dan sat across from me. "So now, what the hell happened here."

"I don't know," I said. "It all happened so fast. I didn't mean for any of this to happen."

"Enough time for that shit," he said. "Just tell me."

I explained the events of the last few hours as best I could, Dan just listening, taking no notes. When I was done, he rested his elbow on the kitchen table and rubbed his forehead. "Oh fuck, Hank. Why the hell did you let yourself get wrapped up in this?"

"Hey," I said defensively. "It wasn't my idea. You said you could use my help."

"Yeah but then I told you to back off," he shouted. "Why didn't you listen to me at that time." He slammed his hand down on the table and came to his feet. He walked to the door and turned back to me. "Get your ass out of the chair. You're coming with me." I followed him out of the door and he shoved me into the back of his police-car.

The next six hours were spent at the temporary police station. I met with Dan again and then waited several hours for the BCI guys to show up. They insisted that I go through my whole story several more times, pushing for more detail and probing for inconsistencies. One thing was clear. Neither Dan nor the BCI people had any sympathy for me. They obviously saw my actions as having gotten in their way and maybe even the cause of the final disaster. I wasn't sure I could disagree.

I was finally released at about five in the morning with clear instructions not to leave town. I walked back to the rectory to get Ellie's car. There was a BCI van on the street and more yellow police tape than I'd ever seen, wrapping around the property and the rectory. One police car sat in the middle of the street and barriers had been set up to block approaching the house from any direction. Jerry Albright stepped toward me.

"Doc," he said. "You can't come in here. This is a crime scene."

"I know, Jerry. I was there."

"Yeah, well, no matter. You can't come in."

"But that's my car at the curb."

"Sorry. I can't release anything 'til the BCI says so."

"How am I gonna get home?"

He shrugged and crossed his arms. It was obvious that he had gotten the message that I was persona non grata. I turned and walked east. I got to the street where Andy's house had been and turned south to walk past it. The house was a total loss, most of it now collapsed into the basement. The garage next to the house was badly singed but still standing. A few pieces of fire equipment were still parked there but there was no longer a fire to battle. A crowd had gathered to gawk at the devastation. I walked on and turned east at the old highway, passing the Pump n" Shop. My mouth suddenly filled with saliva and the idea of stopping in to buy a bottle of something potent filled my mind. After what I'd been through, I deserved a drink. Didn't I? I suspect that I would have ended up in a drunken stupor if not for the fact that the store wouldn't be open for another two hours.

Next, I walked past the temporary municipal building again and the sight of it and the BCI car still parked out front, filled me with a burning mix of rage and guilt. I'd been treated like a criminal there. I'd needed reassurance and gotten only rebuke. Then again, maybe I'd gotten what I deserved. I saluted the building with my middle finger before starting the northward climb up Ellie's hill.

That's when it really hit me. Ellie. How was I going to tell her? She and Sam had had a special bond. Would she resent me the way the police did? Would this be the end of our relationship just as it was starting to heal? I certainly hoped not but, then again, I wouldn't be at all surprised. As I climbed the hill in the gathering light of early morning, I tried to formulate a strategy. At this I was not very successful, considering what I'd been through in the last eight hours and having had no sleep for twenty-four. I resolved to just wing it.

CHAPTER TWENTY-EIGHT

I got to Ellie's driveway, out of breath from the uphill climb. I surveyed the house. Nothing looked disturbed. The outside lights were still on but none inside. Everything looked secure. I approached slowly, not sure if I wanted to go in, or to go back down the hill and wait for the Pump n' Shop to open. I even considered getting back to my RV as quickly as possible and hitting the road. But the thought of Ellie alone in there, needing my help, needing my explanation, drove me on. That and my feelings of guilt and shame. I walked up the little ramp and opened the front door with my key. I stepped inside the dark house and closed the door as quietly as I could. If Ellie wasn't awake yet, maybe I could take a few minutes to rest and to gather my thoughts. I considered looking for a bottle but knew there wasn't any in the house so instead I headed to the hall, hoping to lay down in the spare bedroom for just a few minutes. Of course, I'd forgotten about my home-made alarm system and slammed into the stacked cans, barking my shin and causing a racket that would have waken the dead.

Ellie called from down the hall. "Hank, is that you?"

"Yeah," I responded.

"What happened?"

I struggled to pick up the cans and set them against the wall. "I just dropped something," I lied. "I'll be there in a second". When I got to her door, I of course couldn't open it. "Ellie," I called. "The door is locked. Can you open it from your side."

I could hear her struggling to get out of bed and to the door. The lock clicked and she opened the door. "Why the hell was this locked?"

She was barely able to stay upright with her crutches so I stepped in and helped her back to bed. "Lay down," I said. "We need to talk."

She looked at me with concern, working her way to panic. "What's wrong? What's going on?"

I sat at the side of the bed and took her hand. "Ellie, something has happened, something bad."

She sat up. "Hank, you're scaring me."

"I'm sorry. I don't mean to." I settled her back down onto the bed.

"So, what is it?"

"Last night I got a text from Sam's phone."

"You mean from Sam."

"Well, not as it turns out. I went to the rectory and Sam wasn't alone. Andy Folger was there, too."

"Why was he there? It must have been the middle of the night."

"Andy was angry. He blamed Sam and me for turning him in to the police. He had a gun."

Ellie gasped and tried to sit up again. "Hank, what happened?"

"Ellie, I don't know any other way to tell you this. Both Sam and Andy...well they're dead. Both of them."

"Oh my god. No!" She pulled her hand from mine and covered her mouth, tears immediately flooding her eyes. "Not Sam, please, not Sam."

"I'm so sorry," I said at least twice, maybe more times. I reached for her but she held me at arm's length.

"How...how did it happen?"

She sat in shock and horror as I once again told the story. When I was done her hand dropped from my chest and she looked at me with wide eyes blinking away tears. "I don't understand," she said. "Why? Why Sam"

"Andy had made a confession to Sam about the murders. He admitted that had killed those women. And he thought Sam had told me. He thought we had gone to the police."

"Is this because of your investigation or whatever it was? Is that why he wanted to kill you?"

All I could do was nod. She swung her arm back and threw her open hand against the side of my face, where Andy had struck me with the gun. The pain was searing and I grabbed her wrist. "Look, I never meant this to happen," I said.

"But it did anyway," she shouted. "And I told you to stay out of it. Hell, everyone did. But no, you had to be the hero. You son of a bitch."

I released her hand. "Please, let me explain."

"No," she shouted. "No, just get out of my house."

"But I can't leave you alone."

"Apparently that didn't stop you last night," she said. "I don't want to ever see you again. Get out."

"But you need help."

"I'll call someone."

"Who?"

"Anyone but you," she said, no longer shouting but with a hateful edge to her voice and steeliness in her eyes.

I backed away, my hands up in surrender. I stood and left the room after making sure her wheelchair was beside the bed. I stumble through the dark hall and back to the front door. Once outside I dropped to the stoop and sat with my face buried in my palms. I think I was too overwhelmed even to cry.

By the time I got back on my feet, the sun had risen fully. I glanced back at the front door but knew better than to go back inside. Guilt and remorse washed over me. Once again, I had screwed up the most important relationships in my life. I was worthless and I should just spend the rest of my days in a drunken stupor. I headed down the driveway and back toward town. I got to the Pump n' Shop and expected it to be open but it wasn't. I remembered that Angie was not only the proprietor of the store but also the mayor of Amber Creek. She had probably been called in on the previous night's disasters. Just as well. If I had gotten my hands on some booze who knows what might have happened. So I just kept walking and beating myself up until I got to my RV. I went inside and dropped onto my bed. In spite of all that had happened, I eventually drifted to sleep.

Some time later I was woken by a knock on the door of my RV. I got out of bed and answered it. Bob stood there with a cloth covered tray. "I brought you some supper," he said, working his way past me to the banquet.

"Thanks," I said. "I could have come over to the house for it. Frankly, I could use the company."

Bob suddenly looked like a kid with his hand in the candy jar. "I don't think that would be a very good idea right now."

"Why?"

"Charlotte and Irene are pretty upset right now. About Sam."

"They know?"

"Hank, everybody in town knows. And they know you were involved...
somehow. It's not that anyone blames you for what happened."

"But they do," I said. "They think that, if I had kept my nose out,
Sam would be alive."

Bob just nodded and removed the cloth from the tray revealing a large
slice of ham, a mound of mashed potatoes and a generous helping of green
beans. He turned to walk away.

"I don't want that," I said. "Take it with you."

"You need to eat something, Hank," Bob said. "You've been in here
alone all day and I doubt if you've had anything to eat."

"You sure there's no arsenic in the food," I said and immediately
regretted it.

Bob turned on me. "So that's what you think. You fuck up and we
decide to poison you. Get over yourself, Hank. My family and I probably
owe our lives to you but you fucked up big time and it'll take a long while
for us to figure out what to do with that. You sitting out here feeling sorry
for yourself is no good. So, eat your goddamn meal." He walked out of the
RV and slammed the door behind himself.

After a minute of indecision, I sat down in front of the plate and began
to eat slowly. Was Bob right? Was I feeling sorry for myself instead of
taking responsibility for the part I had played in the tragedy of last night?
I didn't want to think about it so I focused on the meal. Turned out, I was
famished and ate it all, in spite of myself.

When I was done with the meal, I washed the plate and silverware in
my sink, set them back on the tray and covered them with the dishcloth.
I weighed just leaving them on the table as if they would somehow get
themselves back to Irene's kitchen. I doubted that anyone would come
to retrieve them. I finally picked them up and carried them out of the
RV to Irene's kitchen door. I stood a minute and considered setting the
tray on the doorstep and just walking away. Instead I took a deep breath
and tapped lightly on the door and, getting no response, knocked harder.
Someone approached the door, the face obscured by Irene's lace curtain.
The figure paused at the door, as reluctant as I had been. After a minute
or so, the door opened and Irene stood in the gap. Her expression was
unreadable.

I cleared my throat. "Thanks for the food, it was delicious. I washed the dish, too." I held the tray out to her and she reached to take it. Tray in hand, she stepped back into the kitchen and started to close the door. I put my hand against it to stop her. "Irene, I need to tell you how sorry I am. Sam was my friend too. I never meant for anything to happen to him."

She set the tray on the kitchen table and walked back to the door. "Hank, I don't blame you for what happened and I'm glad you aren't dead too, but...I can't do this. I can't pretend that things haven't changed. You're just going to have to give me time. Okay?"

I nodded and backed away. "Anyway," I said." Thanks...for everything." I turned to walk back to the RV. The door closed softly behind me, but I could still hear Irene sobbing behind it. I knew her tears were for Sam but a part of me wished that they were for me, for what I had been through. I supposed that was too much to ask. After all, Irene didn't really know me. Not like she'd known Sam. It was just that I felt like she had accepted me into her circle. She had made me feel like family. Then again, she had also warned me to stay out of the police case. And I hadn't listened. Because of that Sam was dead and I had endangered Irene's friendship and Bob's. No. This shouldn't be about me. I was about Sam and the people who loved him but, like usual, I was looking for ways to make it about me. I was overwhelmed with disgust over my own behavior. If I'd had a bottle right then, I would not have lasted but a few minutes.

CHAPTER TWENTY-NINE

After getting back to the RV, I'd taken a sorely needed shower and collapsed back into my bed. In spite of having slept most of the day, I was still exhausted and fell quickly to sleep. The next thing I was aware of was the ringing of my phone. I jumped out of bed to answer it.

"Hank, It's Dan."

"Oh," I mumbled. I checked my watch. "Good morning."

"I'm sorry if I woke you," he said, stiffly. "The BCI is done with your car. You can pick it up at the municipal building."

"Thanks," I said. "And Dan, I don't know if I already said this but I am really sorry how this all turned out."

"Yeah, well...When do you plan to pick the car up. I have some statements for you to sign."

"I can be there in twenty minutes."

He said "Fine" and just hung up. The conversation had been very brusk and I could tell that Dan had wanted as little contact with me as possible. I couldn't blame him for his anger because I shared it. I was angry at Hank Pressman too. I was angry at his arrogance, his intrusiveness and his need to be right, at whatever cost. The problem was, being Hank Pressman myself, I had no one else to chastise or give the cold shoulder to. And it looks like I had no friends left whose shoulders I could lean on. Not in Amber Creek at least.

I dressed quickly, grabbed a packet of pop tarts and left the RV heading to the municipal building. I considered calling Ellie and letting her know that I would drop her car off but decided to just show up with it. I didn't want to give her a chance to make other arrangements that wouldn't include me.

The same young woman was at the front desk of the municipal building. As soon as she saw me walk in she picked up her phone. I could hear one ringing somewhere in the back of the offices. After a curt exchange, she hung up and smiled at me, business-like. "Chief Gilmore will be here in a second." She went back to whatever work was on the desk before her. Dan walked into the reception area seconds later.

"Hank," he said formally. "Will you come this way?" I followed him and he directed me to a chair beside his desk. He sat, removed a set of car keys from the desk drawer and handed them to me. I had forgotten that he had taken them from me at the rectory that awful night. I smiled in response and he pushed a stack of papers toward me. "I'd like you to read these and, if they are an accurate representation of your statement, I'd like you to sign and date each page." He sat back in his chair. I picked up the papers, slowly read through them and signed each one before sliding them back across the desk. He took them, slipped them into a manilla folder and started to his feet.

I grabbed his elbow. "Dan, come on," I said. "Can we at least talk?"

"Everything I want to talk about has already been covered." He waved the envelope before me.

"Give me a break, Dan. It's not like I did anything with the intent of getting someone killed."

"And yet, here we are," he sat back down. "You know, the BCI guys wanted to charge you."

"With what?"

"I don't know. Interference with official acts or something. I don't think they even knew.

But I talked them out of it."

"Well, thanks for that anyway," I said.

"So, we're square. And I don't want to see or hear from you again unless it's part of my official duty. Got it?"

"I thought we were friends."

"So, did I. But then you did everything possible to undermine me, my case and my standing with the BCI."

"That's ridiculous."

He stood again. "Is it ridiculous that your interference got two people killed and left the serial killer case in limbo. Is it ridiculous that this town, that has already lost so much, now has to deal with losing its priest? Does none of that matter to you?"

"Of course it matters," I said "I've been through a lot too, if you haven't noticed."

Dan clenched his fists at his sides and his eyes bore into me. "Get out of my office, you self-important son of a bitch."

It was clear that he meant business so I nodded and left the office feeling angry and ashamed at the same time. The receptionist directed me to the lot at the side of the building where I found the car. I climbed in and drove out of the lot. Passing the Pump n' Shop I reassured myself that it was now open, just in case, and drove past. Minutes later, I pulled into Ellie's driveway. I killed the engine but sat there for a good five minutes considering my options. I could drop off the keys and just leave. I could ask to come in the house to collect what belongings I'd left there, hoping Ellie would take pity on me. I could demand that Ellie talk with me. Force her to hear me out. I got out of the car unsure of which tack I would take. I stepped to the front door and knocked. Soon the door opened part way and a middle-aged woman in hospital scrubs stood there. "May I help you," she said.

"Hi, I'm Hank Pressman. I'm returning Ellie's car." I held the keys out for her.

"Oh, thank you", she said, taking them from me and smiling at me as if waiting for me to leave. "Was there anything else?"

I cleared my throat. "Ah, well, no. Not really. I'd better go." I turned to leave when I heard Ellie's voice from inside. "Carol, ask him to come in, would you."

Carol stepped back and opened the door fully. I nodded and walked inside. She followed me into the kitchen. Ellie was seated in her wheelchair at the table, a coffee mug and the newspaper in front of her. "Carol is from the home health agency in Mt. Carter. She'll be staying with me for a while."

I extended my hand to Carol but, with a nod from Ellie, she left the room. Ellie looked up at me with a pinched smile. "Thanks for bringing the car back, finally. Not that I'll be driving much for a while yet."

"The police kept it. I guess they wanted to make sure it had nothing to do with...well, you know."

"Yeah, unfortunately, I do," she said. "I'm glad you're here anyway. Please, have a seat."

I pulled a chair out and lowered myself into it, uncertain why she had asked me to stay.

"I wanted to apologize for the way I reacted the other day," she said.

"Oh, no. That's not necessary." I said,

"Yes, it is. I blamed you for what happened. But I know that the blame is Andy's. You didn't want to kill anyone."

"No, I didn't."

"And yet, one of my best friends is dead." Her eyes moistened and she cocked her head to the side. "I have to admit that, illogical as it is, I'm so very angry with you. And I don't know what to do about it."

"It's okay," I said. "I understand. Emotions aren't always logical. When someone loses a person who.."

"Please Hank," she interrupted. "Don't play psychiatrist with me."

"I'm sorry...about everything."

"I know you are," she said. "But that doesn't make it better. Not yet. Maybe someday."

"I hope so, Ellie because you are very special to me. I don't want to lose what we have."

"I'm not sure that we have anything left, Hank. I just want you to know that I do care about you but, for now, I can't have you in my life."

At this point, we were both fighting back tears. "I understand," I said, reaching across and placing my hand on hers. "If ever you need me for anything you just have to call." I stood, walked back out the front door and headed downhill toward town, on foot.

My mind was abuzz with remorse and guilt and self-loathing. I had once again screwed myself out of all the things I had come to value. My need to prove myself, to show everyone how clever I was had driven those I'd cared about away from me. Again. Hell, it had gotten a friend killed. I'd fooled myself into believing that I was a new man, a better man. Now the truth was apparent. I was still Hank Pressman, a self-important liar, a cheater and a drunk.

I got to the bottom of the hill and saw the Pump n' Shop again and it was finally open. I knew it was a bad idea. I knew I would regret it. But I walked into the store and picked up, not one, but two cheap bottles of booze. I was glad that Angie's granddaughter was behind the counter. I was pretty sure Angie herself would have kicked me out. At my request the clerk double bagged my purchases in opaque plastic bags that I hoped would disguise their contents. I left the store and walked around the back of the building to have the first sip. My mind flashed back to the last time I had done this exact same thing. You think remembering the results later that day would have deterred me. But no. I, the smartest guy around, the trained mental health professional, I went ahead and opened the bottle. I put it to my lips and took in a mouthful, spitting it out almost immediately. It tasted like gasoline. I looked at the bottle. The white label just said whiskey, 90 proof with a little red square warning me to not drink while pregnant or driving. I wasn't planning either so I took a more measured swig and swallowed it fast enough that I wouldn't taste it for long. Then I took another and a third, each bigger than the last, before recapping the bottle and slipping it back into the plastic bag. I took a deep breath and started walking back to the RV.

CHAPTER THIRTY

I woke in the dark on a wet bed smelling of urine. Scuttling to the end of the mattress, I got to my feet. Instantly, my head swam and I fell back again, landing in a puddle. I sat up more slowly and ran my hand through my hair, damp with what I was pretty sure was piss. I reached my arm out and touched a wall. Examining it I found the light switch and hit it. The light was blinding for a moment but as my eyes adjusted, I could tell that I was in the RV. That was a good thing, I supposed. I stood and hurriedly bundled the bed clothes and put them on the floor. Thankfully, the mattress had a waterproof cover which I wiped down with a dry corner of the otherwise sodden blanket. Doing this brought on a wave of dizziness forcing me to grab onto the wall to steady myself. Then came the nausea. I was lucky to be standing beside the bathroom door and made it to the toilet before my stomach ejected what little was in it. After several dry heaves, I decided I was done and sat back on my haunches. This all seemed so incredibly familiar. When had I experienced this before? Then I remembered the day I'd heard about Carla's death in prison. I'd gotten so drunk I'd blacked out. And here I was again.

I tried to remember how I had gotten here. The last I could recall was ...was meeting with Dan and, oh yeah, with Ellie. Then what? I drew a blank. I looked at my watch. It was nearly midnight. I'd left Ellie's around, what was it? Ten in the morning maybe. I'd lost over twelve hours. I hoped to hell that I'd spent most of it sleeping.

I got to my feet and stripped out of my wet clothes. Still woozy, I decided to wait before taking a shower, so I wrapped a towel around my waist and walked into my kitchenette. In the sink lay an empty whisky bottle. Its twin stood on the banquette table, only a quarter empty. Beside my recliner was a tumbler, a small amount of brown liquid in the bottom. I picked it and the bottle up and walked them both to the sink. I started to empty the bottle. The whiskey vapors wafted back to my face. In spite of how lousy I felt, the appeal of the alcohol was magnetic. I knew it was a bad idea. Booze had never been my friend, not really. Then again, what did I have to lose? I'd already alienated everyone I cared about both here in Amber Creek and back home. What the hell. I lifted the bottle to my lips. I took a swig and a new bout of retching hit me. When it was done, I tipped the bottle in the sink and let it run down the drain. Unsteady on my feet again, I stumbled to the recliner and plopped into it.

My head was too foggy to think. I needed to figure out what I had done since that morning but I couldn't make my brain work. Well, that's not quite true. It could work well enough to replay, over and over again, my inner voice yelling *You Fucking Idiot*. I slammed my hands against my forehead trying to get the thoughts to stop. When that didn't work, I got to my feet, steadying myself for a moment against the low ceiling. Then I guided myself to the wardrobe and pulled on a t-shirt, a pair of shorts and flip flops. I hoisted the pile of soiled bed clothes and carried them wavering through the RV and to the stairwell. I somehow got myself down the steps and outside where I dropped the laundry. At least it and its stench were out of the RV. Then I just started walking. No particular direction and certainly not in a straight line. I'm not sure how long I walked. I was on the town square when a police car pulled up and a voice called out to me.

"Hank, is that you?"

I looked into the car. It was Jerry Albright. "Yeah. It's me."

Jerry climbed out of the car. "What the hell are you doing out here at this time of night."

"Just taking a walk, that's all," I mumbled.

Jerry approached me. "You've been drinking."

"Yeah, so?"

"You know I could arrest you for public intox, right?" he said.

"Go ahead," I said. "I've done just about every other fucking stupid thing. I might as well spend a night in the drunk tank."

"I oughta do it," he said. "You've made a real mess of things around here." He took me by the arm and put me in the back seat of the squad car. He climbed in behind the wheel and made a U turn. A minute or so later he pulled up in front of Irene's house. He guided me out of the car and into my RV. Then he walked me back to the bare mattress that was my bed and told me to lay down. "And don't get back up till morning," he said, adding, "There's an AA meeting in Halston tomorrow at noon. I'll pick you up at eleven."

He must have left then because he wasn't there when I woke with blinding sunlight streaming in the window beside me. I lowered the shade and sat up before sliding to the edge of the bed. The mud in my head seemed to have drained out. I wasn't as confused though I still could not recall what I had done the previous day. I walked into the kitchen and filled the coffee machine. I took the last of the pop tarts out of the box and sat at the banquette eating it while waiting for the coffee to brew. I reviewed what little I could recall. The meetings with Dan and Ellie, neither of which had gone well. And then Jerry found me wandering outside. He could have arrested me. Hell, he should have arrested me. But he hadn't. He brought me home. And he was coming to take me to an AA meeting. Somehow, he was able to overlook all the crap and extend his hand to me. I guess that was the fellowship they always talk about in AA. The acceptance and assistance I had never offered to another alcoholic. I suddenly felt so inadequate, so... what was it Dan had said...self-absorbed. And he'd been right.

I'd dealt professionally with many people in this kind of position. I'd always said they had a choice to make. They could say 'I'm a hopeless drunk and I might as well keep going and drink myself to death'. Or they could say 'I made a mistake, after doing well for so long. So, I need to learn from my mistakes and build on my success'. Now I was in the position to make that decision. It would have been so much easier if drinking had been my only mistake but I had made so many more. I would have probably sat there ruminating for hours if Jerry hadn't knocked on my door. I got up and opened it.

"I told you I was picking you up at eleven," he said. "You sure as hell don't look ready."

"I'm sorry," I said. "Just woke up. Come in and have a cup of coffee while I get ready. It'll just take a few minutes."

He complied and sat at the table. I poured him a mug of coffee. "Sugar, Cream?"

He waved me away and I walked to the closet, picked out a change of clothes and closed myself in the bathroom. After a quick shower and some very basic hygiene, I was back with Jerry, dressed in khakis, a button-down shirt and loafers. Without a word, he downed the last of his coffee, stood up and headed out of the RV. I followed and got into his squad car, beside him.

The trip couldn't have taken more than thirty minutes though it seemed a hell of a lot longer. Jerry wasn't interested in conversation. I tried to engage him a few times but gave up after his one-word responses got me nowhere. We pulled up to the same small church in the rundown town of Halston. This gray brick and limestone edifice had been one of Sam's churches. I couldn't help but wonder what the future held for it and for the other two, thanks to me.

I followed Jerry to the side door and into the cramped church basement. It was dimly lit by low basement windows around the periphery. Jerry found a light switch and bare fluorescent fixtures came to life. There was a circle of chairs and a long table with a coffee machine and Styrofoam cups. Jerry took the coffee pot and filled it in the little bathroom near the door. At his direction, I filled the filter basket with coffee and put it in the machine. Jerry poured water in and turned it on.

"Now what?" I asked.

"We're early so we sit," he said. We took seats in the circle. I fidgeted and Jerry looked at messages on his phone. Finally, without looking at me, he said "I wish you'd never come to Amber Creek."

"I'm sorry to hear that," I said. "I really felt like I was starting to fit in. I like the place."

"I've got to admit that you have been helpful, to a point but," he shook his head. "Then you fucked up big."

"I know," I said. "And I really am sorry. I know that doesn't help much but that's all I have." We sat in silence for a few minutes then I turned to Jerry. "Why are you doing this?"

"Doing what?"

"You obviously don't like me, especially not after what happened but still, you're helping me. You could have put me in jail last night. You didn't have to bring me here today. So, why?"

He looked me straight in the eye for the first time that day. "I'm doing it because it's the right thing to do. A couple months back, somebody helped me out for no good reason. And so here I am, sober. I helped you not for you but for him. He told me to pass it on and that's what I'm doing."

"Who, who helped you?"

His eyes bored into me and I could see rage in them. I suddenly knew. "It was Sam. This was one of his churches. He brought you here."

Jerry shook his head in disgust, got to his feet and moved a few chairs down from me.

We sat quietly for another ten minutes then another man, about my age entered the room. He greeted us, deposited a box of donuts on the table, poured himself some coffee and took a seat. By the time the noon whistle sounded from the town square, four more people had joined us. A woman of maybe thirty, heavy set but neatly dressed in slacks and a blouse, called the meeting to order. She led us in the Serenity Prayer and then each person in the circle said his or her first name followed by the inevitable "I'm an alcoholic". That phrase had always seemed silly to me. Of course, you're an alcoholic, why else would you be here. Maybe for the first time, It sank on that day. As I introduced myself, I realized that I was not telling these people that I was an alcoholic. I was telling myself. And that was something I needed to do every day for the rest of my life. Not because it made me a bad person or because I was sick but because accepting my flaws opened me up to dealing with them. And because they can't always be fixed, I would need to deal with them every day.

The meeting progressed with discussions of personal successes and failures, followed by accolades and reassurances. I admitted to a relapse but gave no details and Jerry let me get away with that though I suspect he didn't want to. After an hour, I felt somehow more in control. We recited the serenity prayer again and the meeting was over. Then we gathered around the coffee table. The coffee was bitter, the donuts were dry but the company was just what I needed. Anonymous yes, but real and caring and unapologetic. Afterwards, Jerry and I got in his car and drove back to Amber Creek. Though he didn't look at me he at least talked a little more.

"What are your plans?" he asked.

"I don't know what you mean," I said.

"Plans," he said. "Are you going to stay in Amber Creek?"

"I haven't decided. Before ...before what happened at the rectory, I was thinking about it. I'm not a small-town kind of guy but I liked the people here and, well, there's Ellie."

"How 'bout since what happened?"

"I don't know. It feels like things have changed and, of course, they have. But what I mean is people don't seem to want to talk to me. They don't give me a chance to explain."

"Maybe that's because all of your explanations sound more like excuses."

That hit me hard. Because I knew it was true. "Okay, so now what do I do?"

"You're the shrink," he said. "But if you ask me, people are gonna need a whole bunch of time. This has been a lot to handle, for all of us. This town is pretty tight-knit but nothing like this has ever happened before."

"What about the tornado?"

"That's different. No one had any control over that. We pulled together because we needed each other. We needed to be a town and that town needed to heal. These murders, they're different. They were choices, they were somehow avoidable. And everyone wants to figure out what they missed, how they could have prevented them. And they want someone else to blame. You're an easy mark."

I thought about what he had said and it made sense. "You're a pretty smart observer," I said.

"For a dumb cop," he said and the conversation was closed.

Jerry dropped me off at Irene's. I thanked him and headed for my RV but then I was stunned to see my bedding draped over the clothes line. I veered to Irene's door and knocked. She opened it and her expression changed instantly from welcoming to pained.

"Irene, you didn't have to do my laundry," I said.

"It wasn't going to do itself," she said.

"Well thanks, and... thanks for everything else you've done for me, Irene. I just want you to know how sorry I am for what happened."

"I know," she said, and took a deep breath. "Sorry doesn't fix it though, does it. I just kept asking myself why. Why didn't you just let it go, let the police do their jobs? But I think I know. Maybe I knew all along."

"Irene, please let me explain."

"No, Hank. You don't have to. My Edie was like you. He had all the answers, or at least he sincerely thought so. He didn't need to listen to anybody, because he knew. But he didn't know shit, not really. And neither do you."

"I told you that I didn't mean any of this to happen. If I had known..."

"What? If you had known you would have stepped back and let the police do their jobs. Be honest with yourself, Hank. You would have come up with a *better plan* then another one and another. Just as long as you never had to admit that you were wrong."

"I admit it, Irene. I do. And I'm as sorry as a man can be."

She shook her head slowly. "You can take your laundry down in about an hour. It should be dry by then." She gave me a tight smile and closed the door. I walked to my RV feeling more alone than I had been in a long time.

CHAPTER THIRTY-ONE

During the next few days, I stayed in the RV most of the time, only going out at night, taking long walks and thinking. I spend a lot of time talking myself out of drinking again. I checked in with Ellie by phone and ran a few errands for her but avoided contact with anyone else. My contact with Ellie herself was superficial and strained. Bob had stopped by with another meal the first night. I thanked him but told him not to bother in the future. His discomfort in being with me was palpable and I decided I'd rather make my own food than put both of us through it again. I did tell him that I was thinking about moving on and he just nodded without comment.

On the third day, I called Ellie to check in. "I need to ask you for a favor," she said.

"Anything," I replied.

"I need you to drive me to Halston... for Sam's funeral."

I sucked in a deep breath and held it for a bit. "Sure," I said. "I'd like to attend the service myself."

"You don't have to if it would make you uncomfortable," she said.

"No, really. I'd be happy to. If it's okay with you, I'll drive my RV up to your place to pick you up tomorrow and we can go to the funeral in your car."

"That would be fine," she said. "The service is at ten in the old high school gym. The church was too small."

"I'll be there at nine," I said.

She thanked me again and hung up. The entire conversation had been superficial and the quavering in her voice told me that she had been on the brink of crying. In the past, she wouldn't have held it back. She would have felt comfortable letting me see inside. Letting me share in her pain. That kind of intimacy was over, at least for the time being.

The next morning, I put on the one suit I had kept. It was a little loose, the result of all the exercise I'd gotten since coming to Amber

Creek. Before driving away, I stopped at Irene's house to announce that I was moving the RV to Ellie's temporarily and then I was planning on leaving town. They were all standing on the stoop, dressed in their best for Sam's funeral. All but Irene. I thanked them for their support and asked if we could keep in touch. To my surprise, Charlotte hugged me, if somewhat indecisively. Bob shook my hand. "No matter what's happened since then," he said. "You did save our lives and I can never express my gratitude for that."

Tears welled up in my eyes. "It was the best thing I've ever done... for myself," I said. I ruffled the children's hair and began walking back to the RV. Irene's kitchen door opened and I turned to see her stepping out.

"Hank," she said. "Take care of yourself." I stepped back to the stoop and reached for her hand. She pulled me in and kissed my cheek. "Be a better man. I know you have it in you."

All I could say through my tears was "Thank you."

I turned away, walked back to the RV and climbed into the driver's seat. It was the first time I'd been behind the wheel in weeks and I'd forgotten about the crack in the windshield. It had happened on the day I first arrived in Amber Creek. It wasn't bad enough to obstruct my view of the road. I considered just leaving it there as a sort of symbol of my messed-up life. I rolled my window down and waved to the family one last time. As I drove away, the little golden angel I had accidentally broken off of my wife's headstone swung gently from the rearview mirror. I couldn't help but wonder if I would ever again have the chance to be part of a family. It had been special and I had blown it. Again.

I pulled onto Ellie's driveway and parked the RV on a slab beside the garage. Ellie was waiting for me at the front door. I gave her a peck on the cheek and, thankfully, she didn't turn away. I wheeled her down the ramp and helped her into the passenger side of her car. I stowed the wheelchair in the back seat and climbed into the driver's seat. I looked over at her. "How ya' doing, really?" I asked.

"Not good," she replied. "I doubt there's enough make up on earth to hide the bags

under my eyes."

"I think everyone will understand," I said. She smiled and pursed her lips, trying to hold the pain inside a little longer. I started the car and drove down the hill through Amber Creek to join a line of cars, all heading west toward Halston.

Ellie directed me to the gym. The parking lot was already full so I stopped by the front door, helped Ellie into her wheelchair and pushed it up a ramp to the door. Then I drove the car to the first parking space I could find, nearly two blocks away. After several minutes I rejoined Ellie and wheeled her into the gym which was already nearing capacity, stacks of full bleaches on both sides of the room and folding chairs on the floor. We found a place near the front that had been reserved for Ellie 'and guest'. Wheeling to it I could sense lots of people looking our way. It was hard to miss the judgment in people's eyes. I placed Ellie's wheelchair at the end of the row and took the seat beside her. Dan came up behind us and whispered in my ear. "If you wouldn't mind, I'd like to meet with you after the service. There's an office space through that door." He pointed to the left, only a few feet away. I said sure and Dan was gone.

The service started just after ten, officiated by the bishop himself. He explained that the actual funeral and burial would take place in Sam's hometown but that he felt a memorial service was necessary among the people he had so loved. He led the group in prayer and song. Then there was a series of readings and testimonials. Ellie was actually called up to speak and when she was done, the entire congregation was in tears. Then more speeches, more prayers and more songs followed. I didn't follow them though they were vaguely familiar to me. When the service was over, Ellie and I waited while the crowd filed out quietly. Then I wheeled her to the little office where Dan was waiting. He greeted Ellie, thanking her for what she had said.

"Take a seat," he said to me. "This won't take long."

"What's this about?" I asked.

"I wanted you to know that the case of the deaths at the rectory is being closed. No charges will be filed. We no longer need you to stay in Amber Creek."

"Am I being thrown out of town?" I said. Ellie grabbed my arm and shook her head in frustration.

"No, Hank," Dan said. "But I understand that you have been considering leaving. The law will not stand in your way."

"But what about you?" I challenged him. "Do you think I should leave?"

"I'm not sure I give a fuck what you do," he said.

"Now guys," Ellie interjected. "This is not the time or the place for a scene. Okay?"

Dan and I both nodded like kids who'd been called to the principal's office.

"Dan," Ellie continued, "is there any more information you can give us about the case?"

"Well, the physical evidence supports Hank's story. Both men were killed with Andy's gun. Fingerprints were his and Hank's. Shoe scuffs on the floor suggest a struggle while Andy was down."

"Anything else?" I asked.

"Well as you know, Andy's house burned down. We can't prove arson yet but it looks like a bunch of papers caught fire in the basement. He had a storm shelter down there and he may have used it for storage or ...for holding his victims."

"Pardon," Ellie said.

"Because of the fire, we couldn't find much useful evidence in the basement but we did find his car, about three blocks from the rectory. He'd loaded a lot of clothes and personal items in it. It looks like he was planning on leaving town,"

"That's more or less what he told Sam and me," I said.

"Well," Dan continued, "among the personal items we found a box, wood with brass trimming and a fancy lock, 'bout the size of a cigar box. We had to break the lock, but later we found the key on Andy's key chain. Anyway, inside he had some...souvenirs. Without going into too much detail, they link him to the serial killings. They may even help us with the body we weren't able to identify."

"Oh God," Ellie said. "So, it was him."

"Yeah," Dan said. "And we found something else in the box. His mother's wedding ring. We aren't sure what to make of that yet."

"Do you know how she died?" I asked.

"She was old. We just assumed natural causes, at the time," Dan replied.

"So, what are you going to do about it now?" I asked.

"Not a damn thing," he said. "What good would it do?" He got to his feet. "So that's all I wanted to tell you. I'd better get going. The wife is waiting in the car."

I extended my hand. "Thanks, Dan. I know you didn't need to tell us this."

He nodded but didn't take my hand. "What do you two plan to do?"

"I think I've worn out my welcome around here," I said. "I think I'll be heading out."

"That's probably for the best," he said. "And you, Ellie?"

"Once I'm on my feet again, it'll be back to the old grind, I guess," she said.

"That's good," Dan said and walked out. I turned Ellie's wheelchair and rolled back into the now empty gym. We got outside and Ellie waited while I brought the car around. I helped her in and we drove home in silence. I pulled the car into her driveway and got out to retrieve Ellie's wheelchair. I helped her into it and rolled her up the ramp and into the house. Once inside, I stooped down and faced her. "You know that I've got to leave, don't you?"

"Yeah, I know," she said.

We looked at each other for a long minute. There was pain in her eyes but, I thought, there was love too. I decided to take a risk. "Ellie," I said, "Come with me."

She blinked back tears, and slowly shook her head. "You know I can't."

"Why?" I pleaded.

"Hank, I'm needed here, I have purpose."

"I need you too. You can't just let me walk away." I pulled back, suddenly very hurt and very angry.

"You're the one who's leaving, Hank."

"So, what you're saying is that you don't really love me, at least not enough."

She reached out and touched my face with the tips of her fingers. "Hank, you're really such a child, and a spoiled one at that. You can't see past your own desires."

My mind flashed back to my telephone conversation with Phyllis. She'd said almost the same thing. Were they right? Was I just a spoiled child? I couldn't be. I was a grown man, a doctor. But still it pained me to realize that maybe they both had a point. Maybe, once again, it had become all about me. I turned my head away so that Ellies wouldn't see the guilt in my eyes.

"Amber Creek is my home," she continued. "And it's lost its priest. It wouldn't be right to take its doctor away too."

I turned back to her and covered her hand with mine. "But you love me, I know you do."

"Maybe I do," she said. "But that's not enough. I suspect that's the difference between you and me. Goodbye, Hank."

I suddenly knew that she was right. I came to my feet and stood for a bit, lost in myself. Finally, I leaned down and kissed her. Her hand caressed my cheek again then she pulled away, a pained smile on her lips and tears streaming from her eyes. I couldn't bring myself to say goodbye so I just turned and walked out of the house. I climbed into my RV. After a few painful minutes of looking back at the house and sketching it in my memory, I started the engine and drove down to the old highway where I turned west heading away from Amber Creek. I was alone again, on the road again, running from the person that I didn't want to be again. But, unfortunately, I didn't know who I did want to be or where I was going to find that person.

Marie's golden angel swung back and forth on its string, sparkling in the sunlight. It reminded me of how I would have disappointed my wife again, even after her death. But it also reminded me of the faith she had had in me. It reminded me that she had seen some fragment of good in me as had Ellie and Irene and, If I was truly honest with myself, so many others. I committed myself there and then to finding that fragment and making it the seed of a new and better Hank Pressman. I hit the accelerator and headed west.

9 798869 268808